Merman's Touch

Dee J. Stone

Copyright © 2015 Dee J. Stone.
All rights reserved. No part of this book may be reproduced or used in any form without written permission from the author.
This is a work of fiction. Names, characters, places, and events are the product of the author's imagination or are used fictitiously, and any resemblance to real life, movies, television, games, or books is entirely coincidental and was not intended by the author.

First Edition.

ISBN-13: 978-1508627449
ISBN-10: 1508627444

Merman's Touch

Chapter One

It feels so good to be wrapped in the arms of the love of my life. Damarian's lips trail down my neck, and I inhale his familiar ocean scent. He sweeps his lips toward my mouth and lightly brushes them against mine.

I moan.

Damarian chuckles softly and leans back on the couch. He focuses his attention on the book in his hand. "I do not believe I can do this."

"Read me a couple of lines."

His eyebrows crease as he squints at the words. "'The young boy…neared the monster. The beast's eyes…were as red as…fire. The boy hes…hes…'"

I bend forward to scan the page. "Hesitantly."

"Thank you, my love. 'The boy…hesitantly approached the monster and…with…withdrew his sword. After a few slashes, the beast was…slain and the village was…s…safe.'"

I clap. "Very good, Damarian! Soon you'll be reading Shakespeare."

"Shaksfear?"

I giggle and peck his lips. Before I can draw back, he locks his arm around my waist and lowers me to the couch, nuzzling my nose. Next, his lips move over mine.

It's been a few weeks since Damarian and I have become an official couple. The first thing he wanted to do was learn to read. I ordered a program online and he tackled it right away. I'm amazed at how quickly he picked up on it. Maybe merpeople are super smart. Or maybe Damarian is just very determined.

He smiles down at me, his eyes filled with nothing but pure love. He strokes my cheek. "I am very fortunate to have you, Cassie."

I cover his hand with mine. "Me, too."

He leans toward my ear. "Forgive me. I have not spoken in a human manner." He sits back and thinks for a few seconds. "I am so lucky to be with you, Cassie."

I force out a smile. "Very good."

"What do I receive as a reward? No. What is my prize?" He laughs and reaches for my lips, but I turn my head. His eyes cloud with confusion and hurt. "What is wrong?"

I look away.

"Cassie?" He runs his finger down my cheek.

Still not meeting his gaze, I say, "I don't like seeing you change yourself. You're so amazing because you're *not* human. You're a merman. The way you talk, the way you carry yourself, that's what makes you special, what makes you *you*. And you're throwing it all away."

He tucks his fingers under my chin, lifting my face so our eyes meet. "But what am I to do, my love? I cannot live on land behaving as though I am a child of the sea." His eyes search mine. "Is it not your wish that I remain on land with you?"

I shut my eyes. "Of course, Damarian. I want more than anything for us to be together."

He lowers his cheek on mine. "Then this is what I must do. I must learn to behave as a human. I must learn to read and I shall seek work."

Merman's Touch

My eyes fly open. "Seek work? You mean, a job?"

"Yes."

I haven't thought about that. I teach a surfing class every morning, but it's summer now. Soon I'll be starting my first semester at the community college here, and Damarian…what will he do all day? I'm so selfish for not thinking about him.

I wish we could run away to a secluded island and just be together, where we won't have to deal with real life issues. Where it won't matter that I'm a human and he's a merman.

He lightly runs his lips across my forehead. "Fret not, Cassie. All will be well."

I keep convincing myself that if we want it really badly, we can make it work. But I don't want Damarian to give himself up. I'll love him no matter what, but he's changing for me. I feel like I'm robbing him of his essence.

He gets to his feet and grins. "I shall return with your worms."

I smile as he heads for the kitchen. Then I reach for his book. He loves me so much that he's sacrificing himself. If only there was a way for me to go into the ocean. At least that way, he wouldn't lose a large chunk of himself.

He returns with a bag of gummy worms and plops down near me. I crawl on his lap, wrapping my legs around his waist. "So…my mom's coming home in a few weeks."

Damarian nods. "Yes, we have discussed this."

"Right. But here's the thing…" I gaze into his innocent eyes, the color of the deep ocean. "I think we'll need to tell her about…about you."

His face fills with alarm.

I wrap my fingers around the back of his neck. "I know it scares you, but I have no idea how long she'll stay. We can't run back and forth to the ocean, can we? I mean, if you want to go home until she leaves, I'll understand, but—"

"My sweet Cassie," he murmurs, resting his forehead against mine. "I understand. It is so very difficult when we are apart. When I am in the ocean, I long for you."

"So what should we do?" I whisper.

He encloses his arms around me and pulls me tight against his chest. "Do you believe she will, as you humans say, 'Freak out?'"

The words sound so natural on his lips. I don't know if I should laugh or cry. I bury my face in his chest. Even though he hasn't been in the ocean for several days and swam in my pool a few hours ago, he smells like sea water. It's a smell I can never get tired of. "Of course she'll freak out," I tell him. "But she's my mom. She'll be okay with it."

He doesn't say anything, but I feel a tremor travel down his body. I clutch onto him. "I'll be here, Damarian."

He nods against my head. "Thank you."

***

Damarian grips my hand as we make our way toward the beach. I squeeze his. I know how hard it is for him to be so close to the ocean. His family and friends are there, his life.

Tightening my hold on my surfboard that's starting to slide down, I say, "You don't have to do this to yourself. You can go back home."

"It is all right."

I tell this to him every morning. I can't stand to see the hurt in his eyes. But he insists on coming. I'm not sure if it's because he's bored and lonely at home or because he wants to accompany me. Or maybe being near his old home eases his mind somehow.

He sits down a few feet away from the shore, far enough that even a drop of salt water can't hit him. I fall to my knees. "I don't like seeing you upset."

Merman's Touch

He twirls a strand of my blonde hair between his fingers. "Do not worry. I am not upset."

"Okay." I kiss him again. "Don't miss me too much."

"That is not possible."

I wink, pick up my surfboard, and run toward the tide. Some of my students are already gathered there. I watch them for a few seconds. Uncle Jim mentioned how good I am with the kids. He used to teach the surfing class before he injured his leg. I haven't really thought about what I want to study in college because I didn't want to deal with it. Being an adult, having all these changes, scares me. I never considered being a teacher. The only thing that comes to mind is how my high school classmates made my teachers' lives a living hell. But maybe teaching younger kids would be different.

I glance back at Damarian. He's observing the many people on the beach with an amused and curious expression on his face. He keeps telling me that humans never cease to amaze him. A lump forms in my throat. Here I am making plans for myself. But what about Damarian? Assuming he learns to read like a pro and how to act like a human, where will he work? I doubt many places are willing to hire someone without proper ID, let alone a high school diploma.

"Miss Cassie!" eight-year-old Timmy yells from the distance, lugging his surfboard as he runs toward me and the rest of the kids. "I'm here on time." He beams.

"Yes, you are."

"How many more days?" he asks.

"About a week," I say with a pout.

He frowns. "I love surfing."

"I know, sweetie."

"I'm gonna be so sad when it's over." He lowers his head toward the sand.

I ruffle his hair. "But when the classes are over, you'll be such a great surfer you won't even need me anymore."

He raises his head. "Really?"

"Of course!"

He beams again.

I clap my hands. "Come on, kids!"

When class is done, I grab my towel and make sure to dry every part of myself. My eyes move to the spot Damarian was in before my class started, but I don't find him anywhere. My heart races. He's been on land for a while now and can take care of himself, but I can't help stressing when I don't see him. Ever since Kyle, another merman and my ex-boyfriend, threatened to expose Damarian, I've become more vigilant. He caught Damarian's transformation from merman to human on camera, and I worry someone else might do the same. Except this time they would go to the media.

I scan around, but don't see him. I grab my surfboard and am about to head to Misty's Juice Bar, the place my best friend Leah works at, to see if he's there, but then I spot him by the ice cream stand. My whole body sags with relief. I smile. He's so cute. He's like a little kid marveling at our world.

I head over, just as the guy hands him a long, rainbow-colored popsicle. Damarian's eyes are bigger than beach balls as he stares at it. He catches sight of me and grins. "This appears like coral. Yet, it is edible." He licks it, and his eyes light up. "Delicious! Would you like one, Cassie?"

I laugh. "Okay."

Damarian hands the guy another dollar, and he gives me a popsicle. I haven't had one of these in years.

As we make our way home, I keep my eyes on Damarian, watching the way he licks the colors of his popsicle, trying to determine if they

Merman's Touch

have different flavors. My view on life has changed now. Damarian looks at everything with innocent, curious eyes. He studies our world the way scuba divers and marine biologists study the ocean. To him, we *are* his ocean. He makes me learn to appreciate our world and everything and everyone in it. We get so busy with life that we never stop to just admire it.

I rest my surfboard against the living room wall and sit down next to Damarian on the couch. He's devoured over half of his popsicle while I'm hardly a third in. He's used to cold temperatures.

He finishes and tosses the wrapper into the bin. "Maybe you should try out for the NBA," I joke.

"NBA?"

"Basketball."

His eyebrows come together. "Yes, I recall that sport."

I hold out my popsicle. "Want? I can't finish it."

His eyes shine. "Gladly! Thank you." He bites off half of it.

I giggle.

He finishes in less than a minute and throws the wrapper into the bin. Merpeople have sick eye-hand coordination.

Damarian leans back, rubbing his stomach. "What shall we do today?"

"Well, first things first. You need to swim in my pool."

He nods. "Of course."

"Then maybe we can do something human?"

His eyes light up. "Yes, please! What shall we do?"

I motion "one minute" with my finger and go down to the basement. I return holding a large box in my arms and drop it on the couch.

Damarian eyes it. "What is that?"

"Open it," I urge.

He carefully does. A new pair of rollerblades sits before him. With a bewildered expression, he lifts one of the black blades and stares at it. He spins the green wheels, then brings his eyes to me. "I do not understand. This resembles shoes, but the wheels…" He spins them again. "Are we to ride on this?"

"Yep. I'm going to teach you how to rollerblade."

He stares at me like I told him I'm going to jump into the ocean with a bowling ball attached to my leg. I can't help but giggle at how adorable he is. "I really want to share my interests with you," I tell him, pushing some of his golden hair out of his eyes. "But since we can't surf together, rollerblading comes close. Maybe one day we can go snowboarding, too."

He continues to finger the rollerblade, staring at it like it's some foreign object that landed from Mars. "I would very much enjoy to participate in activities that interest you as well. But it frightens me."

I close my fingers around his wrist. "I'll be there to make sure you don't get hurt. It'll be a lot of fun."

He nods slowly. "Yes, I believe it shall be fun." He grins. "Shall we go?"

Chapter Two

Damarian and I spend the rest of the day rollerblading in the park. As soon as he gets his blades on, he speeds away like he's been doing it for years. *I* fall more times than he does. I'm really glad he's having a great time. I know deep down I'm trying to make his human life as best as possible. I'm practically tearing him away from his real life. He constantly tells me he doesn't need or want anything as long as we're together, but I can't help feeling like I need to compensate. Maybe in time things will fall into place. I hope.

As he takes a shower, I lie on the couch, stretching my arms. I know I'll be a little sore tomorrow from the rollerblading.

A strawberry scent fills my nose. I sit up and pull Damarian closer, causing him to fall on me. Ever since he took a shower at my house the first time, he insists on continuing to use my shampoo. It makes goose bumps pop up all over my body when I think about it. Nothing says true love like a guy using his girlfriend's girly shampoo.

He nuzzles my temple and reaches for one of my braids. He unties it, then does the same to the other. My hair tumbles down my shoulders in small waves. He runs his fingers through it, his expression turning serious. "Cassie, I have been thinking while I bathed."

"Yeah?"

"I believe it is time I visit my family."

A lump forms in my throat. Of course I want him to see his family and friends, but every time he leaves I feel like a part of me goes with him. Not to mention how dangerous it is. Going back and forth to the ocean, switching from one form to the other, makes it that much easier to get caught. If only there was a way to make this easier.

His warm lips slowly slide down my throat. "If it is all right with you, Cassie."

"Of course it's all right." I lock my arms around him and squeeze him tight.

He buries his face in my neck. "I wish it were not so difficult. Perhaps…perhaps I shall lessen my visits."

"No." I pull away and look into his eyes. "Absolutely not."

"Are you certain?"

"I'm *very* certain. We'll be extra careful, like always."

He swallows hard and nods.

I touch his cheek. "You need to see them, Damarian. Especially little Zarya." I bite down on my cheek to prevent tears from entering my eyes. More than anything, I want to meet his family. I've met his younger brother, Kiander, king of the merpeople, and his sister, Doria. But I'm dying to meet his littlest sister, Zarya. "Would…" I clear my throat. "Would your family ever consider coming on land?"

Damarian blinks at me.

I shake my head. "Never mind."

He gathers me to his chest and whispers into my ear, "I shall ask them."

"You will?" My voice is above a whisper.

"I have not considered it before. But perhaps they shall wish to visit land. Mother is very much interested in the female I have chosen as my mate."

Merman's Touch

I slowly untangle myself from him. "She is?"

"Yes."

"She'll come back with you?"

He holds out his hands. "I am not certain. Perhaps."

I'm about to jump for joy, but hold myself in place.

Damarian laughs and kisses me. "How I enjoy seeing you happy."

"I enjoy seeing you happy, too."

"I know, my beautiful, sweet Cassie. I see how you try hard to please me." He rests his forehead against mine. "Thank you."

I close my eyes. "We have a few hours until we need to go to the beach. I'll take a shower, we'll eat something, and then we'll head to bed, okay?"

He squeezes my hand before I leave for the bathroom. Like always, it smells like the ocean mixed with strawberries. I can stay in here for hours, enjoying the smell. It's almost like he's in here with me.

My cheeks burn at the thought.

When I step out of the bathroom, I smell something. Something good. I walk to the kitchen and find Damarian standing by the stove, mixing a pot. I come up from behind him and wrap my arms around his middle. "Are you cooking?" I practically moan into his neck.

"I observed a man preparing this feast on the TV yesterday," he says. "It is…" He glances down at a piece of paper he scribbled on. "Mushroom soup."

"Mmm. And when did you buy the ingredients, you little sneak?"

"This morning as you educated the fry."

I love how he still uses his merman terms. "Ah. So while I taught my little fry how to surf, you decided to surprise me with dinner?"

He nods.

I peck his cheek. "I love you, my merman."

"And I love you, my human."

I help him with dinner, and after we finish eating we go up to my room and lie down next to each other. Damarian puts his arm around me. "I am exhausted."

"Get as much sleep as you can because you have a long journey."

He nods and his eyes close. Soon, I hear him breathing softly. I brush some hair off his forehead and watch him sleep. My heart fills with love. It's the kind of love I read about in books and have seen in movies. I never thought I'd get to experience it. It's the most amazing thing in the world. To have such a deep connection with someone, to know he will always be there for me and do anything for me, even risk his safety and the safety of his people.

I lean toward his ear. "I love you so much, Damarian. I'll love you until the day I die, and I will do everything, absolutely everything to make you happy. All I ask is that you be mine forever."

**

Someone taps my shoulder. My eyes snap open. Damarian stares down at me, his eyebrows creased. "I believe it is time, Cassie?"

I blink the sleep away and glance at the clock. It's nearly four AM.

I sit up and reach for clothes, but Damarian puts his hand over mine. "Will you swim with me in the sea?" he asks.

We swam together in my pool this afternoon, but I understand it's not enough for him. It's like only eating tofu. He wants to swim with me in the ocean, in his world. I tighten my fingers around his hand. "Of course."

We haven't swum together in the ocean in weeks, since before my mom left for New York. I dress into my wetsuit while Damarian only wears shorts. He takes my hand and we head for the beach. Normally, I'd drop him off at our usual spot—a place on the beach with many rocks that most people don't wander to. But because I'm going to join him in the ocean, we head to the dock.

Merman's Touch

I triple check to make sure no one's around and nod to Damarian. He shimmies out of his shorts, then dives into the water. The waves crash into each other as he undergoes the change from human to merman. The ordeal is extremely painful and lasts about thirty seconds.

When it's over, Damarian's head breaks the surface and he holds his arms out. I cannonball into the water. It feels good against my skin. Since it's in the middle of the summer in Florida, the water's temperature is perfect. I feel the stickiness of his tail as it whooshes against my legs. It kind of sucks that it's in the middle of the night and I can't see him well. I wish I could take in his sapphire tail, the way it looks like crystals as it gleams in the moonlight. He looks so different when he's in the ocean, more magical.

I fasten my arms and legs around him, and we float in the water. The waves wash over us, but they're not too violent. I lay my head on his chest. "This feels so good." To be in his arms when he's in his true form. He feels so alive, like the ocean provides him with key nutrients, just like humans need oxygen.

"I agree, my Cassie."

My eyes slowly adjust to the dark. I can make out some of his beautiful face. I touch his cheek, and he leans his face into my palm. "There is so much I wish to show you, my love," he whispers. "So much of my world."

It's a good thing he can't see my face clearly because tears seep out my eyes. "It's okay."

He lifts me onto his back and tells me to hang on and to take a deep breath. He submerges into the ocean. I can't see anything, but feel him swim fast. Soon, we're at the sandbar, the one we used to meet at when my mom was home.

I climb onto it and Damarian closes his hand around my calf. I take his other hand and lay it palm-up on mine. I love his webbed hands.

They make him who he is.

"How long until you must return?" he asks.

I have no idea what time it is, but it should be getting close to five, when the fisherman start their morning catch. "Soon," I say, my voice laced with regret.

He cups my face between his hands. "I will long for you."

"I will, too."

"Will you allow me to hold you close as I swim?" he asks.

"Of course, Damarian."

I slide into the water and he takes me in his arms, pulling me tight against his chest. His silky hair brushes my face. I run my fingers through it, softly tugging on the strands. He doesn't dip into the water. He keeps our heads above the surface as he rushes through the ocean. He's going at such a fast pace that large amounts of salt water enter my nose and mouth. Being in his arms as he surges through the water is like sitting in a racecar. It pumps me up with so much adrenaline that I feel like I can do anything.

Things bump into us as we continue to speed. Seaweed, fish, crabs. Damarian cradles me close and mutters into my ear, "I will not allow any harm to come your way, Cassie. Take in some air."

I nod.

He dives into the ocean and, while I still can't see anything, I feel. He spins around, faster and faster, like propellers of a ship. The next second, I'm soaring in the air.

My eyes open to see the black sky. As I plummet toward the water, I take in a large gulp of air. I land in Damarian's arms.

We rise to the surface and he grins at me, his eyes hopeful. "Did you enjoy that?"

I hug him. "That was amazing. I felt like I was a breaching whale. It scared the crap out of me, but it was so fun!"

Merman's Touch

His chest rumbles as he laughs. "I am glad. But I am afraid we must part now, Cassie."

My arms remain around him. "Damarian…" I can't hold back the sob.

He rubs my back. "I understand, for I feel it as well. Shall I remain on land? I do not need to return."

I shake my head. I won't do that to him. I won't deny him the chance to see his family.

His lips press into the hollow space between my neck and shoulder. "Farewell, my love."

My head snaps back as he trails kisses from my throat to my face. When they reach my lips, our mouths press into each other like the world is coming to an end and we're saying goodbye forever. Each kiss holds so much passion and yearning. I don't know if we'll ever stop.

The sky is getting light. I push my body away from Damarian, but my lips are still attached to his and my arms still cling to him. Damarian doesn't let go. The waves thrust our bodies closer to each other, as if the ocean wants us to remain together.

My lips unfasten from his and I lay my forehead against his. Our chests heave. This doesn't get easier, no matter how many times we do it.

"I shall imagine you with me in the ocean," Damarian whispers. "Lying with me in my bed. Holding you close."

I shut my eyes and nod, swallowing the lump forming in my throat. "Don't go meeting other human girls," I joke, like I always do when we part.

"Never."

"Spend time with your family," I tell him. "Come back in two nights."

He looks into my eyes. "Are you certain?"

I nod. "You need to see them for more than just one day."

He caresses my cheek. "If that is what you wish, Cassie."

"It is."

"Thank you."

He positions me behind him, and I climb on. He brings me close to the dock. Our arms are wound tightly around each other as we squeeze our bodies together, nearly fusing as one. "Bye, my merman," I say softy.

"Farewell, my human."

We kiss one final time. I yank myself away from him and swim toward the dock. When I reach it, I look back. Damarian waves before diving into the ocean. Next, his sapphire tail rises in the air. He waves it, then quickly pulls it underwater, out of sight.

I heave myself onto the dock and sit on it, my eyes on the calm ocean, my toes touching the water. The sun is already rising. Damarian is on his way home.

I stay here until I'm drier than the sand.

Chapter Three

Leah and I sit on our surfboards in the middle of the ocean. The waves are too flat for surfing. A part of me wonders if Damarian might tease me and grab my foot, maybe sweep his tail past my legs. But he'd never venture this far out—the water is too shallow and there are too many people around.

It feels good to love someone so much that I miss him after only a few hours. But I know it's not healthy for me to absorb myself in my fishman and only my fishman. Time apart is healthy for a relationship. Just like Damarian needs to spend time with his family and friends, I need to spend time with mine.

"You'll have to tell him, you know," Leah says, playing with her dark brown hair. Her eyes flick to mine. "I feel like a fraud every time I look at him."

I keep my eyes on the water. After I rescued Damarian and returned him to the ocean the first time, I never expected him to come back, which is why I told Leah his true identity. She's the only one who knows.

I've kept the secret from him all this time. I'm scared he'll feel hurt and betrayed if tell him the truth.

She nudges her toe into mine. "Hey."

I look up and force a smile. "Sorry. I guess I just freak out about losing him. Because we're from two different worlds and are so different, I can't help but worry that our relationship is doomed and we'll break up. Sometimes I feel that his family is just waiting for him to come to his senses and ditch me."

"He promised himself to you, Cassie. He says he wants to be with you for eternity. Didn't he say you're his mate?"

I scoff. "Sure, I'm his mate. We never..." I clear my throat. "We haven't..." I shake my head.

She rests her hand on my arm. "You will. When the time is right. I see the way Damarian looks at you. He loves you to death."

"I know," I whisper.

"You've got to stop worrying about him leaving you. He won't. Once you two take that step, you're stuck with each other." She nudges my toe again, forcing a small smile to climb onto my lips.

Merpeople mate for life. When Damarian and I finally...or *if* he and I finally reach that point, we'll be bonded forever.

That's what I desperately want. To be that close to him, to finally have that eternal link. But Damarian still hesitates, which makes me freak out even more when he goes home—to other mermaids. I hate having these insecure thoughts. I want to drown them out of my head.

"How are things with Jace?" I ask Leah.

She plays with her hair again. "Okay."

I raise an eyebrow. "Just okay?"

She sweeps her legs back and forth in the water. "We're going through a rough patch."

Now I rest my hand on her arm. "What happened?"

"I guess we're not on the same page on certain things." She sighs. "Maybe we're too different."

"Do you love him?"

Merman's Touch

"I think so. I mean, I really like him."

"You can make it work. When you love someone, you can't give up."

She nods slowly, continuing to sweep her legs in the water.

"Damarian didn't give up on me, and I didn't give up on him. We have such a complex relationship. But we make each other feel good and have such a deep connection. I know commitment is hard, but if you guys truly care for one another, you have to try to make it work. I mean, I'm not an expert on this sort of thing, but I don't want to see you give up on Jace. I know he makes you happy."

"Yeah." She smiles. "If *you* can make a relationship with a fish work, I need to make my relationship with a human work. Unless Jace is secretly an alien. Who knows? Merpeople exist. Next we'll hear that vampires secretly roam the streets at night, and then we'll hear werewolves howling on a full moon and—"

I splash water on her with my legs. She squeals and does it back. When I splash her again, this time harder, my board tips and I crash into the water. Leah laughs and raises her fist in triumph. I tip her board, sending her into the ocean with me.

***

The house is too quiet. I rest my surfboard on the wall and make my way upstairs to my room. Damarian and I have been sleeping in my bed every night, nestled in each other's arms. I fall back and stretch my arms, running my hands across the bedspread, wishing he were here with me. The bed smells like him. Actually, my whole room smells like him. No, the entire *house* smells like him, as though he's taken a permanent residence here.

I wonder what he's doing. Is he playing squid wars with Zarya and his twin brothers, Syd and Syndin? Maybe he's showing off all his human knowledge to his merfriends. He told me that even though his kind doesn't try to open any sort of communication with humans, they are extremely curious about us. I'm pretty sure he's boasting how he can read, write, and use money.

My palm flattens on his spot on the bed. I close my eyes and whisper, "Damarian."

Something rings. My eyes slowly open. My phone. I sit up and head downstairs to the couch, where I threw it. A voicemail from my dad. "Hey, Cass Bass. Sheila and I would like to have you over for dinner Thursday night. Bring your boyfriend."

Things have been going pretty well with my dad. I've been spending more time with him and his family. His wife, Sheila, is really sweet and his kids are adorable. But they haven't met Damarian yet. I guess I've been pushing it off because I'm not really sure what will happen once I introduce him into their lives. Will that put Damarian at risk? I need to tell my mom the truth about him, but what about my dad?

Chapter Four

I balance the bag of "essentials" on my knees as I sit on the rocks on the beach, waiting for my man to come home from the sea. The bag contains a few towels to dry Damarian off to speed up his transformation from merman to human, a sheet to cover him in case someone is lurking in the shadows, his pajama pants, and candy to help him feel better.

My whole body beats with anticipation. It's been two days. Two *long* days. I don't know how military wives do it.

I squint at the waves, hoping and wishing to see something in the water, but I don't see any movement. It's pitch black out here, though my eyes have somewhat adjusted. I squash the negative thoughts trying to surface in my mind. Damarian is on his way. He's *not* ditching me. He never will.

Glancing at my watch, I see it's well past four. I tell myself that doesn't mean anything. Merpeople don't have a sense of time like we do. I can't hold him accountable for being late. I reach for a gummy worm and bite it in half.

Every part of me wants to dive into the ocean and search for him, but that would be the most stupidest thing on the planet. First of all, I'll drown. Second, the ocean is so vast and he could be anywhere.

Stop freaking out.

My head snaps up when I notice the waves getting a little violent. I stretch my neck and squint. An arm. I see an arm!

Just as I scramble to my feet, his golden head sticks out of the ocean. I jump in my place and wave. He waves back. Holding the bag close to my chest, I hop down the rocks, nearly losing my balance. When I reach the tide, Damarian is already heaving his body out of the water.

I leap toward him. He catches me by the waist and rolls onto his back, tucking me close and pressing his lips into the side of my neck. He murmurs my name over and over as his lips kiss every inch of my face. My arms are wrapped so tightly around him, my chest practically merged with his, that I can hardly breathe.

"My beautiful Cassie," he whispers.

I lock my legs around his middle, feeling the scales of his tail. I dig my face into his bare chest, inhaling his fresh, ocean scent. "Damarian."

"I do not believe I can withstand two days apart from you," he says.

I raise my head. "Did you not enjoy yourself?"

He cups my cheek in his webbed hand. "Yes, I did enjoy myself. But how I longed for you."

"Me, too."

I spent a lot of time with Leah and had a lot of fun, but I missed him terribly.

"Zarya has presented you with a gift," he says.

"A gift?"

He points to a small object near the shore. The waves crash over it, almost dragging it back inside. I crawl toward it and sweep it off the ground. It looks like a piece of coral. It's so pretty, with bright blue and pink colors in the shape of a flower. I can't imagine something so exquisite like this actually exists.

I also can't believe Damarian's sister took the time to get me a present. It makes me feel really good, like I've been accepted into his family, into his life.

"It's beautiful," I tell Damarian. "Zarya is so sweet. Please tell her thank you the next time you see her."

He nods. "Will it die on land? Zarya was concerned it would not live out of water."

I study it. "I'm not sure. We'll put it in my pool and hope it survives in the salt water."

I find myself smiling as I hold the coral tightly in my hand. I really want to meet Zarya. I feel such a connection to her, and I feel like I know her so well because Damarian's told me so much about her. Out of all his siblings, he's the closest to her. She's about five years old and loves to explore the ocean, just like her older brother. As the baby of the family, her parents spoil her rotten and she knows she can get away with whatever she wants. But she's such a sweet little girl that anyone would do anything for her.

I hope I can meet her pretty soon and not have to wait until she's an adult. Damarian made it clear that his parents don't allow the younger children to leave the ocean, but maybe they'd be willing. I mean, I am part of the family, aren't I? I'd like to think so.

I fall back on my knees and gather the items from my bag. After we dry Damarian to the best of our ability, I throw the sheet over the two of us, and settle down in his arms. Holding him as he shifts takes away some of the pain. As much as it hurts me to see his face break out in a sweat and his eyes roll over as he writhes in agony, I want to do anything I can to comfort him.

There's always this hope in me as I watch him wait for the wave of pain to hit—hope that one day it won't hurt as much. But the pain doesn't seem to lessen after each transformation, almost like the universe is telling me to let him be who he's meant to be. It seems that sometimes the universe fights for us to be together while other times it gives me the finger.

He grunts as his body begins to convulse. His eyes snap shut. I hug him as close as possible as I mutter words of comfort into his ear, brushing my lips across his face. It's drenched in sweat. I grab one of the towels and gently dab his face.

Then it's over. His head falls toward his shoulder as ragged breaths escape his mouth. His eyes flutter for a few seconds before they open, and they light up the second he sees me. Lifting his hand, he presses his palm to my cheek. "The pain is worth seeing your beautiful face," he murmurs, his voice so weak I barely hear it.

I lower my head and touch my forehead to his. We just lie here for a few minutes, with Damarian's chest rising and falling—first heavily, but gradually decreasing to a slow, steady rhythm.

After not having to shift in two days, I'm pretty sure it was really difficult this time. I look into his face, pushing some hair out of his eyes. My whole body gets engulfed in a warm feeling as I watch him sleep. It starts at my heart and expands throughout my bloodstream, hitting every organ.

I lean forward to whisper in his ear, "Damarian."

He stirs.

"We need to leave the beach."

His eyes slowly open and scan around. It looks like it takes him a few seconds to gather his bearings. I help him sit up and hand him a few gummy worms, which he gobbles down. He pulls on his pajama bottoms and stands on shaky legs. Usually, he rests for a few minutes after his transformation, but we have ten minutes worth of walking to

Merman's Touch

do.

"Almost forgot," I say, sweeping the coral off the ground.

I link my arm through Damarian's as we trek home.

After placing the coral in my pool filled with synthetic sea salt, we make our way to the living room. Damarian grabs me by the waist and collapses on the couch. I snuggle up to him, once again breathing in that fresh ocean scent.

I pass out with my arms and legs tangled in his.

***

Someone's kissing me. I open my eyes and look into Damarian's face. With a loving smile, he dips his head and closes his mouth over mine. My arms hook around the back of his neck as I pull him closer to me. His lips are soft, warm, and taste like cinnamon mixed with salt water. They move over mine so softy, as though he's rubbing a feather against my mouth.

I don't think of anything but how amazing and right this feels.

When our lips come apart, my eyes stay closed as I savor the moment. I feel Damarian caress my cheek. With a moan, I open my eyes and stretch my arms, giving him a warm smile. That's when I realize I'm lying in my bed. "You carried me?" I ask.

He takes my hand and lightly kisses the back of my fingers. "I awakened a few hours ago. You were so beautiful when you slept, but you did not appear comfortable on the couch."

"Thanks. That was so sweet of you." I squeeze his hand. Then I sniff. "What's that delicious smell?"

He gestures to a tray sitting on the night table. Two pancakes are piled on there, along with a glass of orange juice and cut-up fruit. "I have prepared breakfast for you."

"You made me breakfast? You're so amazing, Damarian."

"I was not certain whether you would like…" His eyebrows

furrow. "Forgive me. It is a word I cannot pronounce easily."

The lingering taste of cinnamon from Damarian's kisses enters my mind. "Cinnamon?"

"Yes!" His eyes light up. "Cinnamon."

God, he's so cute.

He reaches for the tray and places it on my lap. "Please enjoy."

"Thanks. Did you eat yet?"

"Yes. I am quite satisfied with my work."

I cut into one of the pancakes. "I know they're amazing." I take a bite and my mouth explodes with all these flavors. I gobble down the rest of it within minutes.

"Did you enjoy it?" he asks.

"I've never tasted anything so good in my life!"

His cheeks turn pink. I stare at him. I haven't seen Damarian blush before. With his pale, translucent skin, I didn't think he could. It makes my heart melt, but I can't stop the feeling of unease creeping up my spine. Blushing makes him seem too human.

"I appreciate when you compliment me," he says, sliding his fingers through mine.

"You don't usually get compliments?"

Damarian's gaze drops to the floor. "Father…he is not one to be very generous with compliments." His smiles wryly. "One must perform a magnificent task to receive one from him."

My thumb rubs circles on his hand. "I'm sorry."

"Mother compliments," he says.

I'm not sure if all merfathers behave the same way as Syren. Maybe it's their culture. If not, if Damarian's dad is strict because that's who he is, I don't see him welcoming me with open arms. I don't want to think about it.

"I promise to compliment you as often as I can," I tell Damarian.

Merman's Touch

"Like now—you made me the most delicious breakfast I've ever had. You are so talented and so determined. So driven to succeed and you don't let anything get in your way. You fight for what you believe in and for what you want. I have so much respect for you."

He gazes into my eyes. "How happy you make me, my love," he whispers. He deposits the tray on the night table, puts his hands on my waist, and lowers me to the bed, climbing on top of me. When his lips touch mine, they are more aggressive, like he can't get enough of me.

I roll us over and am on top of him. I kiss him just as aggressively, more desperately, showing him how much I love and appreciate him. How much he means to me. How I don't want to ever lose him. I want him to understand that all he does for me—for us—all he sacrifices, is worth it. Because our love knows no bounds or limitations.

His hands roam all over my body. As his lips travel down my neck, causing heat to shoot throughout me, I place my palm on his chest and gently push him a few inches back. "I'll be late for work."

His lips latch back on mine. Between kisses, he mutters, "Screw work."

A laugh bursts out of my mouth. "Did you just say, 'Screw work?'"

His heavy eyes suddenly fill with shock. "Forgive me. Did I say something inappropriate?"

I giggle. "No. Where did you hear that from?"

"From the TV. The man spoke in such a manner."

"Come here." I haul him toward me. "You are so cute. Human slang works for you."

"I spoke it in the right manner?"

I giggle again. "Yes, you did."

He pecks my forehead. "Screw work and stay here with me in the bed."

I gnaw on my bottom lip. Oh, how tempting. There's nothing more

I want to do than spend the entire day in bed with Damarian. But Uncle Jim would kill me if I were to ditch. The surfing class is his baby, not to mention lessons are almost over for the summer.

Do I spend my morning teaching little kids to surf, or do I spend it with my totally sexy merman?

Damarian touches both sides of my face. "I declare myself to you, Cassie Price. For all eternity. I wish to seal our bond."

My mouth drops. My heartbeat pounds in my head. When I try to speak, only a croak comes out. I swallow a few times before I find my voice. "You...you mean...are you saying...?"

He nods, his eyes shining. "Yes, Cassie. I am prepared."

I just stare at him, completely dumfounded. I have to be dreaming. He said—he wants. After waiting so long...after begging him all this time.

I throw my arms around him and yank him to me.

Screw work.

Chapter Five

The bed feels like a cloud. My body wakes up, but my eyes stay asleep. I don't remember ever being this comfortable.

It might have something to do with the man lying beside me, his arm draped over my stomach as he holds me close. His soft breath tickles my ear. I turn to my other side so I can look into that face that is mine and will be mine forever. My movement causes him to stir, and his eyes open.

As soon as they land on me, the biggest smile I've even seen crawls on his face. He reaches toward my forehead to brush some hair off. "Cassie," he murmurs.

My cheeks heat up. "Damarian."

Our gazes are locked on one another. There are so many emotions swirling around in his eyes. Everything he feels for me. It's like he's baring his soul.

"How do you feel?" he asks, stroking the side of my face.

My entire face and neck flame. "Really good. You?" My eyes search his. This was his first time.

His grin couldn't be wider. "Magnificent."

A sigh I didn't know I was holding leaves my mouth. "Yay." I laugh.

He laughs, too, then leans forward to press a light kiss on my lips. "I am so happy, my sweet Cassie. I did not know I could feel in this manner." He nuzzles my nose. "We are mated."

I can't believe we've actually reached this point. What he and I shared…it was the most amazing thing I've ever experienced in my life. Now we're officially official, and nothing and no one can keep us apart.

I take hold of his arms as I stare into his face. "I love you."

"As do I." He brings his lips to mine again and gives me a sweet, loving kiss. When we come apart, I realize my lips are extremely dry. I lick them a few times, but they are still parched. Damarian's eyes move to them for a second before focusing on my eyes. "What is the matter?"

"It's nothing." I swallow. My throat is so dry I think I'm going to choke. "I'm just really thirsty."

"I will acquire a drink for you," he says, sitting up. The blanket drops and I see him. All of him—his naked body. I've seen him naked many times, and considering what we just did a few hours ago, I shouldn't feel embarrassed, but I do. It means something different now, something huge. All this is exciting, but pretty scary.

Damarian must notice my discomfort, because he looks down at himself. His eyes fill with guilt. "Forgive me, Cassie. Would you like me to—"

"No," I assure him. "It's cool. It's all cool." I wave my hand, feeling another blush. "Walk around naked. Yeah, it's fine with me."

His eyes are on me for a few seconds before he chuckles. He gathers me to his chest and kisses my temple. "How sweet you are."

As a merman, he doesn't understand what nakedness means to humans. I felt a little uneasy with Kyle, but my relationship with him was so gradual that I had time to mentally prepare myself. I fell in love with Damarian so fast, and I feel so much stronger about him than I did about Kyle. I wish Damarian and I could take things slower, but at the same time, I want to take things fast, too.

Naked, Damarian makes his way downstairs to the kitchen. I sit up, cloaking myself in the blanket. That's when I feel a pounding headache. I rub my forehead. It's so strong that I whimper.

A few seconds later, his hands are on my face. His voice fills my ears. "Cassie? Are you all right?"

My eyes immediately spring to the glass of water in his hand. I grab it and gulp down the water. The headache lessens, though I still feel a light pounding. The water is refreshing. "Thanks," I tell him.

He sits down near me, his hand still on my face. "Do you feel ill?"

I close my eyes and take in some air, letting it out slowly. The headache is gone. I open my eyes and find Damarian's worried ones examining every inch of my face. "Thanks, I'm better now," I say. "I just needed a drink."

He nods unsurely, his eyebrows creased with concern. "You were pale."

I force a smile. "I'm okay. Don't worry." I kiss his forehead.

"Forgive me if I behaved toward you like you are a fry. I do not wish to see you ill or in pain. It causes me to feel ill."

I rest my forehead against his. "Thanks. But I'm really okay."

My phone rings. My heart sinks. Great, I know who's calling, and I don't want to deal with him. Maybe Damarian should explore the ocean and see if he can find a secluded island we can run away to. Then I won't have to deal with Uncle Jim.

I stretch for my phone to confirm it really is him. I let it go to voicemail.

"Is that not important?" Damarian asks.

"Too important," I mumble.

He looks confused.

"Uncle Jim," I explain. "He's probably busting a vein."

He nods slowly. "For you did not go to work."

"Yeah. But screw work, right?" I smirk.

He smiles widely. "Mating with you is wonderful."

Another blush creeps up my face. Damarian can be really direct sometimes. I hope one day I won't feel this embarrassed.

"It is," I say, then hide my face under the blanket.

Damarian's arms come around me and he holds me close to him. My nose is smashed into his chest with the blanket between us. "Do not be ashamed. Mating is a beautiful activity between two beings."

I pull it off my face and stare at his chest because I can't meet his eyes. "I know. I'm sorry for acting so weird. It's just a little nerve-wracking for me. It's not easy for me to be so open."

He tucks his hand under my chin and raises it so our eyes meet. "I understand. I wish for you to feel comfortable. I do not want to cause you any pain."

"You're not." I push him to the bed and climb on top of him. With a grin, I say, "And I'll prove it to you."

Chapter Six

After Damarian swims in the pool, he settles down on the couch with a bag of pretzels. I swipe my keys off the counter. "I'll be back soon, okay?" I say.

"Are you certain you do not wish for me to accompany you?"

I wave my hand. "Thanks, but it's okay. You don't need to see Uncle Jim lose it."

He throws a pretzel in the air and tries to catch it in his mouth. It hits his nose and bounces on the couch. "Will he be terribly upset?"

Probably. I shrug.

"How do you humans say it? 'Good luck?'"

"Yeah."

"Good luck, my love."

"Thanks." I give him a quick kiss and head to the beach. I plan on getting my head chewed off by my uncle, but I need to make a very important stop first. I enter Misty's Juice Bar and hear Leah's voice. She's yelling at this high school kid who is under the impression that their names are written together in the stars.

I laugh to myself and watch for a few seconds, debating whether I should continue enjoying the show or take her out of her misery. I choose the latter. As soon as she sees me, her eyes light up like I'm her savior.

"Cassie!" she practically cries out. "Scram, kid." She shoves a smoothie toward the guy and pushes him aside, then reaches for my arm and yanks me closer. The kid drops a few bills on the counter, places a few more in the "Tips" bowl, and walks out with his smoothie, his head raised in confidence.

I drop down on one of the stools. "I see someone is persistent."

She groans. "Were we like that at that age?"

"You do know we're only a year or two older than him."

She walks to the smoothie machine to work on an order for another customer. "True, but don't you feel like you've grown so much since we graduated high school? I feel like I'm twenty years older."

I know what she means. I also feel like that. I just committed myself to a guy for the rest of my life. If that doesn't say maturity, I don't know what does.

"Want anything?" Leah asks.

"Yeah, thanks. I'm so thirsty."

She works on my smoothie and hands it to me. I grab a straw and chug half of it down. Leah holds out her hands. "Hey, the world's not coming to an end yet."

I close my eyes and almost moan in pleasure as the liquid continues to slide down my throat, cooling every inch of me.

"Should I prepare another one?" she asks.

I finish the last bit and shake my head.

She rests her elbows on the counter and looks at me. Her eyes narrow. "What happened?"

"What do you mean?"

Her eyes narrow even more and her eyebrows scrunch together. "No, seriously. Except for the freaky gulping-your-entire-smoothie-down-in-less-than-two-minutes-with-no-brain-freeze thing, something

Merman's Touch

happened. You look different." She raises an eyebrow in a you-are-so-busted way.

My cheeks burn. Is it stamped on my forehead that Damarian and I did it? I mean, Leah's my best friend and can read me too well, but is it really that obvious?

I lean forward. "Okay. Something *did* happen."

She rubs her hands together. "Ooh. I love me some juice." She cups her hand around her ear and bends forward.

"Damarian and I had sex," I whisper.

"You WHAT?"

"Shh." I motion her with my hands to keep her voice down.

She raises the counter and runs out, grabbing my arm and dragging me out with her. She brings me to a secluded area on the beach. "Okay. Tell me *everything*!"

I do. When I'm done, she squeals, takes hold of my arms, and jumps around. "I can't believe it!"

I jump along with her, and we spin around in a circle, laughing like we're two drunken girls on the beach. I trip over some sand and we crash to the ground, tumbling over each other. Still laughing, we roll onto our backs and stare at the sky. The sun is not too strong this morning and the sky is clear.

"Was he a human or a merman?" Leah asks.

My head snaps to hers. "What? Of course a human! I told you we were in my bed. And, um, sleeping with him when he's a *fish*? That's a little…weird."

She shrugs. "You never thought about it? I'm pretty sure your man would rather be a merman when he does the deed. He does have the works in that form, doesn't he?"

"Yeah, of course. But I never…I haven't thought about *that*." And I'm not sure I want to. Does Damarian want to be in his true form? I don't know what it would be like. I'm a human and he's a merman. It wouldn't be right. Would it?

I decide to change the subject. "I was so awkward after. I don't know why. Most of the time I feel so comfortable around him, but sometimes I feel shy."

She's quiet for a few seconds. "It's probably because you really like him. This was a huge step for you guys and you wanted it to be perfect. It's normal to freak out."

"Yeah, I guess. And it was also his first time."

"Not to mention you basically married him."

"Yeah." I flatten my hands to my sides and gather some sand.

"Was it good?"

My whole body heats up. "Amazing."

She grins. "So fishboy knows what he's doing?"

I sit up. "He was so cute, Leah. So nervous and excited, but mostly nervous. Just thinking about it makes me want to hug him." I draw my knees to my chest. "I wish it was my first time, too. It would have made it more special."

Leah sits up. "Don't think like that. I'm sure Damarian was glad his woman had some experience." She raises her eyebrows suggestively.

I throw some sand on her lap.

"Hey!" She grabs a handful.

"Not at my eyes!" I jump to my feet and race around the beach, with Leah chasing after me. After a few minutes, something gets caught in my throat and I fall to my knees, coughing.

Leah huffs as she catches up to me. "Damn, I need to work out more." She wipes sweat off her forehead.

"I'm so *thirsty*."

She snorts. "No one told you to run around like that. Oh, crap." She smacks her forehead. "I just ditched work. My ass is going to get fired because of you." She reaches for my hand and hauls me to my feet. "Come, I'll make you another smoothie."

***

To say Uncle Jim was furious would be an understatement. He told me I should thank the sacred sand that he's my uncle, or else I'd kiss my job goodbye. I do feel guilty that I left him and my students hanging, but…yeah. I would not have traded what Damarian and I shared this morning for anything.

Damarian's flipping through a photo album when I walk in. His eyes brighten. "Cassie!"

The fact that he's so happy to see me makes me feel really good. I join him on the couch and kiss him. I look at the album that's opened on his knees. "I hope there are no embarrassing pictures in there."

"Is it customary for humans to capture their reflections and place them in books?"

"Yeah. It's making memories."

He nods slowly. "I understand." He points to a picture of Mom holding me as a baby at the hospital. "Is this you as a fry?"

I nod.

"Humans appear quite peculiar as fry." He flips through the pages. "Studying your growth is fascinating." He closes the album and places it on the coffee table. "Was your uncle upset?"

I wave my hand. "Yeah, but it's no big deal."

He takes my hands in his. "Forgive me if I am to blame for causing a rift in your family."

"A rift? No, it's okay, Damarian. Really. I told you Uncle Jim is high maintenance. Besides." I play with some of his hair. "I'd choose you over my students any day." I kiss his forehead. "I'm going to grab a drink. The smoothies Leah gave me just made me more thirsty. Want some juice or water?"

"No, thank you, my love."

I return to the living room with my glass of water and sit down near Damarian. "I need to tell you something," I say. I've been pushing it off long enough and he needs to know this. I can't keep it from him.

I move a few inches away from him so I can give myself some space as I formulate the words in my head. I'm so scared for his reaction. "I hope you won't be upset with me."

Damarian's eyebrows furrow. He runs his fingers through my hair. "Never, my sweet Cassie."

I take a sip from my water, then clear my throat. "So you remember when I first rescued you and helped you get back in the ocean?"

"Certainly I recall. It is something I shall never forget, for it brought us together." He kisses my temple. "What a spectacular day it was."

"Yeah. Um. So." I clear my throat again. "I didn't think I'd ever see you again. So I told Leah. She's known about you all this time."

His expression changes. His face falls. I see the emotions racing across his face. Confusion, disbelief, betrayal. "Leah is aware I am a child of the sea?"

"I didn't want to tell you she knew. I didn't want to upset you. Had I known you'd come back, I wouldn't have told her."

He doesn't say anything. His lips are pressed in a tight line and his gaze is locked on the floor. He doesn't look mad, just confused like he's not sure what he should be feeling.

I take his hand and slide my fingers through his. "You know you can trust Leah. In fact, she begged me to tell you that she knows. She doesn't want to have any secrets."

"I understand, Cassie. You share a unique bond with Leah. It is natural that you would confide in her. I gather you were baffled by the appearance of a child of the sea."

"You have no idea."

He pulls me to his chest and his lips trail down my neck. "Thank you for telling me." He continues brushing his lips down my throat.

"Damarian?"

"Yes?"

"Did you talk to your parents about coming on land?"

His lips draw away from my skin and his eyes meet mine. They are full of regret. I guess I know the answer.

He tilts my head up so our eyes are on one another. "Do not fret. In time, I am certain they will wish to come on land." He can't hide the uncertainty from his eyes

I nod, though my throat constricts.

He puts his arm around me and holds me close, his lips skimming down the side of my face. This gesture alone tells me everything. We'll stay together no matter what, no matter who tries to stop us. Hopefully, his family will accept me one day—accept us. But we're not going to live our lives constantly wondering what the future holds. All that matters is right now, that we're together and happy.

Chapter Seven

I park the car in Dad's driveway and take a deep breath. I've been here a few times, but I've never brought Damarian. I really want Dad to like him, and for Damarian to like my father. Having the love of your life's parents not accept you is not a good feeling. I don't want to put Damarian through that. Mom adores him, and I hope Dad will feel the same.

Damarian lays his hand on mine. "All will be well."

I force out a small laugh. "*I* should be the one calming you down."

His eyes smile. "Humans have extremely volatile emotions."

I slap his chest. "I'm sure merpeople freak out just as much as humans. You're always a gentleman and put my needs before yours." I stretch my neck to give him a quick kiss. "And that's what makes you so damn irresistible."

He moves to pull me closer, but I sit back. "I don't think it will make a good impression on my dad if he finds us making out in his driveway." At least, that's what I think. I didn't have a dad when I went through the teenage years, where I'd fight with him about the guys I wanted to date. The thought of what could have been makes my heart sting a little, but I push it away. All that matters is that I have a relationship with my father now. I can't wallow in the past.

Merman's Touch

"His wife, Sheila—my stepmom—makes these lemon cookies," I say. "They are so good. They're very chewy, so if my dad says something that makes you uncomfortable, eat the cookies, okay?"

His head bobs with a nod. "Are we informing him that I am a child of the sea?"

I shake my head. "I think we need to hold off on that one for now. My dad's head is still reeling from the shock that he and I have reconnected after all these years." I don't want anything to keep us from forming a close relationship. I feel like I lost my dad for six years. Telling him my boyfriend is really a merman would definitely put a strain on things.

We get out of the car and, holding hands, step up to the door. Just as I raise my hand to knock, the door flies open and Ruthie rams herself into me, slamming her face into my stomach. "Cassie's here!"

I cough and pat her head. "You're going to kill me, kid."

She grins up at me. Then her eyes move to Damarian. "Who's that?"

"This is Damian. My boyfriend."

Her nose twists. "Ew."

She's only seven and thinks boys have cooties. I pinch her cheek. "Just you wait. When you bring your boyfriend to meet me, I'll say the same thing."

Her nose twists even more. "Gross."

Laughing, I take Damarian's hand and lead him into the house. I scrutinize his face. He looks confident, but I see the anxiety in his eyes. I squeeze his hand.

Sheila and my dad are in the kitchen, putting together a small snack. Dad takes me in his arms and kisses my cheek. His wife does the same. "We're so happy to have you."

"Thanks," I say, my lips feeling dry. Damn, I need a drink *again*.

Dad's eyes land on Damarian. "You must be Damian." He holds out his hand. Without hesitating, Damarian shakes it with a strong grip. I smile to myself, thinking back to the first time he encountered a hand shake.

Sheila elbows me. "He's hot."

My heart swells as I watch him talk to my dad. He's trying so hard to make a good impression, sometimes stuttering over his words as he attempts to sound more human. I wish I could pull him into a closet and kiss him.

My throat is so dry I feel like I might die if I don't get some liquid in my system. "Can I please have a drink?" I ask.

"Sure," Sheila says. "Soda, tea, water, juice?"

"Water, please. Thanks."

She hands me a glass.

Eight-year-old Bobby saunters into the kitchen, his eyes glued to his handheld game. "Hey, you," I say. What he gives me can hardly count as a nod. I ruffle his hair.

"What is this?" Damarian asks, pointing to the object in Bobby's hand.

I stand still. As a twenty-year-old guy, he should know what a handheld game is. My dad and Sheila give him confused looks.

"Raiders of the Moon," Bobby pipes up. "It's about these kids who land on the moon. You have to fight the Moon Men, see? And you get lots of treasure, and get stronger. You have to be careful because the Moon Men can steal your treasure." Bobby holds the thing out to Damarian as he plays. Damarian watches it with eyes bigger than the lemon cookies sitting on the counter.

"That is fascinating," he says.

Dad and Sheila exchange a look.

I clear my throat. "The cookies look amazing, Sheila."

Merman's Touch

She smiles. "Please help yourselves."

I grab two and hand the plate to Damarian. His eyes meet mine for a few seconds, and we share a silent understanding. These cookies are our weapons. Damarian takes three, bites one, and his eyes look like they're going to explode. "These are scrumptious!" He puts the whole thing in his mouth and chomps it down.

"Damian, be caref—"

He grips his throat and heaves a little, his face turning red, his eyes tearing. I shove my glass into his hand, and he chugs down the water. His body relaxes and his face returns to its natural, translucent color.

He's still not used to human food. He's been eating fish all his life and isn't used to the kind of foods that can dry out your throat, like bread, grains, and baked goods.

"You okay?" Dad asks, clapping his back.

Damarian nods, still chewing some of the cookie. I reach to place a quick kiss on his cheek.

"Gross," Ruthie says.

Sheila elbows me again. "He's adorable. And the way you take care of him is just precious. I can tell you two love each other very much."

"We do," I say softly.

The six of us settle down in the living room with the refreshments. Ruthie bounces on my knees. "Mom said she'll let you teach me to surf when I'm older."

"I'd love to."

"And me, too!" Bobby says.

"Of course."

The room grows silent.

Dad shifts on his recliner. "So tell me, Damian. Are you starting college in the Fall?"

Damarian's eyes trek to mine. He looks alarmed. Damn, I should have anticipated this question. We prepped a bit before we left the house, but Damarian assured me he would be fine.

"Um, maybe," I say. "He's still trying to figure things out."

"What do your parents do?" Sheila asks.

This we prepared. Damarian answers confidently, "My parents catch fish. Forgive me—I'm sorry. My parents are fishermen."

Dad's face brightens. "I used to be a fisherman. Maybe I know them."

Oh, crap. Did that seriously slip my mind? "Probably not," I quickly say. "So, um, Sheila. How's the basement coming along?"

As she tells me the struggles they're dealing with, Damarian and I exchange a glance. I give him a reassuring nod and smile. We'll get through this.

But when I look at Dad, I see he's watching Damarian suspiciously. I swallow. Will he accept Damarian? Or does he suspect something's off with him?

"Do you have a job, Damian?" Dad asks.

"Dad," I mutter. "Stop interrogating him."

"I'm just trying to get to know him better, Cass Bass."

I'm about to tell him he doesn't need to make up for the times he should have been playing police over my potential boyfriends back in high school—not that I had many—but Damarian says, "I will search for work."

Dad nods. "That's great. What kind of work are you looking for?"

Again, Damarian's gaze shoots to mine, totally alarmed. Well, if you can find a place that doesn't require a high school diploma…that would be great.

Dad scans Damarian from top to bottom. "You're in good shape. Do you have any experience in construction?"

Damarian looks like Dad asked him a difficult math equation.

Merman's Touch

"Er...sure?" I say.

"A friend of mine is looking to hire a couple of guys. I can talk to him, if you'd like."

"Really, Dad? That would be great!"

"Anything for my girl." Dad winks.

"Hey!" Ruthie says.

"I'm sorry, sweetie. Anything for my *other* girl." He winks to her, too. I squeeze her tight and bounce her on my knees.

Suddenly, my throat gets parched again. I stand, placing Ruthie on the couch. "Please excuse me. I'm going to get some water."

"There's juice and tea here," Sheila offers, gesturing to the refreshments on the table.

"Thanks, but I'd like water."

In the kitchen, I fill up a glass with cold water and take a long sip. Why am I so thirsty all the time?

"Cass?"

I spin around and find Dad standing behind me. "Hey, Dad."

He steps closer and leans against the counter. His eyes are locked on mine.

"What?" I ask, a hint of fear rising in my stomach.

He folds his arms. "This Damian guy..."

"Dad. Don't call him 'this Damian guy.' C'mon."

His eyes narrow a bit. "How well do you know him?"

A lump forms in my throat. I drink some more water. "Really well. Why are you asking me all these questions and being hard on him? Do you not like him or something?"

"I like him. He seems good to you."

"He is. He's really a great guy. And different."

His forehead wrinkles. "Different?"

I want to bang my head against the counter. Why did I say that? "I mean...you know. He doesn't really care what other people think and likes to do whatever he wants and he's just really sweet and warm and caring and romantic. He's cool like that." If I babble any more, I'll lose my vocal chords.

"Where is he from originally?"

The middle of the ocean? I shrug.

"He has a distinct accent."

I take another swig of my water. Too bad I didn't bring a cookie with me.

Dad moves closer to me and rests his hands on my shoulders. "Cassie." I look into his face. There's concern and wariness floating in his eyes. "Are you happy with him?" he asks.

"Of course, Dad. I wouldn't be with him if I wasn't. I..." I clear my throat. "I really love him. Like really, really."

His eyes soften for a bit, but then they get guarded. "He's treating you okay?"

"Dad!"

He pats my shoulders and takes a step back, shaking his head. "I'm sorry. I'm probably behaving like an overprotective dad right now, worrying about my little girl. As long as you're happy, I'm happy."

I rub his arm. "I am. Very."

He nods and kisses the top of my head.

Chapter Eight

Damarian lifts the blanket and climbs into my bed. His leg touches mine, causing electricity to shoot through every cell in my body. His scent envelops my senses, a mix of masculine soap and salt water. Butterflies gather in the pit of my stomach and chills crawl all over me. I wonder if he'll have the same effect on me sixty years from now.

"May I read this to you?" he asks, holding out a notebook.

He's been having a much more difficult time writing than reading, so I advised him to keep a journal where he could write anything he wants. I promised I wouldn't read it. The fact that he wants to share some of his private thoughts with me sends a jolt of excitement up my spine.

"Sure." I gulp down some water from the glass on my night table, then sit up and give him my full attention.

"It most likely contains many errors. My apologies in advance."

I wave my head. "Don't worry about it."

He nods, his face twisted in nerves. I rub my hand on his knuckles. He takes a deep breath and lets it out slowly. After flipping through the pages, he settles on one that has a lot words crossed out. Like he's been working on it for days. He looks at me, and I nod.

Holding the notebook tightly, he begins, stuttering a bit, "When I was a fry, I did not understand love. I did not understand duty. I was not aware that they were not one and the same. I was told it was my duty to take the crown. I was told it was my duty to take the princess as my mate. No longer a fry, I dreamed of many things. I longed to meet a female, one that would take my heart. One that would gaze upon me in a manner in which no other being would gaze upon me. One that I would wish only to please. One that I would love and cherish for all eternity." He swallows. "I witnessed her sailing on the waves. She was a creature like no other, her beauty and grace captivating my soul. I was taught not to engage with her, for she was dangerous and would only cause me harm. But as she sank to the bottom of the sea, the life gradually leaving her body, I knew what I was required to do—save her at all costs."

Damarian looks at me. "Do you wish for me to stop?"

I realize my eyes are brimming with tears and my hand is lying over my heart. Blinking, I shake my head. "Please continue."

He nods and focuses his attention back on the notebook. "I feared I was too late, for she lay unconscious on the stone. I did not understand the ways of the humans. I did not wish for her to die. The very thought caused my chest pain. I took her hand in mine, felt the warmth of her skin, and I knew deep in my heart that this human would live, because I wanted it to be so."

Damarian glances at me, like he's worried this will offend or hurt me. I nod for him to go on.

"She stirred," he continues reading. "She opened her eyes. Such beautiful eyes, the color of the earth, which I did not see often. In that moment, I understood there is a fine difference between love and duty. And that it was my duty to find love." He raises his eyes to mine. "And I have found it in my sweet Cassie Price."

He closes the notebook and grins, his lips quivering slightly. I taste salt on my lips. After sweeping my arm across my eyes, I take him in my arms and squeeze him to me. "That was so beautiful, Damarian. Thanks so much for sharing it with me. For a merman, you know how to melt a human girl's heart."

He turns his head so his lips graze my ear. "I am glad you enjoyed it."

"Very much." I bring my lips to his and give him a deep, loving kiss. We fall on the bed and continue to kiss each other with nothing but passion and urgency, like no matter how many times we kiss, it's never enough and it never will be enough. Even if we live a million years. My nails dig into his skin and his hands knead my back. I moan as he fills me with feelings only he can give me.

When our lips come apart, our breathing heavy, our chests heaving, we just stare into each other's eyes, reading what lies in our hearts. I stroke his cheek. "You're such a wonderful person, Damarian. I feel so lucky to have you."

"You are mistaken, my love. It is I who is the lucky one."

I shake my head. "No, I am."

"It is I."

"Me."

"I."

I laugh and roll us over so I'm on top. "Damarian?"

"Yes?"

"I'm sorry about what happened with my dad."

He places both of his hands on the sides of my face. "To what are you referring?"

"He was being very hard on you."

"It is all right. I find I like him very much."

"You do?" I ask, totally shocked. I thought he scared Damarian away. I reach for the glass of water and drink.

"Certainly." His eyebrows crease. "But I do not understand what he was referring to when he suggested a location where I am to work."

I sit up and cross my legs. Damarian sits up, too. "Construction," I say. "It's building houses and stuff."

He scratches the back of his neck. "It did not occur to me that humans build their houses." He laughs sheepishly. "How little knowledge I have of humans."

"It's okay. I love teaching you."

"And I love learning from you." He kisses the back of my hand. "This building houses sounds intriguing."

I avert my gaze from him. When Dad first mentioned being able to get Damarian a job in construction, I was excited. He's not the type of person to be cooped up all day in an office. But then something dawned on me. Damarian being out in the sun practically the whole day. Heat and lack of water causes his body to change into a merman sooner than usual, which is about twelve hours. He could always work part time, but what if something goes wrong? What if he desperately needs a pool?

But I can't take care of him my whole life, can I? What am I supposed to do?

Damarian leans back with his arm around me. "The prospect of working and providing us with pay thrills me."

I can't help but giggle. "Providing us with money," I correct.

He kisses me. "Forgive me. Providing us with money."

He lies down and tucks me close to him. After a few minutes, I feel his breathing getting heavy. My eyes are wide awake as thoughts and worries crowd my head. Living in the real world just plain sucks. I can't keep Damarian inside and protect him forever. This is just another thing we're going to have to figure out.

I rest my chin on his shoulder and stare straight ahead. The future

Merman's Touch

is one big unknown, but I'm really glad I have someone to travel down that road with.

Chapter Nine

After dressing into my wetsuit and tying my hair into two braids, I head downstairs to make breakfast. Damarian is still sleeping, and it's my turn to treat him like a king. I've been his queen for too long.

I tap my finger against my chin as I scan the contents in my pantry and refrigerator. I settle on omelets, but this time I'm spicing things up with a recipe I found online. As I work on the food, I hear movement from upstairs. A few minutes later, Damarian comes down, rubbing his eyes. His hair is disheveled and his pajama pants hang low on his hips.

"Someone had a good night's rest," I tease.

"You are the cause of it. With you in my arms, it is possible for me to sleep for all eternity."

I smile. "Please sit down."

He eyes the omelets frying in the pan. "I wish to prepare breakfast for you. I very much enjoy it."

My heart soars. "I know. But I want to do this for you."

"Are you certain? For I don't mind—"

I walk over to him and kiss his cheek. "A relationship is about giving and taking. Let me give to you, okay?"

"All right." He puts his arm around me and tugs me to him. Leaning in close, he whispers, "Thank you," in my ear. Then his lips rub against it. I shiver, despite the warmth radiating off his naked chest. Once he steps away, I feel cold.

When the omelets are done, I slide them into plates and join Damarian at the table. "They look scrumptious," he says.

"Thanks."

We clank forks and dig in. I have to say, this is delicious. The flavors work perfectly together, hitting all my taste buds. Damarian's devouring his omelet like he's been starving for days. I smile as I watch him, feeling giddy like I did the first time I cooked for him. It's strange how even the smallest things like cooking for my fishman can make me feel so good.

Once he's a third in, I ask, "Would you like another?"

He lifts his head. "If it is no bother."

"Nothing's a bother for you." I walk over to the stove and get to work.

Just as I'm folding the omelet, Damarian's arms come around my middle from behind. He digs his lips into the side of my neck. "You are too kind, Cassie. My love for you is as vast as the sea."

I kiss the top of his head. "My love for you runs all the way to Earth's core."

His lips skim across my jaw. "I do not know what that is."

"I'll tell you all about it later."

We return to the table, Damarian with his omelet and me with a banana. "We need to go to the mall after work," I tell him. "There are still a lot of things you need to buy."

When he decided to remain on land the first time, we bought only a few articles of clothing and other necessities, since he planned to stay only for a short while. But now that he'll be here for a long time, we'll need to buy other things, like another pair of shoes, more clothes, and whatever else he may need or want.

"All right," he says. "Thank you."

We get to the beach and I start my class. But halfway through my lesson, I start feeling dizzy and nauseous. I fall to my knees, grabbing hold of my head and heaving.

"Cassie?" Damarian's scent fills my nose. His arms come around me. "Are you all right?"

"Miss Cassie?" Timmy asks.

"I'm thirsty," I moan. And nauseous and dizzy, but I don't want to worry Damarian.

"I will acquire water for you," he says.

"You can have from my water bottle," Timmy says, shoving it in my face.

I smile. "Thanks." I don't mean to, but I chug all of it down. Timmy's eyes widen at the empty bottle. "Sorry," I say.

"It's okay," he says with a wide grin.

Damarian takes my arm and helps me to my feet. "You are ill. Perhaps we should go home."

I look at my students standing in front of me, their faces pinched with worry and confusion. I can't leave them hanging like this. "I'll be fine," I assure Damarian. "Don't worry."

I feel okay when I continue the lesson, but about fifteen minutes later, the nausea returns and my head throbs. All I want to do is curl up in bed, but I owe it to my students to finish the lesson. I push my pain aside and get through it.

When the lesson is done, I head back to Damarian, forcing a smile. I'm about to tell him to wipe the concern from his face, when I feel a sharp pain near my pelvis. I double over, and Damarian catches me in his arms.

"I'm fine," I tell him.

He searches my eyes. "How I worry over you, my sweet Cassie."

Merman's Touch

I touch his cheek. "Can you please get me a drink?"

He nods before lowering me to the sand and heading for the drink stand. I force away the tears of fear that are forming in my eyes. What's going on with me?

Damarian rushes back with a water bottle, uncaps it, and hands it to me. I thank him before swallowing half of it down. The headache disappears and so do the pelvic pain and nausea. "All better, see? It's probably the heat."

Damarian doesn't say anything as he studies the other people on the beach. I know what he's thinking—that they don't look sick like me. I take his hand. "Come. We have shopping to do, remember?"

As we're on our way home, my palms get clammy. The nausea comes back, but this time it's more intense. I jab the key into the lock and throw the door open. I make it to the bathroom just in time.

I slump against the wall, my eyes heavy and ready to close any second. But then I see Damarian standing in the doorway. I've never seen him look so scared. I raise my hand toward him. "It's probably a stomach virus. Totally normal for humans."

It would explain the nausea and thirst, since I'm probably dehydrated. I think. I hope.

Damarian gets down on his knees before me and sandwiches his hand between mine. "I do not enjoy seeing you ill."

"I'm sorry. I don't enjoy being ill."

I want him to smile, but he just looks even more worried.

"It's a virus, Damarian. I'll be fine. I just need to rest and drink lots of fluids and wait for it to pass."

He nods unsurely. "Shall I take you to bed?"

My head is spinning and I'm still nauseous. "Bring me to the couch?"

Lifting me in his arms, he carries me to the couch. He lays me down, then throws a blanket over me. He sits down on the corner and kisses my forehead.

I smile weakly. "You're acting very human now."

He presses his cheek to mine. "I wish to take care of you."

My eyes start to droop. The last thing I feel is his soft lips on my skin.

***

My stomach is rumbling so hard that I wake up. Peering at the clock, I see it's nearly three AM. If I don't put something in my mouth, I think I might die.

After sitting up, I realize I'm on the couch. Damarian is slumped on the recliner adjacent to me. The events of this afternoon come back to me. My stomach virus. Have I really been asleep all this time?

My stomach rumbles again, so sharp it knocks me to my feet. I head to the kitchen. After flicking on the light, I open the pantry. The only things in there are cans of sardines.

The fridge is stocked with lots of food, but as I peer at the different options, my nose twitches. Nothing appeals to me. It's weird to be starving but not in the mood for anything.

I close the door and straighten up. That's when I see the mess on the floor.

That's weird. Why are opened sardine cans littering my kitchen? Did Damarian come down for a snack?

"Damarian?" I call.

No answer.

I look into the living room. He's sound asleep. I get back to the kitchen and stare at the cans. If Damarian didn't eat the sardines, then who…?

Something smells. It's too close to me. I sniff my hands and yelp in disgust. "Ew, fish!" Why do my hands stink? I hate all kinds of fish,

Merman's Touch

except for the one who stole my heart.

My head thumps as my eyes move from the sardine cans to the pantry. Images fly through my head. Me standing at the panty, my hand reaching for one of the sardine cans. Scooping a handful and dumping them into my mouth. Moaning like I've never tasted anything so good in my life. Tossing the can aside and reaching for another.

I stumble back. "No," I whisper. "It couldn't have been…"

I fall to the floor and grab one of the cans. There's nothing in here except for a small fish stuck to the side of the metal. My stomach recoils as I take it in my hand. Closing my eyes, I throw it into my mouth.

And spit it out in the garbage. I rush to the sink for a glass of water. Did I eat those sardines? How could I when I can't stand the taste of them?

The extreme thirst, the nausea, the dizzy spells, the headaches, and now a craving for fish. My heart sinks. Maybe something really is wrong with me.

With shaky knees, I go up to my room and plop down in front of my computer. Placing my hands over the keys, I type in Google, "I'm always thirsty and have headaches." A few links come up. I click on a medical one. My eyes widen and my insides swirl as I see the possible diseases. I minimize the screen and grab hold of stomach.

After a few minutes of heavy breathing, I click back on my Google search page and type in, "Sudden craving for fish." I check out a few sites, but I don't find anything useful. I fall back in my chair.

Maybe it's time I make an appointment to see my doctor.

Chapter Ten

When I open my eyes the next morning, Leah's face is in mine. I yelp and nearly fall off my bed.

"Morning," she greets.

I blink a few times. "What time is it?" I ask, stifling a yawn.

"Almost eight." She touches my forehead. "Your sweet merboyfriend told me you're sick, though I don't think you have a fever." She leans in close. "I think human illnesses scare the crap out of him. He thinks you're going to die." She holds out a container. "I made you some chicken soup."

My headache is starting to come back. "You cooked?"

"Fine, my mom made it. But I was the one who brought it."

The smell reaches me, but instead of my mouth watering, bile rises in my throat.

Seeing my expression, Leah lowers the container onto my night table. "Maybe later."

I scan the area and find Damarian standing in the doorway, his eyes uncertain, and again, full of concern. He approaches me and gets down on his knees, taking my hand. "How do you feel?"

"Fine," I lie. "Can I have a drink, please?"

"Certainly." He dashes down the steps.

Merman's Touch

I try to sit up, but the pain in my head is so strong, my vision gets spotty. I fall back with a groan.

Leah whistles. "Damn, are you sick." She springs back. "Are stomach flus contagious?"

"No idea," I mumble. "God, I feel like hell." Bile rises in my throat again. I leap off my bed and grab the garbage bin from under my desk. I puke. When I'm done, I fold myself into a ball on the floor as tears seep out of my eyes.

"Cassie?"

"I've had stomach viruses before, but they've never been like this."

"What are your symptoms?" she asks, her voice holding a hint of panic.

"My head kills." I cover my face with my arms. "I'm thirsty all the time—but only for water. I'm dizzy and last night, I had this crazy craving for fish and ate a crapload of sardines. You know how much I hate fish. I'm nauseous, and as you just witnessed, I puked."

She gasps. "*Cassie.*"

The hairs on my arms stand up at the sound of her voice. I lower my arms. "What?"

Damarian runs back into the room. He crouches down near me, holding out a glass of water.

I'm too nauseous and weak to accept it, even though my body's begging for it. I just continue to lie on the floor.

"Um, Damarian?" Leah asks.

"Yes?"

"Do you mind if I speak to Cassie privately?"

I open an eye. "Why?"

She gives me a face. "It's just one of those things I need to talk to you in private…"

Glancing at Damarian, I see he's confused and a little hurt, but he nods and leaves the room. Leah scoots closer to me. "Cassie?"

The sunlight peeking through my window makes it hard for me to keep my eyes opened. "What?"

"You…you're nauseous. You threw up."

A feeling of terror nestles in the pit of my stomach. "It's a virus," I say.

Her face gets even paler. "Cassie. You could be—"

"It's a *stomach virus*."

"Cassie—"

"No." I bury my face in my hands. "I'm not. I can't be."

"And why not? I'm sure you're aware that sort of thing could happen…"

"He's a *merman*."

"You probably know more than me that mermen have reproductive organs."

"We slept together only a few days ago!"

"Maybe merbabies develop quicker than humans."

New tears rush out of my eyes. No, no, no. I can't be pregnant. This can't be happening.

"Maybe that's why you're craving fish. Because the baby—"

I jump to a sitting position, ignoring the pain shooting through the back of my head. "I'm *not* pregnant!" I hang onto my bed as I try to catch my breath. "We were careful." I squeeze the mattress. "We *were*."

The room gets silent, until Leah says quietly, "What if it doesn't work on merpeople or something?"

"Lea—"

"And that could explain why you've been drinking so much. Because the baby needs water."

I bang my head on the floor as more tears stream down my cheeks. "I can't be pregnant." Not only am I too young and will be starting

Merman's Touch

college in a few weeks and have no means to support a baby, but the baby would be half mermaid, or merman. "Leah," I moan. "I'm not pregnant. I'm not." I reach for the garbage bin and throw up again.

"Why else would you get sick like this?"

I wipe my mouth. "Wouldn't the baby need *salt* water? I'm pretty sure I've been drinking tap water."

"Let me hop over to the pharmacy to get a pregnancy test."

"No."

"Cassie…"

"I'm not pregnant! I'm not. I'm *not*."

She doesn't say anything.

"I have a doctor's appointment tomorrow morning. He'll tell me what's wrong with me."

"Or he can confirm that you're pregnant."

"How many times do I have to tell you I'm not frickin' pregnant!" My eyes shut tight and a breath escapes my mouth as I feel that sharp pelvic pain again.

"What happened?" Leah asks.

"Nothing."

"Cass, I'm worried about you. If you really are pregnant…"

"What?" My head snaps to hers. "Do you know what would happen? I'd go to a doctor and he'd see a fin in the ultrasound." I cover my face and rock back and forth. "I can't be pregnant."

I continue to rock. If a half-mermaid, half-human baby is really in there, I don't even know what to think. She'd have to live in the ocean. But what if she doesn't have a fin? Or what if she turns out to be something we could never expect or imagine?

I won't believe it. I won't.

"Cassie, just let me get the test before we jump to—"

"No tests." I don't want to find out the truth. Because the truth may be the answer I don't want to hear.

"That's the best option for—"

"Leah, please. I just want to…can I be alone?"

She eyes me carefully, her forehead creased with concern. "Are you sure?"

"Yeah. You have to get to work."

"I can call in sick."

I would shake my head, but I'm scared my head will explode. "I think I'll just sleep it off. I'm sure I'll feel much better after a nap."

"You just slept."

"I'll be okay. Please, I need to sleep. And Damarian is here."

She gets up and walks over to me, getting down on her knees. "Let me help you to the bed."

I let her put her arm around me, pick me up from the floor, and drag me to my bed. My body sinks into the mattress and it's so soothing. "L-Leah?" My teeth chatter as a sudden chill passes over me.

"Yeah?"

"Thanks. You're a really good friend, you know?"

She forces a grin. "I know." She tucks my blanket under my chin and rubs my arm before heading to the door.

"Please don't tell him," I say.

She looks back at me. "I promise I won't. If you feel really sick, call me, okay? I'll run over right away."

I nod. "Thanks."

A few minutes after she leaves, Damarian sits down near me on the bed. "Is all well, my love?"

Tears slide out of my eyes. I can't tell him. What would he say?

He places his hand over mine. "Cassie?"

I feel the sharpest pain I've ever felt in my stomach. I suck in a large gulp of air. Damarian scoops me up. "I am taking you to the…what is that place? The hospital."

"N…no," I moan. *You can't. I might be pregnant.* "D…Da…" I'm so weak I can barely get a word out.

The room spins. I don't know where I am. I think I see the stairs. Is Damarian carrying me toward the door? He can't!

"Da…"

"It is all right, Cassie." I feel his lips on my damp forehead. "All will be well."

"W…water," I choke out.

He glances down at me. He has two heads. "What?"

"W…water."

"You…" He freezes. "You require water?"

I'm so weak I can only manage to nod.

When I open my eyes, I don't see the kitchen. I don't see the sink or a glass of water. I see steps. Steps that lead to the pool room.

"D…Dama…"

I see the pool. Damarian tightens his hold on me. Then he jumps inside.

At first, my legs feel tingly, but then I cry out. It feels like someone's slicing the bottom half of my body with a chainsaw. I thrash and yell and flail and splash water as I continue to cry out in pain. I've been thrown into a pit of fire, its flames swallowing me up until there's nothing left but ashes.

Make it stop, I say to no one. *Please, just make it stop.*

And it does. My arms float above me as I sink to the bottom of the pool. Then I see black.

Chapter Eleven

The first thing I see when I open my eyes is blue, then tiles. I'm in my pool.

Except, something's different. Normally when I open my eyes in the pool, my view is a little blurry due to the water. Now I see everything clearly, like I'm wearing goggles. No, it's better than wearing goggles.

My heart skips a beat when I realize two things at the same time: I'm too far away from the surface—which means I'm sitting on the floor in the deep side—and I can breathe.

The bottom half of my body doesn't feel right. It feels foreign. When I drop my gaze to my lap, I let out the loudest shriek I've ever yelled in my life.

I don't have legs. There's a tail there instead.

I jerk myself back, which causes the—the anomaly to lurch upward, taking the rest of my body with it. It flaps up and down, like I'm a baby bird learning to fly. Uncontrollable screams come out of my mouth as the tail tows my body in all different directions like it has a mind of its own. Like it's a creature that can't be trained.

I'm a mermaid. A *mermaid*. I wasn't thirsting after water and craving fish because I was pregnant. It was because I was...I was turning into a

Merman's Touch

fish.

How is this possible?

Strong arms come around me and tug me upward. Something soft brushes against my legs—no, not my legs, my *tail*. My head breaks the surface. I stare into Damarian's face.

"Cassie," he says softly.

His arm is looped around my waist. I stare down at my hands. They're webbed, just like his. Looking lower, I see two sapphire tails swaying in the water, though the one attached to…to *me* is a lighter shade than his.

They're stroking each other, and it feels really good.

I see objects floating a few feet away in the pool. At first I don't know what they are, but then it hits me. Our clothes, ripped to shreds.

My hands grip his shoulders. "D-Damarian." My whole body is shaking. Convulsing.

"Cassie," he says softly again, his hand rubbing my back. "It is all right. Do not fret."

"What's…what's going on?" Tears burst out of my eyes. "I have a…a…" I can't even say it.

I'm trembling so hard, my tail whips around, throwing me from right to left. It smacks Damarian in the face, then hauls me back, out of his grasp. I crash into the wall of the pool.

My head rings.

"Cassie!" Damarian speeds toward me and gathers me in his arms, cradling me close. His lips press into my forehead, my nose, my eyes. They skim the side of my face. "It is all right. I am here. I am here to protect you and make sure no harm comes your way."

My arms lock around him and I clutch him tight as the lower half of my body flails around. I can't catch my breath.

"Relax, my love." He caresses my cheek with the back of his

fingers. "All will be well."

How can I relax? I have a freakin' tail!

His fingers dig into my scalp as he holds my head steady, his eyes boring into mine. He doesn't have to say anything—I see it in his eyes, the eternal love he has for me. That causes my muscles to relax, my breathing to grow more even. After a few seconds, my hold on him loosens.

Damarian's hands fall away from my head, settling on my waist. He draws me closer to him, his eyes warm, loving. Leaning in close, he whispers, "My love. You are so very beautiful as a child of the sea."

My breath is knocked out of me. Slowly, my gaze moves to the bottom half of my body and I see myself, really see myself. The sunlight shining off the tail makes it look like crystals, just like Damarian's.

It *is* beautiful.

My gaze slides upward, to my chest. I expect to see myself naked. But I'm not. Sapphire scales cover me. I remember Doria's chest splattered with scales in the same manner.

Mermaid.

"How?" I croak.

Damarian's hand closes around the back of my neck and urges me forward, until my head rests in the hollow space between his neck and shoulder. A feeling of serenity takes over me, like his energy is soothing me.

Our bodies fit perfectly together.

"I do not understand it," he says into my ear, "But it is so lovely." He touches the area near my left eye. "Your eyes are as blue as the sea."

My eyes changed colors? A shiver travels down my spine. "Damarian. I'm scared."

Merman's Touch

"I understand." His hand moves from my waist and laces with mine. "Come." He dips into the water bringing me down with him. Our tails sweep the floor of the pool. I see Damarian in a whole different light. I can't really describe it, but he looks more ethereal, more magical. My hand lightly treks up his arm. He feels different, too. Smoother, electrical.

Our hands interlock. "Feel the ocean water," Damarian says. I've never heard him speak underwater before. His musical voice sounds so majestic, touching every part of me. He closes his eyes. "Feel it, Cassie." My eyes flutter closed, too. "The way it caresses your skin. The life it provides you."

I feel it. It's as though every particle of the water is nurturing me, giving me strength.

Opening my mouth, I take in a large gulp of water through my gills—holy crap, my *gills*—and feel the oxygen flow through my body. I've never felt so rejuvenated.

My hands jump to my hair. I pull a strand and study it. It's golden, not hay-like. But it's a different kind of golden than Damarian's. Less vibrant, though still gorgeous. And it doesn't lay limp on my shoulders like it used to, rather there's life and volume, and the way it floats in the water is breathtaking.

Taking a closer look at my hand, I realize my skin is the same translucent white color as Damarian's.

"Damarian," I say, my own voice musical. I feel my lips lift into a small smile.

His eyes open and he returns the smile.

Sliding my hands out of his, I kick off the floor and break the surface. Taking in a gulp of air feels weird. As a human, it's an amazing and cherishing moment, especially if I've been underwater for a bit. But as a—God, I can't even think it—it's secondary, and not as precious.

Dee J. Stone

As my eyes study the room I've been in a million times, I see things I've never noticed before. Like the dirt between the tiles, the dry blood near the ladder where I cut my toe on a few years ago. I'm pretty sure Mom and I scrubbed that thing until the metal shined. There's a small spider near the window. Everything is much more focused and clear. It's actually pretty incredible.

I hear a buzzing sound. No, not buzzing, but more of a rumble. Like a washing machine. No, like a refrigerator. My eyes widen. I can hear the refrigerator from all the way down here?

A memory attacks my mind, the one when Damarian shifted into a merman in my pool for the first time. He heard the phone ring from down here. Merpeople have acute hearing. That means…I have acute hearing, too. And voices. I can hear them perfectly. Little kids are on their way to the park. They're bouncing a ball. It reverberates in my ears.

And there's more. The construction work being done a few blocks away, the ticking of all the clocks and watches in the house, the water dripping from the bathroom faucet. Even my sense of smell is much stronger. The musty odor from the basement mixed in with laundry detergent from the washing machine. The garbage in the kitchen that should have been thrown out days ago. The smell from the light bulb that burned out last night.

I start to swim. My arms move differently, more gracefully and effortlessly, as if it's second nature. My tail pumps me forward. I'm going at such a fast pace that I bang into the opposite wall. I flip over and swim toward the other end of the pool. The water feels amazing on my skin, more so than when I'm a human. I've never felt so free, so liberated. I've always loved the ocean and surfing, but now it's as though it's an integral part of me, a necessity I can't live without.

Pumping harder and faster, I swim at an extremely fast pace. It thrills me, inflates me with adrenaline. I raise my arms in the air and only use my tail to propel me forward. It's like I'm sailing on the sea. Flying.

I kick off and fall on my back. I've never felt so alive. No wonder Damarian looks like a total different person when he's submerged in the water. The water is our life.

Did I just say *our* life?

Damarian's head breaks the surface. We swim toward each other, and when we're a few inches apart, he puts his hands on my waist and pulls me to him. We spin around in the water, like we're dancing. The whooshing of our tails sound so natural, like it's something I hear every day. Something I love.

Without knowing what I'm doing, I fall on my back and raise my tail in the air. Damarian does the same. Our tails wrap around each other in a loving embrace. I've never felt so close to him, not even when we slept together.

Our hands find each other's and we smile, sharing something secret and special.

I'm still scared as hell, but I also feel a bit awesome. I didn't think I could get any closer to my merman.

Our tails drop back into the water, still wrapped around each other, and our bodies come together. Damarian's hands are on my back, and my nails dig into his shoulders. Our foreheads touch. "This is amazing," I whisper.

"I agree." His voice is barely audible. I can hear his heartbeat. It's racing just as fast as mine. Maybe faster.

We stay like this for a few minutes. Damarian takes my hand. "Come."

"What are we doing?"

"Do you trust me?" he asks.

"Of course." I don't know how I would do this without him.

He tightens his hold on me and dives into the water. I follow. The next second, he kicks off the floor. It's like we're connected through our minds and hearts, because I find myself doing the same. We leap in the air, in unison.

The ceiling is so close to us, and when I stretch my arm, I graze it, just like I did the time I rode Damarian as he soared in the air. It's almost like we're moving in slow motion. I see the way the sunlight coming in through the windows creates rainbows on the water, the way our tails look like crystals as it reflects off them.

We hit the water with hardly a splash and dive deep. Our hands come apart, and mine sweep across the bottom of the pool. My tail surges me forward, alongside Damarian. We swim like fish in the ocean.

When we come up to the surface, I launch myself into Damarian's arms and laugh as he showers me with kisses. "I do not understand it," he says between kisses, "but I am glad you have a tail."

Although every part of me beats with fear, at this moment I'm surprised to admit that I agree.

Chapter Twelve

I don't know how long we swim and play in the pool. It could be minutes, it could be hours. We soar in the air. We race one another. Our tails hug. I forget that I'm a human who turned into a mermaid. I forget that I should be scared as hell. All that matters is what's going on between the two of us.

When the room starts to grow dim, I realize it must be pretty late. Damarian says, "Perhaps we should leave the pool."

I nod, my throat tight. The reality begins to dawn on me. I have to face the world now, face...*this*. Whatever it is.

Damarian leads me to the edge of the pool and puts his arms around my middle. "I will lift you," he says.

"Okay."

He hoists me up, and I use all my energy to drag my—my tail over the edge. As soon as I leave the water, I feel like I lost something dear to me. I feel naked.

Damarian's hands clutch the edge of the pool. He swings his tail with so much force that he leaps over the edge. I don't feel as strong of a connection to him as I did in the water. It's still there, but weak.

I crawl closer to him and he throws his arms around me. It takes a few seconds for me to find my voice. "We're going to change."

He nods.

I stare off into the distance, my heart pounding in my ears. What does all this mean? Am I going to have to swim in my pool twice a day like Damarian? How the *hell* did this happen?

Damarian's arms tighten around me. "We shall hold each other. Comfort each other." His mouth is on my temple. "Persevere, my love. It will end soon."

I nod, forcing my tears at bay. What if I don't change? What if I doomed to stay like this forever?

He whispers things into my ear as we wait. Romantic things. It chases away some of the terror creeping up my back, but it's not gone completely. How can it be? In just a few minutes, I might feel agonizing pain.

When I'll change back into a human, I'll be naked. The second time in front of Damarian. Right now, the two of us are going to share something so intimate, something I'll never share with anyone for the rest of my life.

He lays me down on the floor and covers me with his body, his face digging into my shoulder, his arms holding me close. "I wish you did not have to undergo the pain," he says, his voice filled with guilt.

"I wish you didn't have to, either."

He's about to say something when I feel acute pain in my lower abdomen. I cry out. My palms flatten on the tiles, trying to grab something—anything—as the pain travels from my stomach to my toes.

"Cassie." Damarian hugs me to his chest and kisses my cheeks and my chin. "My Cassie."

Through the fog of pain, I realize I'm smaller than him, which means I'm drying faster. It starts to get more intense. It burns down there. No, worse than burns. It doesn't compare to the pain I felt when

Merman's Touch

I shifted into a mermaid. It's like someone's peeling the skin of my legs off like an orange, little by little, piece by piece. My vision is blotchy and I don't realize I'm knocking my head against the floor until Damarian puts his hands beneath my head. From far, far away, I hear his soothing, comforting voice.

Just when I think I'm going to die, it's over.

My entire body is drenched with sweat, and my heart is beating so fast I think it may fly out of my chest. When I open my eyes, it takes a few seconds until they get into focus. Damarian is on top of me, his own body convulsing. I try to raise my hands, try to comfort him, but they fall to my sides. I'm so weak.

As my eyes droop, there's only one thing on my mind: I can't believe my merman goes through this twice a day.

***

I wake up with something pressing into the side of my body. Not something—someone. I'm too weak to open my eyes. My hands snake up his back, over his shoulders, up his neck, his face, until my fingers tangle in his hair.

A few seconds later, his hands move along my body, one wrapping around my neck while the other laces with mine. His soft breath is on my cheek. Then his lips sweep down my throat. He murmurs my name.

I whisper his, my eyes slowly opening. His face comes into my view, and he smiles, stroking my cheek.

My hand tugs on some strands of his hair. "You're so strong, Damarian. So brave. To go through this twice a day. *Every day*. All for me."

He lowers his forehead to mine. "I would do anything for you. I would cut my tail for you."

"Don't you dare. That's like cutting off your manhood."

His eyes light up as he chuckles. "My sweet Cassie. Despite your exhaustion, you make me laugh."

He sticks his arm underneath me and helps me to a sitting position. The cool air hits my body. My cheeks warm up. Here we are, entwined in each other's arms, totally naked. I can't help but laugh at how absurd this situation is. I'm naked because I was a *mermaid* ten minutes ago.

Damarian stands on shaky knees and helps me up. I stumble against him. It's like I forgot how to use my legs. But after taking a few steps, I'm back to normal, like nothing happened.

We climb up to my room, dress into pajamas, and sit down on the couch. I wring my hands in my lap while Damarian stares at the blank TV screen. After a bit, he reaches for the remote. I don't pay attention to what channel he turns to. I hardly even hear it. The same thing runs over and over in my head. *I'm a mermaid.*

Damarian draws me to his chest. He kisses my temple. "You are trembling."

Looking down at my hand, I see he's right.

"I do not understand it," he says. "I…" He bends forward to plant a light kiss on my lips. "Please forgive me, my love. I am sorry. So very sorry."

"For what?"

"You are a child of the sea…" He scratches his head. "I do not understand how that is possible." He fingers my bottom lip. "I see the fear in your eyes. It pains me."

His words cause tears to well up in my eyes. "I'm so scared, Damarian." I bury my face in his chest. "Is this something permanent? Will I have to swim in my pool twice a day like you? Will I change when even a drop of salt water hits me? Does that mean I can never surf again?"

He holds me tight, his lips skimming along my jaw. He doesn't say anything because he can't possibly know what to say.

"You stood at my side," he says. "From the very first moment. I shall be here for you, my Cassie." He lifts his hand and wipes my tears away with his thumbs. "I shall let no harm befall you."

"Has…" I sniff. "Has this ever happened before? A human turning into a merperson?"

He shakes his head. "I have not heard of such an incident occurring."

My heart plummets to my toes. "Then…how did it happen to me?"

He stares at the floor. "I do not know." He looks at me, his eyes holding so much pain it makes my heart tear in half. "I am so sorry." He digs his head into my neck. "So very sorry."

I squeeze him tight as I rock us back and forth, trying to comfort him. The fact that what happened to me hurts him shows me how much he loves me. I pull back, put my hands on either side of his face, and raise his head so he looks into my eyes. "I'll be okay. Let's try to figure it out." Now I wipe away his tears.

He nods.

"Okay, let's think. The first sign was when I wasn't feeling well. When did I first get sick?" I rack my brain. Has it only been these past few days? Damarian's face turns white. "What?" I ask.

"After we mated…you fell ill."

I stare at him. I got a headache and was thirsty after we slept together. I bet my own face is pale, too. "So you're saying…" I swallow.

"Our mating caused your shift." He's even whiter than before.

I flatten my palms on my knees. How does that make sense? If a person has dark hair and sleeps with a guy who has red hair, does she get red hair? Or if she loses her arm and sleeps with a guy who has an arm, she'll magically grow one back?

Damarian yanks on some of his hair, his eyes troubled. "It is all due to me. I was hesitant to mate with you, for I did not know what would result. Now I have taken your humanity." He covers his face and his shoulders heave.

I put my arms around him. "No, don't think like that, Damarian. Mating with you was the best thing to have happened to me."

His shoulders continue to quake. "All I ever wish is to make you happy. I am not concerned with myself, just for your well-being."

"I know." I kiss the side of his neck.

"I wished to mate with you, for I love you so very much. But I should have been aware of the consequences. How upset I am with myself."

I shift over on the couch so I can force his gaze to meet mine. "Listen to me, Damarian," I say softly. "Don't be upset with yourself. We knew from the beginning that our relationship would be hard. I'm freaked out about all of this, but we have something so amazing together. And we are going to deal with whatever bumps we have along the way. So I'm a mermaid. It's not my first choice, but so much good can come out of it." I press my lips to his. "I can finally see your world now."

He stops weeping and looks at me. "You...you are able to swim in the sea."

I nod.

Some light comes to his eyes. "I have always dreamed of showing you my world."

I envelop him in a hug. "And I've always dreamed of seeing it."

"But you are not able to swim in the sea as a human. It is something you love dearly."

I touch his cheek. "But I love you more."

A small smile crawls onto his mouth. "You are not upset?"

Honestly, I have no idea how I feel. A part of me is still in denial, but the logical side assures me it sure as hell happened. I didn't hallucinate, not to mention Damarian is my witness. It scares me to the very core. But there's another side of me that is excited and looking forward to what will come out of this. Damarian's been part of my world all this time. I wanted to desperately be part of his. Now I can be.

Not wanting to make Damarian feel any worse than he already does, I say, "A little. But I'm also excited. I want to go into the ocean with you."

He leans his cheek against mine. "I wish it, too."

He lies down, tucking me close. I try to keep my thoughts positive, but I can't push away the fear and uncertainty climbing up my back. How can I live like this? I'm the one who takes care of Damarian, remembering to stock up on the sea salt, changing the pool water every few days, making sure he remembers to swim, being there for him when he shifts, saying goodbye when he swims home, and waiting for him when he returns. How can I continue taking care of him if I need to take care of myself, too? How can I live my life if I have to swim in salt water every twelve hours?

Chapter Thirteen

As soon as I wake up the next morning, I know it wasn't a dream. Lifting the blanket off me, I swing my legs over the side of the bed and stare at my toes. No headache, no nausea, no extreme thirst. I feel completely normal.

Except for the fact that I'm in the mood for raw fish.

I look at Damarian, who's breathing softly, his chest rising and falling in an unsteady rhythm. His face is contorted in guilt. I wish he wouldn't take this to heart. I know he feels responsible for what happened to me, but the truth is that he's not. I chose to be with him, a creature from another world. I knew things wouldn't be simple. Nothing ever is.

A chill passes through me and I hug my arms. I don't know if I'm ready to deal with all of this, but I guess I don't have a choice. I need to be strong. For me, for Damarian, for the future of our relationship.

My stomach churns. I'm not sure if that's my body telling me that my tail is on the way, or if it's due to the anxiety flowing through my bloodstream.

My phone beeps. Glancing at the screen, I see it's a text from Leah. **How are you feeling?**

I need to tell her about all of this, but not right now. Not until it sinks in and when I fully accept it and understand exactly what's going on with me.

I text her back. **I'm okay now, thanks. Got some stuff to talk to you about later.**

You're pregnant.

Not even close. **Not pregnant. We'll talk later, k?**

Sure.

Putting my phone aside, my stomach churns some more. How will she react to all of this? She's my best friend and loves me, but will this do something to our friendship? And who else do I need to tell? I planned on telling Mom about Damarian—I guess I need to add a footnote that I'm a mermaid, too. And what about Dad? I don't want to scare him away.

I rub my temples.

"Cassie." Damarian's arms come around me. Just by his contact, I immediately feel better.

I turn over and hug him, then kiss him. "Good morning."

His worried and guilt-ridden eyes search my face. "How do you feel?"

I try to muster a reassuring smile, but I'm not sure I succeed. "Good. You?"

He looks away. "I feel well."

Taking hold of his chin, I turn his face toward mine and say gently, "I'm okay, Damarian. Come here." I hug him closer and kiss the side of his neck. "We'll get through this."

"Forgive me for my behavior," he says. "I wish to be comforting you."

"It's okay. I know how hard this is for you."

"It is more difficult for you," he says.

"Sometimes the person not going through it feels worse," I say, laughing lamely. "Like the way a husband freaks out when his wife's giving birth."

I'm not sure he understands the analogy, but I feel his body relax a little. I'm so focused on making him feel better that I don't care how I feel, ignoring the thoughts and concerns swarming my mind.

"I wish to be here for you," Damarian says. "Just as you were there for me when I came on land. I wish to ease your mind."

"You are," I tell him. "Just holding me like this is enough."

He nods. "Your feelings match mine."

We probably sit like this for ten minutes, not saying anything, just folded in each other's arms, our hands caressing, our lips touching. In this moment, I feel like nothing could hurt me, that no matter what, we will get through this because we are one. Together, forever.

But unfortunately, we have to face life. I pull out of his arms and brush some hair away from his eyes. "I need to get ready for work."

He nods, his face cloudy. "We will require to enter the pool."

My chest tightens. I almost forgot about that.

He sandwiches my hands in his. "Perhaps you will not shift."

"What do you mean?"

"Perhaps..." He swallows. "Perhaps it was an error. Perhaps..."

He's so sweet and amazing for wishing and hoping I won't turn into a mermaid. A part of me feels the same. But who am I kidding? All I want to do is eat raw fish and every single cell in my body yearns to feel the cool, soothing sea water of my pool.

"Maybe," I say.

With my hand in his, he leads me down the stairs and to the pool room. My body perks up when I smell the salt water. A hunger brews deep in my stomach, not one for food, but for something else. Sustenance. Life.

Damarian pulls down his pajama bottoms. "May I hold you?" he

Merman's Touch

asks, reaching his hands out toward me.

"Of course." I tug my tank top over my head, then slide out of my pants. Taking a deep breath, I step closer to Damarian.

His arms come around me, pressing me close to his body. "Forgive me, my love."

We jump into the pool.

The tingling starts only a few seconds before I feel the sharp, burning pain in the lower half of my body. I twist out of Damarian's arms, but my hands try to grab hold of him. His own thrashing pushes me away, but he clutches my hand before I'm tossed to the other end of the pool. As our bodies flail around in the water, I force my eyes open so I can look into his, to let him understand how much I love him.

I see the way he fights through the pain to bring his other hand toward me. I try to do the same. When they finally touch, we grip each other in a firm lock, our bodies tumbling over each other. We don't let go.

Then it's over.

We sink to the bottom of the pool, our hands still fastened together. Damarian's heavy and wild breathing matches my own. After a short while, his hands leave mine, and I'm in his arms. He murmurs soothing words against my temple, his musical voice stroking my skin from top to bottom. Like last night, the salt water makes me feel refreshed, like I just woke up from a good night's sleep. I tighten my hold on him and kick off the floor, shooting up in the air like a missile. Damarian is yanked up with me, and together we soar in the air. I keep one hand in his and raise the other one. We're only midair for a few seconds, but it feels like forever. My eyes lock with Damarian's, and I see the guilt, nerves, and worry leave his face and are replaced with joy, delight, wonder.

When we land in the water, Damarian flips over on his back and places me above him, chest to chest, my tail pressed to his. Smiling sadly, he twirls a strand of my hair between his fingers. "How I enjoy this."

"Why are you sad?"

He shakes his head. "I cannot help but feel such an abundance of guilt for causing this to befall you."

I lay my head against his chest. "It would make me feel so much better if you stopped feeling so guilty. What we just experienced together was amazing. Yes, it was scary and painful and in those few moments, I would have rather died, but look at us now." I raise my head and give him a smile. "We're swimming together in my pool. In the same form."

He's trying to fight the smile forming on his lips. I lean forward to kiss them. He rests his forehead on mine. "Thank you for all you do for me, my love. I am so thankful that I met you."

"Me, too."

We stay in the pool for another fifteen minutes before I reluctantly tell Damarian I need to get to work. As he helps me out of the pool, I try not to think about my class. It's the second to last lesson, but I won't be able to get in the ocean. I won't be able to even stand close to the shore. My shoulders droop at the fact that I'll most likely never surf again. I guess I need to look at the positive—there is still snowboarding and roller skating. Not that they can compare, but I want to look at the bright side. I don't want to let my changing into a mermaid make me bitter.

Once we're all dried up, Damarian and I go upstairs to change—he in a T-shirt and khakis, me in a long-sleeved dress that reaches my knees and covers most of my neckline. My aunt bought this for me when I was a sophomore in high school, and I've never worn it. I

Merman's Touch

didn't think there'd ever be an occasion appropriate for it. Until now.

Hand in hand, we make our way to the beach. Even from a distance, I can taste the salt water on my lips, feel the ocean air settle on my exposed skin. I close my eyes as I take it all in. The ocean has always made me feel good, but this is a whole different level.

Ten-year-old Gail runs up to me as soon as we walk in. "Why aren't you in your wetsuit?"

After making sure she's completely dry, I play with one of her pigtails, which look like mine, just light brown. "I need to stay out of the water for the next few weeks," I lie. "Doctor's orders."

She frowns. "That sucks. How are we going to finish the lessons?"

I tug on her hair. "We will. I promise."

She nods and runs off.

Most of my students have already arrived. I part with Damarian, then make my way to one of the lifeguards, asking him if he can sit with me while I give the surfing lesson because I'm unable to get into the water. In case of an emergency, I need to know someone will be there to jump into the ocean, if needed. I sigh in relief when he agrees.

The lesson begins. Most of my organs sink to my toes as I watch the kids paddling into the water and popping up on their boards. As much as I'll miss surfing, I know I'll miss my students more. Even though we've only been with each other for a short while, I've gotten to know each and every one of them personally and have grown attached to them. I remember being in third grade and my teacher fighting tears on the last day of school. I didn't understand what being a teacher meant. Once we're done with our classes, we cast our students off into the real world, hoping and wishing we gave them enough tools to thrive. Okay, I've just been teaching them a surfing class, but I feel it. I don't know how teachers do this year after year.

Luckily, the lesson goes well and it's over in no time. I wish my students a good day and am about to go to Damarian, when Timmy rushes to me, his body dripping with water. I jump back.

"I'm gonna miss the lessons," he says, moving closer. I bite my lip as I step back, guilt eating away at me. "And you," he adds.

I wish I could hug him. "I'll miss you, too, Timmy."

He gives me a confused look, like he expects me to ruffle his hair like I always do. Biting my lip some more, I wave and walk to Damarian. I don't want to look back and see the hurt expression on his face.

Damarian slings his arm around me as we leave the beach. His lips brush my cheek. "Are you all right?"

"I'm going to miss them."

He nods.

"I guess I'll have to look for a new summer job," I joke, though it doesn't feel like a joke.

He doesn't say anything, but I feel the tension in his muscles. They stay like that until we get home, where he takes me in his arms and brings me to the couch, snuggling close. "Perhaps you would like to swim in the ocean with me? As a child of the sea."

My heart beats with anticipation, excitement, and anxiety. "I would love to."

He smiles and kisses me. "I feel so much joy when you are happy. But it may be wise for us not to venture too deep. Not until you grow familiar to swimming as a child of the sea."

I'm bouncing in my seat. Even though I'm nervous as hell, I'm also excited. It'll be like scuba diving without the gear. Total freedom to swim in the ocean together exploring his world, without having to worry about anything.

"Let's go."

Chapter Fourteen

I hug the bag of essentials close to my chest as Damarian and I head for the beach. The contents inside are doubled to accommodate the both of us. I hide the bag near the rocks, where hopefully no one will find it. We'll need the sheets and towels when we return from the ocean.

We walk to the marina. A few swallows make their way down my throat as we near the many docked boats. The vast ocean. Am I ready for this?

Damarian squeezes my hand.

I look for Ian, Leah's cousin, who hooked me up with a boat a few weeks ago as I met Damarian at the ocean. He's more than happy to provide us with a boat again. After starting the engine, I press my knees together. This is so exciting, yet so nerve-wracking.

Without realizing what I'm doing, my arm reaches over the edge of the boat, my hand sweeping toward the water. Damarian snakes his fingers through mine, pulling my hand away. "Your body yearns for the sea," he murmurs.

I blink at him, then laugh. I remember Damarian doing the very same thing when I brought him to the ocean by boat. He runs his lips across my knuckles. "I shall protect you in the sea. I will not allow any harm come your way."

"Should I be scared?"

"No," he quickly says. "You will not be in danger. But nonetheless, I am here to protect you."

I give him a long, deep kiss. "Thanks."

We reach the familiar sandbar. I raise my eyebrow at Damarian, asking him if this is far enough, or if we should travel deeper. He nods that the location is okay. I kill the engine and sit back, wringing my hands together. This is it, the moment I've been dreaming about for so long. To swim with Damarian in his natural habitat.

"The sea will feel different than the sea water in your pool," he tells me.

I nod. I assumed so.

Damarian holds out his hand for mine. "Would you like to go first?"

Staring out at the beautiful calm water, a shudder creeps down my spine. If for some reason I don't change into a mermaid, I can very well drown. But I have Damarian. He won't let anything happen to me. "Okay," I say.

He holds me steady as I strip out of my clothes. I'll have to return here with another boat to bring this one back to the marina.

I've been scanning the area since we left to ascertain that no boats are around. I do it one final time, then take a deep breath, letting it out slowly.

"I will join you shortly," Damarian says.

I raise my hands and dive into the ocean. The tingly sensation is the same, and so is the pain. I feared it might be more intense, since it's the ocean as opposed to synthetic sea salt.

As I writhe and splash around, I feel Damarian in the ocean. I don't see him or feel him physically, but I know he's there. It's as

Merman's Touch

though our souls are connected.

The pain stops and I float vertically in the water, my tail flowing in the current. Damarian was right, natural sea water feels amazing. It's like I can live weeks, maybe months, without food as long as I can swim in the ocean.

Damarian comes into my view, looking exquisite. I've never seen him clearly in the ocean like this, just blurry due to my human eyes. He looks slightly different than when he's in my pool. A beautiful creature of the ocean.

He gathers me in his arms. "Do you feel it?" he asks, his voice even more musical. "Children of the sea have the ability to sense one another, even on land. But it is much stronger in the sea." He nuzzles my neck. "How I love the way it feels."

My arms come around his neck, my hands tangling in his hair. "I love the way it feels, too."

I stare down below. We're a good few feet from the ocean floor, but I can see all the way down there. The crabs and fish skimming along it. The coral. Raising my eyes higher, I see the many colorful fish swimming around, the seaweed, rays, turtles. Even frogs. It's all so beautiful and magical. I've always loved watching documentaries about ocean life, but now I feel like I'm actually part of it. I can spend weeks here.

Damarian's tail wraps around mine. A feeling of warmth and love envelops me. In the merpeople world, doing this is probably equivalent to hugging, maybe more. It feels really good, and I find my eyes rolling over as I moan.

His lips are near my ear. "Come." Locking his hand through mine, he dives deeper into the ocean. I follow. Our tails swoosh behind us, so powerful and strong. The surface draws farther and farther away.

I hear a low hum. It almost sounds like a swarm of bees. Maybe it's my ears adjusting to the pressure of the water? But as we go deeper into the ocean, the humming gets stronger, and when we pass a school of fish, it gets even more intense. Is it the fish? Do I hear them? Damarian can communicate with any living thing in the ocean. Does that mean I can, too?

We stop and wait for the school to pass. They don't pay attention to us, but I hear the humming. Straining my ears, I try to make out what they're saying, but I have no idea. Once they pass, I turn to Damarian. "Can you hear them?"

He nods. "But they are too numerous in number to hear precisely what they are saying."

A small fish swims up to my shoulder. I look down at it. It just floats next to me. I raise confused eyes to Damarian. He smiles. "I believe she enjoys your company. Attempt to communicate with her."

I stare at it for a few seconds. What exactly do you say to a fish? "Um…hi?"

The fish doesn't answer, but I see something in its eyes. Like it understands me.

My lips curve into a smile. I reach for it, expecting it to dash away, but it moves closer to me. Just as I'm about to brush my finger across its middle, something large swoops toward it, catching it in its mouth.

A startled shriek escapes my mouth as the fish swims away with my little friend. Damn, that thing almost bit my hand off.

I clutch my thumping heart. Damarian covers my hand with his. "I am sorry. But that is life in the sea."

As my heart slows down to a normal pace, I realize he's right. Things are different here in the ocean. It's a dog-eat-dog world—well, a fish-eat-fish world. And the little ones are most likely to be chomped.

I search the area, studying everything. The different kinds of fish, the way they swim and how they eat one another. I'm not an expert on fish, so I have no idea what species they are, but there are so many of them. I can't help but marvel at how amazing all of this is. My eyes are soaking it all in faster than my brain can process what I'm actually seeing.

"Come," Damarian says, gesturing further into the ocean.

As we swim, he suddenly dives deeper until he's a few feet beneath me. Raising his head, he smiles, then spreads out his arms, his tail pumping behind him. My hands spread out as well, my own tail propelling me forward. We swim in sync like this, like we're attached by strings. Like we're flying in the ocean. When he pumps faster, I do, too. When he turns, I turn. It's like we're connected through our minds.

Then without warning, he shoots up, his arms coming around me. He's moving at such a fast pace that it takes a second for me to understand what's going on. We're somersaulting in the water, first dropping toward the floor, then shooting up. Just as we're about to break the surface, we flip over, our tails thrusting. We do it over and over. As a human, I would probably get dizzy, but I'm not. In fact, I don't want it to end.

Damarian turns me around so that our fronts are pressed into one another. As we continue to somersault, his lips find mine. I feel him smiling as we kiss, our hands gripping one another. Kissing him underwater like this feels different, too. More sensual, more enticing. Damarian told me that his hormones are more intense as a human, but right now, I'm finding it hard to believe. I've never felt like this before.

When our lips finally part, Damarian smiles warmly. "I am having a magnificent time with you, my love."

My lips latch onto his for a long time before I say, "Me, too."

We explore more of the ocean, touching the coral, the ocean floor, even say hi to a few fish. I don't know how long we stay under, but I'm guessing quite a few hours. My body starts to slow down, my tail not pumping as fast as before. My arms feel weak and I sink a little. Damarian clasps an arm around me. "Forgive me, Cassie. Your body is not accustomed to swimming in the sea for such lengths. Perhaps we shall return to land."

I'm about to protest, tell him I want to stay down here forever, but my eyes get heavy.

"I do not think it wise to rest here," he says. "It is only safe in the colony, where we are well guarded."

"From what?" I ask.

"Humans. Other creatures as well. Come, we shall return to land."

I lean into him as he steers us toward shore. "What about visiting your family?" I ask. The thought makes me want to puke everything I ate today, but at the same time, every cell in my body fills with anticipation. I want to meet his family so badly, even though I'm scared as hell.

"It is a lengthy journey," he says. "Perhaps once you grow accustomed to swimming in the sea."

"Aww." But I know he's right. I am so wiped out right now. All I want to do is curl up in my bed and sleep for days.

I must have dozed off, because the next second, Damarian is dragging me onto the wet sand. My body wakes up when it dawns on me that we're on land—two merpeople on land. In broad daylight.

My eyes search for my bag. Where did I put it? I see it a few feet away. Laying my hands on the sand, I groan as I heave my body toward the rocks. Damarian gives me a light push. I snatch the bag and open it, yanking out the two sheets and tossing one to Damarian. After we cover ourselves, I hand him a towel, all the while keeping my gaze on my surroundings. Hardly anyone comes to this area because there's nothing here but a pile of rocks and some garbage, but I don't want to risk anything.

Merman's Touch

Damarian draws me close. "Are you prepared?"

"As ready as I'll ever be."

The pain is unsurprisingly just as bad as the last time. And just like the last time, being in Damarian's arms makes it more bearable.

Chapter Fifteen

I wake up to the sun shining in my face. Moaning and stretching my arms, my eyes open. I'm lying on my bed.

Moving my gaze to my left, I find Damarian sitting next to me, his face brightening when our eyes lock. I stretch my arms again and yawn. "What time is it?"

"Seven in the morning."

I squint. "Seven in the *morning*? How long have I been asleep?" The last thing I remember is changing into a human after having such a great time with Damarian in the ocean.

"Since the shift," he says.

He carried me home. He must have been pretty tired himself. I sit up and take him in my arms. "You're so amazing. I love you. So, so much."

His lips sweep across mine. "Not as much as I love you." He nuzzles my nose. "I wished to allow you more rest, but I did not want you to miss your final lesson."

Final lesson? I pull out of his hold. "The party!" I want to throw a small picnic party on the beach for my students. I slam the heel of my palm against my forehead. "I totally forgot to buy supplies."

Damarian grins.

Merman's Touch

"What?" I ask.

His grin grows wider and he holds out his hand, motioning that he has something to show me downstairs. Keeping my curious eyes on him, I give him my hand and let him lead me downstairs. The table is cluttered with a picnic basket, food, drinks, snacks, and paper goods. Perfect for a party.

I gape at him. "You bought all this?"

He nods, still grinning.

Throwing my arms around him, I squeeze him as tight as possible. "How did you remember?"

He dips his head so our lips touch. "I try to remember all that you tell me."

I press my cheek to his and I hug him even tighter. "Thank you so much! How did you know what to buy?"

"Leah assisted me."

He did it all for me, after carrying me home from the beach, even though he must have been exhausted. He and Leah are so great for doing this for me. I'm really lucky to have them.

"After your celebration with the fry, I wish to swim again in the sea," Damarian says, skimming his lips along my jaw. "I very much enjoyed it."

"Me, too."

We go about our usual morning routine, swim in the pool, and make breakfast. I once again dress into the long dress, my throat constricting. Today is the last day I teach my surfing class and I won't be getting in the water. But this is my life now, and I can either embrace it or mope around. I choose to embrace it.

Damarian offers to carry the basket. There's a skip to my step as we walk to the beach. I'm excited to throw this party for my students, to see their shocked and surprised faces. Damarian keeps the basket with him while I ask the lifeguard to sit with me again when I teach my class. Then I head to my students. Most are already there, and as my gaze sweeps over them, I feel proud. A few weeks ago, they were nervous, afraid, had no confidence that they could ride a wave. But today, most of them can. And the ones that haven't mastered it will one day. I don't know if I had that determination at their age.

"Miss Cassie!" Timmy runs, carrying his surfboard. A little girl chases after him.

"Hey." I wave.

When he reaches me, he grabs the hand of the girl and pulls her forward. "This is my sister."

She looks no older than six, with the same dirty blond hair as Timmy. "Hey," I say. "What's your name?"

"Kayla."

"She wanted to come because it's the last day," Timmy says. "Can she watch?" He bounces on his feet like he's had too much sugar.

"Of course you can," I tell her. She smiles shyly.

I gather my students and give them a short speech, telling them how proud I am at what they've achieved and how if they keep at it, they can be great one day. Gail says, "Are you gonna surf today?"

I shake my head.

"Aww," her friend, Wes, says.

On the first day of lessons, I let them watch me surf. I'm not the greatest surfer out there, but they loved watching me. I know many of them want to see me again, and I want to do it for them. It kind of sucks.

I tell them that since today is our final lesson, they could do whatever they want. Most try to show off, and I find myself laughing at how adorable they are. Uncle Jim is right—I think being a teacher is what I'm supposed to do.

Merman's Touch

Someone tugs on my dress. I look down to find Timmy standing next to me, his body soaked. I stumble back. "Timmy."

"Can Kayla come into the ocean with me?"

I glance behind him to see Kayla standing there, her face pinched with excitement, a surfboard in her hands. "She doesn't know how to surf, Timmy."

"She'll just sit on her board and watch me. Please, please!"

I look out at the waves. They're pretty calm today, and if Timmy and Kayla stay close to the shore and away from the other kids, she should be okay. "Just a few minutes," I tell them. "Stay close to the shore and away from the others, okay?"

He nods and runs off, followed by his sister.

I sit down on the dry sand a good few feet away from the shore, hugging my knees. It's when I'm alone that I'm forced to think and face everything in my life that I try to avoid. Like the fact that I'm a mermaid. I always push away the reality and focus on the fantasy—how amazing it is to swim with Damarian in the ocean. But the reality is that I am going to have to deal with it, probably for the rest of my life. What exactly does that mean? Will I be forced to live in the ocean because of how hard it will be to live on land as a human? With the constant need for salt water, what kind of job will I hold? I guess I can always do part-time, but who knows what can trigger the change? What if I put Damarian's life—and the life of all the merpople—in jeopardy?

An ear-splitting yell nearly bursts my ears. I leap to my feet, my eyes on the ocean. Timmy and Kayla are flailing around like they're in trouble.

"Timmy?" I call as I sprint toward the water. "Kayla!"

They continue to yell and thrash around. The other people in the ocean start rushing to the shore, yelling, "Get out of the water!"

I race to the ocean and am about to dive in, but stop myself, nearly falling face-first into the water. I can't get wet.

The lifeguard comes running toward the shore and dives in. He surges to the kids, grabs them, and drags them to the shore. Then I see it…the blood in the water. And when the lifeguard draws closer, I see more. The sharp end of bone where Kayla's arm should be. Bone that was chewed off.

I collapse to my knees. A shark.

More lifeguards rush to them. I hear an ambulance in the distance. They haul Kayla onto a board. Blood pours out of her. A hysterical Timmy is clutching onto the lifeguard, and all I want to do is hold him in my arms. But I can't. I stand and move backward so none of them could spray me with water.

I can't comfort Timmy.

I dash to Damarian, who reaches for me with a confused expression on his face. I grab my bag and rummage inside for the large towel I brought with me. Just in case.

"Cassie?" Damarian asks, touching my arm.

"Be right back."

With the towel in my hand, I race to where the commotion takes place. The lifeguard is trying to pry a still-hysterical Timmy off him. I don't know what they're doing to Kayla because they're blocking my view, but the EMTs are trekking into the beach with a board.

"Timmy," I call, holding out the towel.

His tear-streaked face lifts and he runs to me. I wrap him in the towel, making sure no part of his wet self touches my skin. I pat him all over, drying him, as I hold him close. "Timmy."

He's crying and yelling and pointing in the direction of his sister.

"Are you hurt?" I ask him.

"What happened to Kayla?" he cries.

"It's okay." I hug him closer as he sobs. "Shh, it's okay, sweetie." I rub his back. I can't believe this. I can't—I just—oh my God.

"Tiger shark," someone says. "I swear it was a tiger shark."

The EMTs load Kayla onto the board and pass by. Her head rolls to the side, her eyes barely opened. My blood turns cold when I see her arm—what's left of it.

One of the paramedics comes over to me. "Are you the girl's parent or guardian?"

I shake my head. When I open my mouth, my voice is so unstable I can barely form a sentence. "Her—her mom. I need to c-call her."

"Is Kayla gonna die?" Timmy yell-cries.

The paramedic tells me which hospital they're bringing her to, and that I should notify her parents immediately. With Timmy still in my arms, I hurry to Damarian, who's standing and gaping at me. "Cassie, what is happening?"

"Shark attack," I say as I retrieve a water bottle from my bag and hand it to Timmy.

"S-shark?"

I take out my phone. "I need to call Timmy's mom."

"She's going to die," he sobs into my shoulder.

Just as I'm about to dial his mom, I see her sprinting into the beach. By the look on her face, I know she knows exactly what happened. "Mrs. Miller," I say running up to her.

"Cassie."

I hand her Timmy. "I'm so sorry. I didn't...I couldn't—"

"Is it true?" she asks, tears pouring out of her eyes. "My Kayla?"

"She's gonna die!" Timmy cries.

I tell her which hospital the ambulance brought her to. Then I throw my arms around her and Timmy and hug them. She holds onto me for a few seconds before fleeing to her car, Timmy wrapped securely in her arms.

I fall to my knees and bury my face in my hands, tears seeping into my palms.

Damarian's arms come around me. "Cassie."

I grip him so tight I lose feeling in my hand. "I—I couldn't get in the water. I just stood there helplessly."

"Cassie." He kisses my forehead. "I am sorry. I do not know what to say. I do not understand…" His voice trails off as his arms tighten around me. "You tremble."

"I…" I untangle myself from his arm. "I need to go the hospital." With shaky hands, I grab my bag. It slips from my fingers and falls into the sand. I pick it up and leave the beach, the same images replaying over and over in my head. Little Kayla, missing an arm, the blood gushing all over. Her terrified eyes. The way she lay nearly unconscious on the board.

How I didn't do anything to help.

"Cassie?" Damarian calls. He reaches for my arm.

"I need to go to the hospital," I repeat, continuing to walk.

He keeps his pace with me. "I will accompany you."

"No. I need to see Kayla and Timmy to make sure they're okay."

"Cassie…"

We reach the house. I get into my car. "I'll come back as soon as I can," I tell Damarian and start the engine.

"Please. Allow me to accompany you."

I finally look him in the face. "I need to do this alone." I reach for his hand and squeeze it. "I'll get back soon."

He nods unsurely and steps away from the car. I press on the gas and drive to the hospital.

Chapter Sixteen

The only time I've been to a hospital was when I was ten and my grandfather had a stroke. He died a few days later. Back then, I thought everyone who was admitted to the hospital died. I hope Kayla doesn't have the same fate.

There are many people entering and leaving the hospital, some carrying balloons and gifts, a few couples with newborn babies. I swallow the lump forming in my throat and force back my tears. I need to be hopeful. Kayla lost her arm, but she'll be okay.

Taking a deep breath, I head to the emergency room. So many thoughts run through my head. I shouldn't have let Timmy and Kayla swim in the ocean. How long was the shark there? I should have scouted the waves to make sure it was safe. As a mermaid, shouldn't I have sensed that a shark was there? What good is it to be a mermaid if I can't protect the people I care about from the dangerous ocean?

One thing lays heavily on my mind. Why was the shark so close to the shore?

When I snap out of my thoughts, I find myself in the emergency waiting room. I rub my head, trying to ease the hammering.

I see Mrs. Miller talking to a doctor, holding Timmy in her arms. His face is buried in her shoulder. I stand still for a bit, watching the exchange. Mrs. Miller covers her mouth and cries out. My heart slides down and dissolves into a puddle at my feet. No…Kayla *has* to be okay.

The doctor pats Mrs. Miller's shoulder and walks away. Dropping Timmy, she falls against the wall, her hand still covering her mouth. Her shoulders quake, her legs wobble. It looks like she's going to collapse.

I rush over and hold out my hand. "Mrs. Miller."

"Cassie," she mumbles, her voice weak, her eyes unfocused. She grabs my hand and holds it in a tight grip, hurting me. But I don't pull away. She squeezes my hand even tighter and chokes out, "She died on the way to the hospital."

My vision gets blurry as Mrs. Miller and I weep. A small hand slides into mine. Timmy. I get down on my knees and hug him closely, rubbing his head as I try to console him.

Damn it. Why didn't I do something? I'll never forgive myself. Or that stupid shark. It shouldn't have killed an innocent girl. They wouldn't attack merpeople, would they? Then they shouldn't attack humans, either.

It needs to pay for what it did.

***

Damarian jumps to his feet the second I walk through the door. "Cassie."

My knees cave and I collapse. He catches me just in time, lifting me in his arms and tucking me close. "Cassie," he says softly, his face pressed to mine.

I never thought it was possible for a person to have so many tears. I hiccup and moan and my body shakes violently. Damarian's arms grow unstable, causing me to sink a little, but he repositions me, securing me against his chest. "She…" I hiccup. "She died."

Merman's Touch

His body stiffens. I raise my face to his, seeing his alarmed expression. His mouth moves, but no sound comes out. He walks over to the couch and gently lowers me on it, sitting down next to me. "I do not understand," he says.

"Can we hunt down the shark?" I ask.

His eyes widen in utter shock.

I swallow the bitter taste in my mouth. "So I can kill it."

He springs back like I slapped him. "You wish to do what?"

"I want to kill it." There's no mistaking the malice in my voice.

"But Cassie…you wish to injure an innocent creature?"

My eyes flash to his. "An *innocent* creature? Are you kidding me? It killed a little girl. An *innocent* little girl."

Damarian holds out his hands. "It is their nature, Cassie."

I scramble to my feet and stare him down. "So we should just pat its head and say 'Good little shark' because it's his *nature*? We don't let stray dogs roam around the streets, because they're dangerous. If a lion or tiger would escape from a jungle and run to civilization, we wouldn't hesitate to shoot it down."

I see him processing what I said, trying to remember what a dog, lion, and tiger is. My chest expands and contracts wildly and more tears drip down my chin, splattering my clothes. Glancing down, I see the picnic basket sitting on the coffee table. I shove it off and its contents spill all over the carpet.

Damarian springs back again, his mouth falling open. He's never seen me lose my cool before. When he seems to find his voice, he says, "It is not the same."

"What isn't?"

"Equating a lion with a shark."

I stare at him. "What?"

He doesn't say anything.

"Because sharks are from your world and lions are from mine?" I swallow. "Or do I no longer belong in my world anymore?"

Again, he doesn't say anything, but I see his eyebrows wrinkle in confusion. We just stand there with our eyes on one another, until Damarian says, "You cannot kill it, Cassie."

I throw my hands up. "Why are you defending it?"

"I am—"

"Don't you understand what happened? That thing killed an innocent little girl!" I yell so loud I swear I hear the wall crack.

Damarian shrinks back like I threw hot water at him.

"Am I just supposed to let it get away?"

Damarian reaches out like I'm a small child needing to be placated. "The shark has a master, Cassie. You cannot kill it. Do you wish to upset a child of the sea?"

I blink at him. The shark has a master. Bile rises in my throat as a sudden thought hits me. "Damarian..."

"Yes?"

"Who do tiger sharks serve? The Emerald clan?"

He nods slowly.

"Do..." My whole body is shaking so bad it feels like it will split right down the middle. "Do sharks who serve the clans act on their own? Or do their masters tell them what to do?"

He eyes me carefully, starting to grasp what I'm getting at. "They abide to their masters' will," he says softly.

More bile rises in my throat. I cover my mouth before I vomit all over the floor. Sweat breaks out at my forehead and the room spins. "You're saying someone sent that shark to kill her?"

Damarian steps closer to me. "Cassie—"

"Tell me, Damarian!"

"I do not know. The sharks who serve the five clans do not behave on their own will. Unless..."

"Unless *what*?"

"Unless they are rogue sharks."

My breathing grows more rapid. "Rogue?"

"Yes. Sharks that have strayed from their masters."

"Is that common?"

He shakes his head. "Extremely unlikely. Sharks are loyal to the children of the sea."

"So you're saying that..." I swallow. "That..."

"Perhaps it was a shark that does not serve a clan."

I look away. "They said it was a tiger shark."

"Are you certain?"

"No. I don't know." I heard someone on the beach say it was a tiger shark, but he could have made a mistake. And what about all those other shark attacks we've had over the years? Usually, the sharks were bull or tigers. Bull sharks serve one of the other clans. Did merpeople send those sharks to kill humans, too?

Damarian takes a few steps closer until he's right in front of me. He reaches for me, but I move back. "Cassie, please..."

"What's going on here, Damarian?" My voice is barely audible.

"I do not know." He reaches for me again. "Please, let us relax and—"

"No, I...I just need to be alone right now."

"Cassie."

I race to my room, jumping on my bed. Tears seep into my pillow. This can't be possible. A merpeson sent that shark to attack Kayla? What for? And why is Damarian taking it so lightly? Sure, the sharks don't attack the merpeople, even the ones who don't serve the clans. He told me that as long as they don't provoke them, they live in peace together. What would he do if a shark would suddenly attack someone he knew?

If this attack was not an accident, what does it mean?

The door to my room opens. Footsteps stop right before my bed. A second later, I feel Damarian's weight on the mattress. His ocean scent fills me. Usually, that excites me. But right now, all I feel is disgust.

"Cassie." His lips are on the back of my neck as his arms come around me.

I scoot over. "Leave me alone. Please."

"Cassie."

Tears continue to seep into my pillow. Kayla's dead. From a shark attack. One that may have been plotted.

"Cassie, please do not push me away."

Fresh tears flood out of my eyes. Guilt and pain suffocate me. This isn't Damarian's fault. But sharks are from his world. They might not be as intelligent as humans, but the merpeople are. They can communicate with them. Surely they could have taught them not to attack humans. I wish he would do *something* instead of just brushing it off.

After a minute or two, Damarian gets up from the bed and leaves, softly closing the door after him.

***

"Cassie…"

My eyes open. The room is pitch black. I sit up and am hit with memories. It all comes back to me—Kayla, the shark attack, the Emerald clan. I grab hold of my head and whimper.

"Cassie?" Damarian's hands close over mine. "Are you all right?"

No, I'm not. I'm far, far from okay.

He hesitantly sits on my bed. "Perhaps…perhaps I should visit the sea. Perhaps I can make sense of all that has occurred."

Merman's Touch

I lift my head to meet his gaze. I can make out some of his features in the dark. He looks very nervous. "You'd do that?" I ask.

"Yes." He strokes my cheek with the back of his fingers.

"Just give me a few minutes alone, please?"

He nods and leaves. I bury my face in my pillow, biting down on my lip to keep the tears at bay. But it's no use—they break free.

After a few minutes, I pull myself out of bed, wipe my eyes, and go downstairs. Damarian's in the kitchen, packing a bag of gummy worms. He usually takes some back for his little sister. My heart constricts. I can't think of the merpeople without being reminded of the tiger shark, of the fact that one of them could have purposely sent it to kill a human.

Damarian turns around. When he sees my gaze on the gummy worms, he says, "Zarya questioned me at my last visit why I did not bring the gummy worms."

I nod, my throat tight. I join him at the kitchen counter and fill a glass of cold water. It feels amazing as it slides down my throat.

Damarian raises his hand like he wants to touch me, but he drops it to his side. We stand there, not saying anything to each other. I put the glass in the sink, head for the door, and open it. Damarian follows. We don't talk as we make our way to the beach. It's very hot out, but my skin prickles as chills run up my spine. The last time I was at the beach, only this morning, Kayla was attacked. I don't know if I can step foot in there.

But my body begs to feel the ocean water on my skin. It's like a tug of war between my body and heart.

My heart wins. I freeze in my tracks.

Damarian stops walking and looks back. Even in the dark, I see the confused and hurt look on his face. "Cassie?" he asks.

I shake my head, moving back. "I don't think I can go in there.

I...I can't."

He comes to me. "It is my home, Cassie. Will you not...will you not say goodbye?"

His hurt voice causes tears to pool in my eyes. I bite down hard on my bottom lip. The pain doesn't compare to the pain I feel in my heart.

I hold out my arms. Damarian rushes into them and lifts me, pressing his body close to mine as he buries his face in my neck. "How I love you," he murmurs.

"I love you, too," I whisper back.

"I will learn all I can."

"Thanks."

He doesn't let go. I don't want him to. I want to go back to how things used to be, when it was just me and Damarian in our little love bubble, when sharks didn't attack little girls. When our worlds weren't being torn apart.

He kisses me, but this kiss isn't like the others. The love is there, but the passion is gone. It's replaced by uncertainty, by the unknown. By the fear of what all this means, what it will lead to, and what it will do to our relationship.

We don't let go of each other. Not until the sky gets light. Damarian slowly and reluctantly lowers me to the ground. My arms stay locked around him. He's my Damarian, my merman. The love of my life. He rests his lips on my forehead, tells me how much he loves me, then unhooks my arms from around him. He trudges into the beach, not looking back.

Chapter Seventeen

I'm eating ice cream. I don't even know what flavor.

Kayla is dead. A shark attacked her. Damarian's back in the ocean, trying to figure out what's going on.

Earlier this morning, I couldn't get anything down. Now I can't stop eating. I feel horrible for the way I treated Damarian. Seeing his hurt expression cuts a large chunk of my heart. He didn't deserve it. I could have behaved differently. The last thing I want to do is hurt the person who means the most to me. But I was so distraught and confused.

I haven't swum in my pool since last night. I can't. Right now, all I want is to be a human. I don't know how long I've been out of the water, but I'm not feeling sick. I don't know what that means, but I have no energy to try to figure it out.

I miss Damarian. So, so much. Probably more than usual because of the way we parted. I can't believe I didn't say goodbye properly. Shifting from a human to a merman is so hard, and being there for him always made things easier. Last night, I just tossed him aside. I hate myself.

On the news this morning, they spoke about the attack and told the whole story. How a brother and sister where playing in the ocean, how the shark was swimming too close to the shore. How the lifeguard saved them. It was confirmed that it was indeed a tiger shark.

I don't know what to think. I don't *want* to think. My head will explode.

Someone knocks on the door. My heart perks up at the thought that it might be Damarian. But that's highly impossible. He just returned to the ocean a few hours ago.

After peering through the peephole, I see it's Leah. My toes feel numb. I still haven't told her about what happened to me. I know I'll need to at some point, but not right now. I don't want to deal with that part of my life. If I belong in the merpeople world now, it means I'm semi-responsible for the shark attack. I know it sounds silly, but I can't help feeling that way.

And I plan on visiting Timmy later today. I'll have to tell Leah everything later—when I'm ready to deal with all that's happened.

I throw the door open and she launches into my arms. "I heard what happened," she says. "How are you doing?"

I step out of the hug. "Super."

She hugs me again. I lean in to her, feeling my body relax. With her arm around my shoulders, she leads me to the couch, sitting near me. She raises her eyebrow at the nearly-empty carton on the coffee table. "How dare you eat ice cream and not invite me?"

That gets a small smile out of me.

She picks up the carton and digs the spoon inside.

With my eyes on the blank TV screen, I say, "It was a tiger shark."

"I'm really sorry, Cass."

My throat closes up and fresh tears prick my eyes. "I shouldn't have let them get in the water."

Leah drops the carton on the coffee table and takes me in her arms. She rocks back and forth as I cry on her shoulder. "It's all my fault," I say, my voice muffled by her shirt.

She rubs my back. "It wasn't."

It is, because I couldn't get in the water. The few seconds between my wanting to jump in and the lifeguard rushing inside could have made all the difference.

But Leah can't understand. Even if I told her I'm a mermaid now and that I can't let a drop of salt water hit me, she wouldn't understand. I don't know if anyone can. Not even Damarian.

I yank out of her grasp. She looks taken aback and a little hurt. I rub my forehead. "Sorry. Just…the tiger sharks serve and protect the Emerald clan."

"The Emerald clan?"

"You know, the merpeople Emerald clan."

"Oh! Right, mermaid talk. So tiger sharks serve the Emerald clan." Confusion clouds her eyes.

I take a deep breath and exhale slowly. "D-Damarian told me sharks that serve the five clans—the Sapphires, Violets, Rubies, Diamonds, and Emeralds—don't act on their own. They only do what their masters tell them to do."

Her eyes fill with understanding. "You're saying…a mermaid sent the shark to attack the girl?"

I return my gaze to the TV screen, pushing my legs to my chest and resting my cheek on my knee.

"Cassie, that's crazy. Why would a mermaid attack a human girl? Was she doing something wrong?"

"She was just playing with her brother in the ocean. I didn't know that was a crime."

"That makes two of us."

I look at her, my eyes filling with new tears. "I don't understand any of it."

"Is that why Damarian went back to the ocean?"

I nod. "We…we got into a fight. I think. I don't know. I said things I shouldn't have. He wanted to go back to find out what's going on."

"That's good. Hopefully, you'll get answers." She reaches for the carton. After scooping some of the ice cream and licking the spoon, she sits up sharply. "Do you know anyone from the Emerald clan?"

I shrug. "Just Kyle."

We gape at each other.

"You don't think…?" I say.

"I thought you and Kyle ended things on good terms."

"We did."

"Then why would he send a shark to attack a human?"

I don't know the answer to that. "If anything, a great white should have attacked *me*. The great whites serve the Sapphires."

She dips her pinky into the carton. "Does Damarian's family want you dead or something?"

I'm not sure if she's joking or is serious. I shrug. Her eyes widen. "Cassie?"

"No, they don't want me dead. I mean, I know his dad doesn't approve of us. I mean, he did give us his blessing, but…" I shake my head. "Forget it. His dad's approval is the least of my concerns right now."

She nods, then says, "Does every single tiger shark serve an Emerald mermaid?"

I can't help but laugh a little. "You keep calling them 'mermaids.' There are mermen, too, you know."

She rolls her eyes. "Sorry. Does every single tiger shark serve a mermaid or *merman*?"

"I guess?"

She shakes her head. "This is so screwed up."

Merman's Touch

"No kidding."

"How's the brother doing?"

"Not great. I'm going to see him later today. Then..."

"What?"

I pinch my toes. "I'll wait for Damarian at the beach. Assuming he actually comes back." Assuming I can muster enough courage to go in there. I can't risk him shifting without me. I need to protect him.

"Why shouldn't he come back?" Leah asks.

I lay my head on my knee again. "Because of our fight? I don't know."

"You two aren't going to let a stupid shark come between you, are you?"

It's more than that, but I'm not sure Leah can understand. Damarian defended that shark because it comes from his world. He doesn't understand what the shark attacking Kayla means to me, how it's nearly destroying me. I know he tried really hard to understand—that's why he wanted to go to the ocean to see if he can learn what happened. Can this tear us apart?

Chapter Eighteen

My stomach twists as I stand in front of the Miller house. I haven't been here before, but the atmosphere is gloomy, like a black cloud hovers above. I lift my eyes to the sky. It's clear and beautiful. That doesn't feel right. It should rain, pour. Like the whole world should mourn Kayla's death along with me and Timmy's family.

My finger jabs the doorbell. A few seconds later, I hear footsteps approaching. The door flies open to reveal a teenage girl, holding some toys. She lifts her eyebrows. "Yeah?"

I guess she's Timmy's babysitter. His parents are probably planning Kayla's funeral. I clear my throat. "I'm Timmy's surfing teacher. His mom said it's okay that I stop by."

She widens the door and motions for me to step in. "He's in his room. Sort of just lying there. I tried to get him into the playroom for some games." She nods at all the toys in her arms. "But he wouldn't budge. Good luck." She disappears into another room.

I guess it's up to me to find him on my own. I take the stairs, my steps muffled by the gray-blue carpeting. The house looks pretty nice. I think Mrs. Miller is a lawyer and her husband is a CPA. They have no other kids. My heart cracks when I try to imagine what it's like to lose a sibling or a child.

Merman's Touch

When I reach the top of the stairs, I scan around. There are so many rooms. But when I hear sniffs coming from a room to the left, I rush over. The door is wide open, revealing little Timmy on his stomach, his eyes pasted on a kid's book. It's obvious he isn't reading.

The floor creaks beneath my feet, and Timmy looks up. When his eyes land on me, he jumps to his knees. "Miss Cassie." Gone is his usual, cheery greeting. It's almost like his words are crying, too.

"Hi, Timmy. Can I come in?"

He nods.

I enter and sit down on the corner of his bed. His eyes are downcast. I reach for his book and scan the title. *The Rabbit Who Lost His Way Home.* "Any good?"

"It's Kayla's favorite," he whispers, his eyes on his bedspread. "She always begs me to read it to her every night. Mom and Dad are always busy."

My stomach gets all knotted. He's referring to his sister in the present tense.

"Will you read it to me?" he asks, his big brown eyes hopeful and full of tears.

"Of course."

I shift on his bed so my back is leaning against the headboard. Timmy shuffles closer to me, and I put my arm over him. As I read him the story, I feel his shoulders relax. His tears dry up. When I'm done, his face is no longer as pained as it was.

"You think she heard it?" he asks in a barely audible voice.

I squeeze his shoulder. "I'm sure she did." I stroke the top of his head.

He nods.

The room gets quiet. I keep my arm around him, occasionally giving him a few squeezes. I don't know what to say. I'm not an expert on kids or anything, but I'll be here for Timmy, even if it's enough that I just sit near him on his bed.

I force the tears that fight their way to the surface of my eyes. I need to be strong for him.

"Miss Cassie?" he says after a few minutes.

I swallow so my voice won't tremble with the tears that are threatening to win. "Yes, Timmy?"

"Do you think…do you think the shark would have bitten me if Kayla wasn't there?"

Now the tears come. I swipe them away with the back of my hand. I lay my chin on the top of his head. "Don't think like that, sweetie. It was just an accident." *Emerald Clan.* I push it away. "It was just an accident, okay?"

His shoulders get stiff. "If-if I wouldn't have brought her to the beach, she would…she would…" A hiccup swallows the rest of his sentence.

This is so hard. I don't know if he has anyone to talk to, other than his parents.

I reposition him so I can hug him close, rocking a bit and patting his back. "This isn't your fault, okay? Don't ever think this is your fault."

His face digs into my shoulder. "She wanted to surf like me. Daddy said she was too young. She always wanted to copy me."

"Because you were such an awesome older brother."

He sobs, his shoulders shuddering. "I don't want to surf anymore."

"Timmy—"

"She's dead because of me."

My tears are making it impossible to see. I blink so they drip down my cheeks. I don't want Timmy to hear me cry. I want to be strong for him. I hold him even closer and continue to rock.

Merman's Touch

"Miss Cassie," he cries.

"She wouldn't have wanted that," I say softly. "Do you think Kayla would have wanted you to quit surfing? She would have wanted you to keep at it. Do it for her, Timmy. Work hard to become the best surfer out there. Make your little sister proud."

He doesn't respond, just continues weeping on my shoulder. His nails dig into my arms.

"You'll be okay," I whisper, brushing my hand through his short hair. "You'll be okay, sweetie."

I don't know how long we stay like this. Maybe ten minutes. Eventually, Timmy separates himself from me and rolls over on his bed. I get up and throw his blanket over him, bending closer to kiss the top of his head. Even as he drifts off to sleep, I see his face contorted in pain. I gently rub his shoulder, wishing I knew what I can say or do to make this easier for him. But I don't think there's anything I can do. Killing the shark won't bring Kayla back.

The babysitter is on the living room couch, flipping through a fashion magazine, her legs folded beneath her. She sits forward when I step in. "How is he?"

"Okay. He's sleeping now."

She nods, a sad expression on her face.

We just stand there looking at one another. The whole house is swallowed in sorrow.

"It kind of makes you rethink things, doesn't it?" she says. "How you treat people. My younger brother and sisters can be such pests, you know? Always bugging me. I hardly spend time with them, but talk on the phone or go to the mall. If something were to happen to them…" She bites down on her lip as her eyes tear up.

I reach out and pat her arm. "Tragedy usually makes you appreciate what you have. It sucks, but that's how it is."

She nods.

I pat her arm again. "Take care of him, okay?"

"I will."

I give her a small, stiff smile and exit the house.

Chapter Nineteen

My eyes snap open. I glance at the time and see it's well past five AM. I overslept.

Reaching for my phone, I try to turn it on. I know I set my alarm before I fell asleep. But it won't turn on—it's dead. The alarm must have rang and rang until my phone died. Did I really sleep through it? I remember tossing and turning as I tried to fall asleep, forcing the memories of the attack out of my head. I guess I was pretty knocked out.

Pushing my blanket aside, I swing my legs over the edge of my bed and stretch. My whole body aches because I haven't slept right.

After slipping on my shoes and grabbing my bag, I head for the beach. My stomach does flip flops as I draw nearer. I close my eyes, taking in a deep breath through my nose and letting it out through my mouth. I can do this—enter the beach. I *need* to do this. I have to be there for Damarian.

He's coming home with news. The thought causes my chest to tighten. What if he tells me something I don't want to hear? What if it's worse than I could have imagined?

My knees wobble. I lower myself onto the path that leads to the beach. Hooking my arms around my legs, I bury my face in my knees and breathe.

A little voice in my head urges me to get up. Damarian could be waiting. I don't want him to think I rejected him. I don't want him to return to the ocean.

I force myself to my feet and enter the beach. Like all the other times, the place is deserted. Double checking is almost second nature to me. When I'm one hundred percent sure not a single soul is lurking around, I climb onto the rocks.

The waves crashing into one another catch my attention. I peer over the edge of the rocks. Damarian's head sticks out of the water. "Cassie." His familiar, musical voice drifts over the water, into my ears.

My whole body swells with relief and joy. All I want is to throw myself into his arms, to hold him close and let him hold me close. I want to feel his sweet, warm lips on my mouth. I want to feel his love and comfort.

"Damarian!" I call, bouncing on my heels and waving both hands in the air. "Damarian!" The moon casts enough light to see his face and upper body. The rest of him is submerged under.

He dives back into the water. I hurry down the rocks to meet him near the tide, but stand a few feet away. As he pulls himself onto the sand, I reach into my bag for the sheet and spread it wide open in my arms. When he's completely out of the water and is lying flat on the sand, I step closer and throw it over him.

Lowering myself to my knees, my heart caves. I won't be able to hold him as he changes from merman to human. My hands itch toward him as I see his eyes roll back and forehead start to sweat. But I plant them firmly on the sand, grabbing hold of some grains and squeezing tight. They dig into my skin as I see him convulse, as I hear him cry out softly. Instinct tells me to leap into his arms and hold him, but I stand

Merman's Touch

my ground.

It takes as much time as usual, but right now it feels like hours. When it's finally over, I move closer to him with the towel and dab his forehead, then his hair that's still slightly wet. I lay myself over him, pressing my cheek to his.

"Cassie," he says, his voice laced with relief, joy, and love.

"Damarian," I whisper, stroking the side of his face.

"How are you?"

I almost forgot about everything that's happened. When I'm with Damarian, it feels like the world is made of rainbows and chocolate bunnies. Swallowing, I say, "I'm okay."

He caresses my cheek. "I apologize, my sweet Cassie. I do not believe I can remain on land."

It feels like he slammed a hammer into my heart. I raise my head and look into his eyes. "What?"

"All is not well in the sea," he says, his voice barely audible. I have to lean in close to hear him.

"What...what do you mean?"

He glances back at the ocean again. "All is not well in the sea."

"You said that already. Damarian, what's *going* on? Does this have anything to do with the shark attack?"

He encloses me in his arms. "You must listen carefully," he whispers into my ear. "Do not enter the sea. Do you understand?"

My body feels numb. "Why?"

He looks away from me. "I did not inform you of this matter sooner, for I did not wish to upset you. But you must be aware of it now. You are in grave danger."

I'm officially spooked. Tears choke me. "Damarian."

"Do not cry, my love. I shall protect you."

"Why—why am I in danger?"

He doesn't answer.

I touch his cheek. "You need to tell me. You can't protect me all the time. I need to know what's going on. Please."

He nods slowly. "Very well." He presses me closer to his body. I feel his heart beating at a very fast pace. "There are children of the sea who do not approve of the union between King Kiander and Queen Flora. They have rebelled against the kingdom."

I can't feel my limbs. No, no, no. Why does this keep happening? All Damarian and I want is to be together. Why does it seem like forces are purposely trying to screw us over?

"But you said they want a Sapphire to rule. Your brother is a Sapphire."

"Yes, but I am the true heir to the crown. The true king."

"What difference does that make?" Every part of me pulses in anger. "Kiander agreed to be the king. What more do they want from you? Isn't anything ever enough for you people?"

As soon as the words leave my mouth, I regret them. I just called Damarian's kind "you people." I'm just so frustrated and hurt. All I want is to be with Damarian. I don't want to have to fight for him all the time. I just want him to be mine.

He rests his forehead against mine. "Children of the sea are very traditional, my love. We are not fond of changing our ways. The battle many moons ago tore the crown from the true king. Many want it returned to where it belongs."

My chest huffs and puffs as I try to regulate my breathing. It isn't fair. None of this is fair. I thought we could finally be together once Kiander agreed to marry Princess Flora and become king. He lifted the banishment off Damarian and Kyler. He's a good king. Why can't the merpeople appreciate what they have?

They aren't that much different from humans.

"They are aware that I have been on land," Damarian says, slowly and carefully so I hear every word. "They believe I pushed my duty aside for a fantasy."

"It's not a fantasy," I utter, tears rolling down my cheeks.

"They wish for me to be ruler."

I grip his shoulders and cry into his chest. "No. No!"

He runs his hand up and down my back. "Fret not, Cassie."

I lift my head off him and stare into his eyes. "That's why they attacked Kayla," I realize. "They wanted to punish the humans. Punish me. Us."

Damarian nods, his lips in a straight line.

Kayla is dead because of me. It *is* my fault. Bitter tears prick my eyes. She didn't deserve it. "Who sent the shark?" Please don't say Kyle. I can't bear the thought that the guy I once loved, and the guy I helped return to his home, would betray me like this.

"I am not certain. It is one of the rebels from the Emerald clan."

"Kyler?" I croak.

His eyes flash with surprise. "Kyler of the Emerald clan? No."

"Are you sure?"

"Yes, he is not a rebel."

My body sags a bit in relief. "Who are these rebels?"

"They are members from many clans. Most belong to the Emerald and the Diamond clans, for they are supporters of the Sapphires."

I can't take this anymore. I don't want to believe any of this. I just want to be with Damarian. Why can't I be with him?

"Do they know about me? That I'm...that I'm a mermaid?"

Darkness conquers his features. "I do not believe so. I fear to think how they would react if they discover you are a child of the sea."

My heart is beating so fast I'm growing lightheaded. "What do you mean by that? You think they'd kill me?"

He looks away. "I do not know." He takes my face in his hands. "Do not enter the sea. I beg you."

Tears pool out of my eyes as I nod.

"Do not fret, my love," he says. "I will allow no harm to come your way." His lips tickle my ear. "All will be well. I shall make it so."

"They…" I clear my throat. "They can come on land."

He shakes his head. "They will not be quick to leave the sea."

"How can you be so sure?"

"It is not our nature or our will to leave the sea."

"Even to kidnap me?" I ask.

He nods.

"So what are we supposed to do now? Stay parted forever?"

His arms come around me. "I will return to the sea and we shall make peace. I am yours, Cassie. For all eternity." His lips graze my cheek. "I shall return to you as soon as I can."

"Will you be in danger? Can they hurt you?"

He hesitates before saying, "No."

"Damarian—"

"They will not harm me, Cassie. I am quite certain of it, for they wish me to be their king."

Fresh tears form in my eyes.

"Cassie," he says softly.

"Kiss me."

He tucks his fingers under my chin and lifts my face to his. Dipping his head, he slowly brings his lips to mine, stopping just a few inches away. I feel his warm breath on my face. My whole body throbs with the anticipation of feeling them once again on my mouth. He inches them closer and closer at a very slow pace. Like he wants to savor the moment because he's not sure when the next time will be.

When his lips finally make contact with mine, my mouth explodes.

Merman's Touch

I pull him closer to me, molding my body against him until every single part of me touches every single part of him. Our lips move over each other urgently and desperately. I feel so much in this kiss. The fear, the uncertainty, the passion and love. The determination not to give up on one another. People want to tear us apart, but we won't let them. I hold my merman tightly in my arms and raise a fist in the air. Nothing and no one will come between us. *Nothing and no one.*

"Cassie," he says between kisses. "Cassie."

We don't stop kissing. We just pause for air and to moan each other's names. I feel protected in his arms and know that no one can hurt me. But what will I do when he's gone? How long is he going to stay away? And will he be able to make peace with the rebels?

He lays me down on the sand and showers kisses all over my face, my neck, my upper chest. My fingers cling to his hair and I pull on the strands. I don't want his lips to lose contact with my skin. I don't want him to return to the ocean. I fasten my legs around him and don't let him go. I won't. He and I are going to stay together forever.

Damarian's lips trek up my neck to my lips, then he lays his forehead against mine. "I shall return to you as soon as I can."

I tighten my legs around him. "Don't go. Please."

"My beautiful Cassie," he says, bringing his lips back to mine. This kiss holds so much love and longing that I'm left breathless. His fingers dig into my waist as he kisses me long and hard. Every time he tries to break away, I yank him back to me. He's not leaving me. He's *not*.

"Do not enter the sea," he whispers against my lips.

"Stop," I say. "We're not saying goodbye."

"Do not allow strangers into your house."

"Stop!"

"In case they are to come on land, be vigilant, my love." He buries his head between my neck and shoulder. "I do not wish any harm to come your way. My Cassie."

My hands play with his hair. "This isn't goodbye, Damarian. Please don't let it be goodbye."

"The sun is in the sky," he says into my shoulder. "I do not wish to part with you, but I must." When he raises his head, I see his cheeks are caked with tears.

I throw my arms around him. "Damarian."

"I must go, Cassie."

"No," I cry. "Please, no."

"Be vigilant." He gently untangles himself from me. "I shall return soon."

"Damarian," I say weakly as he dives into the ocean. "Damarian!"

I'm still lying on the sand. I'm too broken to sit up. I only manage to lift my head. His head peeks out of the water. He blows me a kiss and waves.

"No," I beg. "Come back. Please."

"I shall return to you, my love," is the last thing I hear. My head falls back and I stare at the light sky. Tears rain down my cheeks and I can hardly breathe through my nose. My chest rises and falls violently as I try to catch my breath.

I curl into a ball and weep into my hands. "Damarian."

Chapter Twenty

I texted Leah to come over as soon as her shift ends. The second she walks through the door, she yanks me in for a big hug. "Are you okay?"

"Not really."

We sit down on the couch and I tell her everything, about the rebels, how they might want to kill me, how Damarian is in the ocean now, trying to make peace.

Her eyes and mouth are the widest I've ever seen. "This sounds like something from a book or a movie."

Sticking my hands under my knees and staring at the floor, I mumble, "That's not the half of it."

"What?"

After taking a deep breath, I say, "Follow me."

I lead her down the stairs and into the pool room. Her eyebrows rise in confusion and curiosity. My fingers reach for the hem of my shirt. "Don't freak out, okay?"

"What are you doing?"

I pull the shirt over my head, then shimmy out of my pants. "Just promise me you won't freak."

She blinks at me. "You're stripping naked. How am I *not* supposed to freak?"

Don't say I didn't warn her. Raising my hands over my head, I jump into the pool.

It hits me at once, the tingling, the pain. I twist and flail around, every cell in my body crying out. In the back of my mind, I know this will end soon, but as I'm burning in an invisible inferno, all I can think about is how much I want to die, just so this will be over.

And then it is. My body falls to the floor of the pool. Kicking off, I break the surface. Nothing could have prepared me for the expression on Leah's face.

She backs away, her eyes so wide they look like they're about to pop out of their sockets. Her mouth opens and closes. She stumbles back, trips over her feet, and hits the ground.

Pretty much the same reaction I had when I saw Damarian in his merman form for the first time.

I prop my elbows on the edge and lift myself a little so I can peer at her. She's splat on her back, her eyes locked on the ceiling, not blinking. It's like she's in shock.

"So as you can see," I say. "I'm not pregnant."

A large breath breaks out of her mouth. She turns her head and gapes at me.

"Surprise," I mutter.

"Mer..." she chokes. "Mer..."

"Mermaid," I offer.

She slowly sits up, her whole body shaking. She blinks, her mouth wide open. She backs away until she hits the wall, mumbling things I can't hear.

I hold out my hand. "Leah, it's okay."

"Are you *insane*? How is it okay? You're a mermaid. Holy shit, you're a freaking mermaid."

Merman's Touch

I flinch. "At least you're no longer in shock."

"Think again." Her breathing is heavy.

The room gets dead silent.

"What the *hell*, Cass?" Leah finally says. "You're a *mermaid*. Look at your hands. They're *webbed*!"

I nod. I almost forgot Leah's never seen a mermaid, or merman, before. I'm so used to how Damarian looks, but she's not. I'm not surprised that she's freaking out like this, though it does make me feel like a freak.

"And your eyes are blue! They look exactly like Damarian's."

"I guess all merpeople have the same color eyes."

"Do you know how crazy this is?" Leah says.

"*I'm* the mermaid, aren't I?"

She shakes her head in disbelief.

I reach to touch her, but she's too far away. And I don't miss the way she cringes. It's a slap across the face, but I guess I don't blame her.

"So you're a mermaid now?" she asks, pressing her lips together like she's scared of my answer.

"I guess."

She hangs her head between her legs. "This is so insane. My best friend is a fish."

"Thanks for making me feel better."

She lifts her head, her expression apologetic and full of regret. "Sorry. I just…you're used to this kind of stuff. You see Damarian change every day. Me…not so much."

I nod. "I understand how freaked you are. But I needed to tell you. You're my best friend."

"How long have you been like this?"

"A few days. I've been in the ocean, Leah. Swimming with

Damarian. It was amazing. Like scuba diving, but with so much more freedom."

She shakes her head in disbelief again. "I can't believe I'm having this conversation." She crawls a little closer, though not too close. "So you need to swim in there twice a day?"

I stare down at the water. When was the last time I swam? Was it two days ago? It was definitely more than twelve hours. If I was Damarian, my body would have been crying for salt water after so many hours without it. Is it different for me?

"I...I don't know," I say.

We're both quiet. I see how Leah keeps her gaze mostly on my face and not the lower half of my body. It stings a little because I don't want this to affect our relationship.

"I guess I'll get out," I say.

I've never gone out of the water on my own before as a mermaid. Damarian always gave me a lift. "Can you help?" I ask.

She looks at me like I asked her to slice off my arm with a saw. "Uh...sure."

As she stands, her knees wobble. She breathes in and out, rubbing her hands down her clothes. I watch as she hesitantly scans me, from head to tail. "That tail is so pretty." She covers her face. "God, I can't believe this."

Again, I don't blame her. I was so blown away when I saw Damarian's tail for the first time.

"Take my hands and pull me," I tell her. "I'll try to swing my tail."

She blinks a few times. "Swing your tail. Right." She looks down at my webbed hands. "Um..."

"It's okay..." I say, holding them out. She slowly brings hers closer, inch by inch, until they're only a few centimeters apart. Then, she slides them into mine.

Merman's Touch

She yanks them away. "Weird. They feel like normal hands yet they don't." She takes hold of both my hands again and yanks me. Her eyes bulge as she stumbles forward, nearly falling into the pool. "What is that thing made of? Stone?"

"Sorry…"

She takes in another large gulp of air. Squeezing my hands, she groans as she pulls me. I try to swing my tail over the edge, but we're not working together, our movements not in sync. I lose all my energy and slip back into the pool. Luckily, Leah lets go before I take her down with me.

I sink to the bottom of the pool.

"Cassie!" Leah's voice is frantic.

I wave my hand, telling her I'm okay.

"I was just about to dive in to save you, then I realized you can breathe underwater. Duh."

When I get some energy, I swim to the surface and rest my elbows on the edge of the pool. "Let's try again, but we need to work together."

"Okay."

It takes a few tries, and maybe ten minutes, but I finally manage to haul myself out of the pool with so much force that I bang into Leah. She gets tangled around me and a chair tips over, falling on top of us.

She rubs her elbow. "Damn, you're strong."

"Sorry."

She stares at me, from the top to my head to my tail. "So…what happens now? You change?"

"Yeah, once I dry up. Can you please bring me a few towels from the upstairs closet?"

"Sure." She heads for the door, then looks back at me, at my tail. She shakes her head in disbelief once again before disappearing up the stairs.

I think she's taking this whole thing rather well.

When she returns with two large towels, I wrap one around my torso and ask her to do the same with my tail. She crouches down to her knees and stares at it for a bit before slowly wrapping the towel around it. I fold my arms over my chest and lean against the wall. A few minutes pass.

"How long does it take?" Leah asks.

"I don't know. It depends on how dry—" I cry out when I feel acute pain in my lower abdomen. My back hits the floor and my palms flatten on the tiles as I try to clutch onto something—anything—as the pain travels from my stomach all the way to my toes.

"Cassie!"

I don't know if I'll ever get used to this, but it does give me comfort that it will all be over soon. When it does, my entire body is drenched with sweat, and my heart is beating so fast I think it may fly out of my chest. When I open my eyes, it takes a few seconds until they get into focus. Leah sticks her concerned face in mine. Her mouth moves, but I don't hear anything, until a few seconds later. "You okay? Holy shit, I thought you were going to die."

I try to sit up, but I'm so weak I fall back down. My vision turns black.

Chapter Twenty-One

"Cassie!"

I open my eyes to darkness. As I move my body, something feels different. There's a bit of friction, like I'm underwater.

"Damarian?" I call. No matter where I look, I can't see a single thing.

"Cassie." His voice is weaker.

"I can't see! Where are you?"

"Cassie." His voice sounds far, far away.

When I wake up, I see Leah's head drooping toward her chest. Glancing around, I realize I'm in the pool room, and the events come back to me—I just showed Leah I'm a mermaid.

Damarian's voice. Was it a dream?

Leah stirs. When she sees me, she smiles weakly. "Welcome back."

"What time is it?"

She shrugs. "Close to six, probably."

Only a few hours until I head for the ocean to see if Damarian will return. I know it's still early and that he couldn't have made peace with the rebels yet, but I still need to go there.

"Let's go upstairs, get you dressed, and sit down in the living room," Leah says. "There's a lot we need to talk about."

Leah settles down on the couch while I change into my pajamas. She's munching on popcorn when I get downstairs. She looks semi-normal, not like a girl who saw her best friend swimming in her pool as a mermaid. Not like a girl who witnessed the mermaid shift into a human. Maybe that means she's more okay with it, or maybe she's acting as normal as possible for my benefit.

I sit down next to her and grab some popcorn. "I won't be able to surf."

Her eyes meet mine. "That sucks."

"Yeah."

"Is there a mermaid Damarian can talk to? Maybe someone who can switch you back or something?"

I snort. "I'm sure there's a long line to the ocean's sea witch."

She slaps my shoulder. "I'm trying to help."

"He said he's never seen it before." I rub my forehead. "Damarian's in the ocean trying to make peace with the rebels because of me. Because he fell in love with *me*."

She pats my back. "He'll succeed, Cass. Everything will be okay."

I desperately want to believe her, but I don't know if I can.

"Want me to spend the night?" she asks.

"You sure? I'm going to wait for Damarian at the beach later, though."

"I'll stay with you until then. That's what best friends are for. It's not every day a girl turns into a mermaid. Those scales—although gorgeous—cannot be good for your skin. I have lotion in my bag."

I laugh. "What would I do without you?" I put my arm around her. "Thanks for being such an awesome friend."

She returns the hug. "Thanks for keeping my life interesting."

***

Leah and I sleep in my bed like we did many times before I met

Merman's Touch

Damarian. It feels nice lying next to her and talking about everything.

We both can't sleep. Leah because of what happened to me, and me because I'm anxious to see if Damarian will show up. And if he does, will he have good news to share with me?

"Tell me how things are going with Jace," I say.

"We went to the arcade yesterday. It's one of his hangouts."

"He got you to go to the arcade? You quit going with me when we were like twelve."

"The place is filled with little kids challenging you, and you know I can't stand when someone calls me a chicken. But…" She shrugs. "The things we do for love."

"*Love?*"

"Sorry. The things we do for guys we are totally into."

I won't look at the time. I won't count how many hours, minutes, and seconds I have until I might be in Damarian's arms again.

I sit up on my elbow. "Last we talked, you told me you guys were going through a rough patch."

She grins and wiggles her eyebrows. "Let's just say there are certain…activities that can fix a lot of problems."

I slap her arm. "Leah!"

She shrugs. "What? I can't help if I'm so irresistible."

I slap her again. "Just make sure you guys have a lot to talk about, too."

She nods. "Thanks."

We continue to talk, and before I can blink, it's starting to get light. Leah glances at the window. "Time to go fishing?"

I roll my eyes.

"Come on. Admit that was a good one."

"Fine. It was a good one. Thanks for spending the night."

She waves her hand. "Don't mention it."

"I'll walk you home."

Her house is out of the way, but it's the least I can do. Leah's such a good friend and does so much for me. I know I haven't been the greatest friend to her because I've been spending so much time with Damarian. I promise myself to make it up to her.

We reach Leah's house. She turns to me and grins. "Well, this is me. Thanks for such an amazing night. Call me?" She winks.

I laugh. "Don't cheat on Jace with me. He's too much of a good guy."

She winks again. "Gotchya." Her face turns serious. "Be careful. If you need me, call me and I'll come right away. Okay?"

"Thanks so much, Leah."

She waves and enters her house.

The quietness of the night envelops me. It makes me feel really lonely. I head to the beach, to the rocks, swinging my bag of essentials. Keeping my eyes on the waves, I wait.

And wait. When my eyes can't stay open, I pinch my left foot, forcing myself to stay awake. I've been waiting at least forty-five minutes, and the logical part of my brain tells me it's highly likely Damarian's not meeting me tonight, but I won't give up.

My skin prickles as the salt water air touches it, and all I want to do is dive in there, but I force the temptation away. Reaching into the bag, I pull out the sheet. I sniff it. It smells like Damarian. It's only been a day, but I miss the smell. Hugging it close to my chest, I lie down on the rocks, staring at the dark sky. The rocks dig into my back and ribs, and I know I'll have to get up in a few seconds, but for now it feels good to just stare at the sky, at the stars.

It reminds me of the night Damarian and I lay on the beach a few weeks ago. It was the first time he was this close to the stars. Usually, on rare occasions, he'd swim close enough to the surface at night and stare at the sky. Being there with him as he experienced it for the first time on land was so special and magical. So intimate.

"It feels like you can hold them in your hands," I told him. "But really, they're huge, some even larger than the sun. It's just that they're far away, like light years away."

Damarian gawked at me. "They are larger than the sun?"

I locked my hands beneath my head. "Yeah. I wanted to be an astronaut when I was younger." I chuckled to myself. "I would have made a hot astronaut, don't you think?" I elbowed him.

"I do not know what that is, but yes, you are indeed 'hot.'"

I laughed. "Astronauts explore space."

"Space?"

I pointed at the sky. "They go up, up, up. All the way there." I turned my head and our eyes met. "Humans are curious creatures. Just like we explore the ocean, we explore space."

His face filled with intrigue. "And what have you discovered up in the space?"

"Many things. Like there are other planets."

"Planets?"

"Yeah. Worlds, just like ours. But there's no life on the other planets, at least not that we know of."

He focused his gaze on the sky. "That is quite fascinating. I have always wished to explore the deep ocean. Perhaps…perhaps if I were born a human, I would be exploring the space."

"Then *you* would have made one hell of a hot astronaut." I climbed on top of him, resting my elbows on either side of him and staring down into his face. "You know what I always fantasized about?"

His eyes flashed with delight. "Please inform me."

My fingers tiptoed down his chest. "Making out with my boyfriend under the stars. It's…romantic," I added with a shy laugh.

He put his hands on my waist and turned us over so he was on top. He touched his nose to mine. "Would you like to know what I fantasize about?"

"Hell yeah."

"Having a female who informed me of her fantasies."

First a blush spread over my face. Then I smiled. I rolled us over so I was on top again and smashed my lips to his. His arms snaked around me and he hauled me closer to his body. I swear the stars smiled down at us.

I blink and the memory is gone. Sitting up, I rub the pain away from my back. Lying on the rocks was *not* a good idea. I creep toward the edge and bend over. The ocean is calm. I don't see Damarian. Straining my eyes at the rest of the ocean, I don't see anything.

Gathering my bag, I stand up. Maybe he'll meet me tomorrow.

✦

Chapter Twenty-Two

Dad calls first thing in the morning. "Hey, Cass Bass. How are you?"

"Hey. I'm fine." If you disregard the fact that I'm a mermaid and it's my fault my boyfriend is in the ocean trying to make peace with some rebel merpeople.

"That's great. How's Damian?"

Well honestly, I have no idea. What if he's in danger?

"Cass?"

"Huh? Oh yeah, he's great. Super. Couldn't be happier."

He's quiet for a few seconds. "O...okay. Listen, my friend wants to set up an interview with Damian."

I grip the phone. "An interview?"

"For the construction job."

The construction job? I totally forgot about that. What's that compared to rebel merpeople? Sometimes I forget about the little things in my human life that are really important.

"He's not here," I tell Dad.

"Will you tell him to call me as soon as he gets in?"

"Um..."

"What, Cassie?"

My fingers plow through my hair. "I, um…I don't exactly know when he'll be back." Could be days, weeks, months, years. God, I hope not.

Dad sighs. It's the kind of sigh I remember getting a lot as a kid, when I screwed up or disappointed him. My eyes well up with tears. I hated disappointing him. "Dad—"

"I pulled a lot of strings to get him this interview," he says in a gentle tone, though I still sense the disappointment. "With no prior experience and no GED, do you know how hard it is to find a job?"

"Yes," I say in a low voice.

He sighs again.

"When's the interview?" I ask.

"Tomorrow afternoon."

My eyes shut. "He won't be able to make it."

"And why not?"

Because he's in the ocean. And if he returns tonight, I doubt he'd be up for an interview tomorrow. "He…he had to take care of some things," I say, hearing how lame I sound.

"Can't he 'untake' care of them so he can make the interview? Job offers like this don't come often and—"

"I know."

"—he needs to find a job if you two will be living together, especially with you in college. You need to learn to take care of yourselves. Your mother and I will always be here to help you, be it financially or anything else, but you need to learn to support yourselves."

"Dad, you can't just come into my life and tell me how to live it."

He's silent.

Dammit. I rub my forehead. "I'm so sorry. I shouldn't have said that. I didn't mean it."

Merman's Touch

He's still quiet.

"Dad?"

"That's okay, Cassie." I can tell by his tone that he's lying. "Try to convince him that having this interview is very important and he should push everything else aside to make it, okay?"

"Yeah. Okay."

"Bye, Cass Bass."

"Bye. And thanks for doing this. Damian and I really appreciate it. And I, um…I love you."

He's quiet. Did he hang up?

"I love you, too, honey."

My hand relaxes. I didn't know it was balled into a fist. I didn't know how desperately I wanted my dad to say those three words to me.

I wish I didn't snap at him like that. He was just trying to help. But everything feels like such a mess. How can Damarian and I focus on our human lives when there's trouble in the merworld? If I want to be honest with myself, Damarian's first priority is to his merman life, not his human one. He was supposed to be the king and he gave it up, abandoning his people. How can I expect him to care about an interview?

But if he misses the interview, what happens? This could be such a good opportunity for him, once we figure out the little details, like how long he can be out in the sun before shriveling up.

I rub my forehead again. Why can't things ever be simple?

***

He's calling my name.

His voice is so far away, like he's on the other end of the planet. But something's different. I don't know what it is, but I can feel it.

"Damarian?" I call out. I can't see anything due to the darkness around me, but it feels as though he's standing right next to me. "Damarian." I reach out, but don't feel anything, only water.

Then in a split second, lightning flashes, too fast for my brain to register it. Damarian cries out in pain.

"Damarian!"

There's another flash, and another shout from Damarian, but I still can't see anything.

"Where are you?" I call.

"Cassie..." It sounds as though all the energy is being sucked out of him.

Ringing yanks me out of my sleep. I spring up on the couch, my heart racing, my palms sweating. The word "Mom" displays on the screen. Placing my hand on my heart, I realize I must have fallen asleep.

The dream. Damarian. Is he in trouble?

The ringing continues. I shake my head and reach for it. "Mom," I say.

"Hey, honey!"

My heart is still running a million miles a minute. Damarian's screams echo in my ears. He's in trouble.

"Cass?"

I blink. "Sorry."

"Are you okay? You seem distracted."

"Yeah." I force a smile. "I'm cool."

"That's great. I'm leaving for Texas tonight and I just wanted to check in. I don't know how long I'll be there, but I have a surprise for you!"

My whole body perks up. "You're coming home?"

She laughs. "As soon as I'm done with Texas, I'm all yours!"

A genuine smile crosses my lips. I haven't seen my mother in so long. With everything that's been going on, I can use my mother's comfort. But things are a little different now. Damarian's not the only merperson—I am one as well. I told him I want to tell her about him being a merman, but will I have to explain that I'm a mermaid, too? That sleeping with him caused me to change? I'm sure she'd be thrilled to hear that.

Pushing my worries aside, I say, "I can't wait! When will you be done with Texas?"

"Probably no sooner than a week, honey."

Cassie!

The hairs on my arms stand up. "Damarian?"

"What?" Mom asks.

Dropping my phone, I stand, my gaze pasted on the spot in front of me. "Damarian?"

Quiet. I strain my ears, but don't hear anything. Could I have imagined it?

I feel a sharp pain all over my body, like someone's shocking me. I'm about to rush to the pool room, but then I realize the shock's not coming from me. It's coming from…Damarian. I *feel* him. I can't explain it exactly, but I just know it's him. And that wherever he is, he is in a lot of pain.

"Cassandra Price! What the hell is going on?"

Crap. I dive for my phone. "Sorry, Mom." I wince as the sharp pain continues. "I can't wait for you to come home, but I have to go now. Speak to you later. Bye!"

I hang up and text Leah to ask Ian to rent me a boat, and that she should wait for me there. I run up to my room and change into an old skirt and shirt. Then I race to the beach.

Leah's at the marina, and waves me over. She gestures to the boat. "Your wish is my command. Now why is renting a boat so important that you took me away from my break?"

"We're going for a ride." I take her hand and pull her with me into the boat. Then I start the engine. When I put enough distance between us and the beach, I focus my attention on Leah. "Damarian's in trouble. I have to help him."

"What do you mean he's in trouble?"

"I don't know. I've been having these dreams about him, and just a few minutes ago, I...*felt* him."

"What?"

"I can't explain it. I just know."

Cassie!

I press my palms to the sides of my head as his cries slam against my mind. "I'm feeling him again," I pant, sweat breaking out all over my body. After a few seconds, the shouts stop and I raise my eyes to Leah.

She's staring at me like I fell off the moon. "Do you have any idea how freaky this is? Your eyes...they turned dark blue for a few seconds and your skin turned, like, clear."

I feel that pain on my body again. Biting back a groan, I say, "I have to help him."

"How are you going to...?" Her face gets dark. "You're not thinking about..."

I nod. "I'm going into the ocean."

"Are you *insane?*"

"I've done this before, remember?"

She holds out her hands. "Let's calm down and think this through."

"There's nothing to think through. Damarian is in trouble and I'm going to help him."

"You're going into the ocean all by *yourself?* You've never swam that deep before. Who knows what kinds of creatures lurk there!"

Damarian's warning to not step foot in the ocean bounces in my mind. I shove it away. I don't care about the rebels. My merman is in trouble.

"But you don't know where the colony is, Cass!"

"Calm down, okay? I'll be fine."

"You…" She groans. "But." She groans again. "Damn, you're so stubborn." Her expression changes, going from shock and bewilderment to concern, and I see her eyes fill up with tears.

"Leah…"

"Don't be reckless," she says in a low tone. "I…" She hiccups. "I get that you want to help Damarian, but I can't let you go. You have no idea what lies there."

My own eyes fill with tears. "I love him so much, Leah. So, so much."

"I know."

"I need to go."

She brushes her tears away, not looking at me. "What if you get hurt?" Her gaze shoots to mine. "You're my best friend."

I take her hand. "Would you try to help if you knew I was in trouble? If you heard me shouting in pain?"

She wipes her nose. "Of course I would!"

"Now you understand why I need to go down there."

With more tears escaping her eyes, she pulls me into her arms. "I'm just so scared something will happen to you."

I squeeze my arms around her. "I know. I'm scared, too. But I need to do this."

She nods, sniffing.

"I'll come back as soon as I can." I pull back and look into her eyes. "I'm tougher than you think."

"I know you are." She laughs lamely and wipes her eyes again. "I suck at goodbyes."

"It's not goodbye," I tell her. "I'll be back before you know it."

She nods.

I get up and peer at the water. My throat constricts. I have no idea what lies in the deep ocean, but Damarian needs me. I need to be strong, for him. For us.

Leah takes hold of the hem of my skirt. "Good luck."

I place my hands over hers. "Thanks." Winking at her, I raise my arms and dive into the ocean.

As soon as I hit the salt water, the familiar pain engulfs me. I twist and flail around, biting hard on my lip and begging for it to stop. When it does, I find myself floating in the ocean, moving along with the current. Like before, the coolness of the water feels good against my skin and fills me with energy, nourishing me. I close my eyes as I soak it all in.

"Cassie?" Leah calls.

I swim to the surface.

She sighs in relief. "Good, you're a mermaid. I mean, not good, but…I mean…" She shakes her head. "I'll shut up now."

I laugh lightly, then swim closer, putting my hands on the edge of the boat. Leah's gaze dips to my webbed hand. She hesitantly puts hers on top of it. "I'll be okay," I tell her.

She nods unsurely. "Okay. But if a shark wants to eat you or something, punch it in the balls."

I laugh. "As if I know where its balls are."

She laughs, too.

"Thanks for everything, Leah."

"*No.* This sounds like goodbye."

I hold back the tears threatening to pool in my eyes. What if this *is*

Merman's Touch

the last time I see her? Damarian warned me to stay out of the ocean, and I'm deliberately putting myself in harm's way.

Not wanting to dwell on it, I say, "See you soon," and dive into the water.

Chapter Twenty-Three

I don't know where I'm going, but my tail steers me deeper into the ocean. As the surface draws farther away, I know I should feel like an alien, and a part of me does—the human part. But the mermaid part feels like I returned home.

Last time, Damarian was with me, sharing the excitement as I experienced swimming in the ocean for the first time as a mermaid. Now I'm alone. Alone and afraid.

I swim past the fish and other ocean life. Like the last time I was in the ocean, I hear the humming sound from all the fish. At any other time, I would stop or slow down to watch and study this amazing, beautiful world. But Damarian needs me.

My heart thumps as I look to my right and left. Anyone can be lurking around. Rebels. I swallow and keep swimming. I won't give up on Damarian, no matter how nervous or scared I am.

Goose bumps crawl over my skin. Damarian—I feel him. It's so much stronger than when I was on land. I spread out my arms and close my eyes, scrunching my eyebrows as I concentrate on the pulse going through my body. I don't feel anything else. I can't sense if he's hurt.

I speed up. After what feels like hours but is probably only minutes

Merman's Touch

due to my pacing, I raise my head and see I'm far from the surface. The area is darker and the temperature is colder, but a nice, welcoming cool. Am I closer to the merpeople colony?

I twist my neck around, scanning the area. That's when I see two dolphins a few feet away. I swim toward them. They squeak when they see me, one rolling over on its back while the other spins around me.

"Hey," I greet.

The one spinning around me, who is slightly bigger than the other, stops and nudges its beak into my palm. The other continues to squeak, rolling on its back again. I smile. I've always wanted to swim with dolphins. I do a small dive and another somersault. The dolphins squeak again and do their own somersaults.

I laugh and rub the top of their heads. "Do you know where the Sapphire colony is?"

They flap their flippers and nod. They motion for me to follow them and they take off. I hurry after them. They lead me farther into the ocean, flanking me on either side. The temperature drops.

I try to push away the fear pricking my nerves. I'm getting closer to the merpeople colony. How will they react to me? I'm pretty sure it's not common for a human-turned-mermaid to drop by. And the thing that scares me more is Damarian's family. What will they say when they see me? What if they don't like me?

When I see something large and dark in the distance, I ask my tour guides to stop. The thing's moving closer. I falter back. Then I realize what it is. A blue whale. It's *huge*. I can't help but gawk. Blue whales are the largest mammals in the ocean. It swims past me, its tail sweeping behind and creating a whooshing sound like I'm in a giant washing machine. It's like I'm standing in front of a ship.

It's so amazing.

One of the dolphins squeaks. I nod. "Let's continue."

We must be pretty deep in the ocean. I see fish I've never seen before in my life, so colorful and bright. The coral here is exquisite. I don't realize my pace has slowed until one of the dolphins swims back to me and nudges me. Nodding, I speed up.

We swim for a little while before the dolphins come to a halt. They squeak and point their beaks in the distance, to a gap between two large rocks. My heart starts to race. The Sapphire colony must be there.

I rub the tops of their heads. "Thanks."

Our pleasure.

My hands freeze. Did they just speak to me?

They flap their flippers again and zoom away. I watch them until they're out of sight, then slowly turn toward the rocks. There it is—Damarian's home. His family. His life.

Taking in a large gulp of water and letting it out slowly, I swim toward it. As soon as I'm out of the rocks, all I see are fish and sharks. Lots of sharks. I saw a few sharks on my journey here, but not like this. There are all different species here, hammerheads, blue sharks, great whites, bull sharks. And tiger sharks. The image of Kayla's bloody body and severed arm flickers in my mind. My stomach clenches. It feels like years since I left land. I miss it already.

I convince myself that the sharks won't hurt me and swim forward. It's as though I tripped an alarm, because at once the sharks surge toward me. I stumble back and whimper. I do a one-eighty and am about to dive back through the hole, but sharks block me.

A large bull shark stops before me, its intense eyes gazing into mine. I swallow. If I was human, I'm pretty sure I would feel sweat breaking out at every area I have sweat glands.

It opens its mouth, revealing razor-sharp, deadly teeth.

Chapter Twenty-Four

The only thing that enters my head is: I'm going to die.

I find myself inching away, but I'm surrounded by sharks. Large and small, deadly-looking and even more deadly-looking. I would scream, but my vocal chords must be frozen.

The bull shark snaps its mouth open and closed. I flinch and cover my face with my arms. Hopefully, the bite will be quick and fast, but who am I kidding? I saw the way Kayla looked after the attack.

No. I won't go down without a fight. I drop my hands and fist them.

They fly to my temples when I feel something scratching the inside of my head. *Who is trespassing?*

I blink at the shark. Did it…?

I said, who is trespassing?

Holy crap. The shark is talking to me. I feel its voice in my head.

Answer me!

Two large blue sharks float on either side of the bull, their intense eyes on me. I try to open my mouth to say something, but I can't move. Those teeth…they look really sharp.

Looks like a child, the blue shark says, *I do not recognize the tail.*

Neither do I, the other one says.

I look down at my tail. It's not the same shade as Damarian's. They noticed. Does that mean they'll kill me?

"I'm here to see the Sapphire clan," I say.

The bull shark exchanges looks with the others. When they look back at me, they have murder in their eyes. My heart hammers in my head. Either they don't give a damn about what I said, or they don't believe me.

"Damarian of the Sapphire clan," I say.

The bull shark moves closer. *We do not recognize you. We will kill you.*

Tears form in my eyes. I know I won't feel them on my cheeks. They'll drip into the water, their salt mixing in with the salt of the ocean.

Damarian. I came here to save him. I risked my life for him. And this is my fate? To die by these sharks?

"Please," I say. "You have to hear me out. Damarian's in trouble. I came to help him. I know my tail is different, but I—"

The bull shark lunges at me, and just as I'm about to yell the loudest one I've ever yelled in my life, I hear someone shout, *Stop!*

All the sharks turn around. A small shark, a baby, swims toward me. A great white.

"Fiske!" I say, my whole body sagging with relief. Damarian introduced me to him a few weeks ago. I've never been so happy to see a shark before in my life.

The bull narrows its eyes. *What do you want, pup?*

Fiske swims closer to me and nudges my hand so I touch the top of its head, feeling the familiar rough surface. *What are you doing here, Cassie?*

I don't know if I can communicate with him without using my mouth. Concentrating hard, I think in my head, *Do you know where Damarian is? He hasn't been to land in a few days and I'm worried he's in trouble.*

Merman's Touch

I'm not an expert on shark expressions, but it seems as though Fiske's eyes fill with regret.

What? I ask, dread soaking my body. *Is he hurt?*

Fiske turns toward the bull shark. *This is the friend of Damarian of the Sapphire clan. It would be in your best interest not to harm her.*

She is not of the sea. She does not belong. She must be eliminated.

My throat chokes up.

The Sapphire clan would have you executed. Fiske turns back to me. *Come. I will bring you to the Sapphire clan.*

I feel like jumping in the air and saying "I'm free! I'm saved! I won't die!" But I rub the top of Fiske's head and say, *Thanks.*

The bull shark and Fiske give each other death glares. I grab onto Fiske's fin and let him draw me away, deeper into the ocean. When there's a good distance between us, I say, "What the hell are they?"

Sentinels. All the creatures that come or go must pass through them first.

That's how the merpeople manage to stay hidden from humans. Other than the fact that they are deep in the ocean, the sharks won't let anyone get past them. If not for Fiske…I'd be a dead fish.

I am in training to be a Sentinel, Fiske says. *Most do not believe I am fit for the job because of my age. But I will prove them wrong.* I swear he's giving me a smug smile.

"That's great," I say, my head spinning. All this…I can't wrap my head around it.

The area we've been swimming through has been mostly empty, with just fish and coral, but soon enough, I see them, and I stop dead in my tracks. Mermaids and mermen, with different tails. Oh my God. I'm actually here in the ocean with merpeople.

A young couple stops swimming and stares at me. Others do, too. They all look at my tail, their eyes and mouth wide. I feel like the spotlight is shining on me.

The Sapphire clan is this way. Fiske gestures to the left, where I see a large cave. Gulping in some more water, I follow him inside. When we emerge out of the other end, I nearly lose my head. All around me are sapphire tails. Mermaids and mermen of all different ages, swimming around. In the distance, I see many more caves. They talk and laugh and eat fish. They're all so beautiful.

Each and every one of their tails is a different shade of sapphire. I don't know how that's possible, but it is. They all have golden hair, but again, each a different shade. The only thing identical about them is their eyes—they are all deep blue.

There are also a few great white sharks around, though most aren't swimming, just floating in place. Like they're on guard.

"Cassie?"

I look to my right and find Doria next to a girl who seems to be around her age. Two boys with the same face are swimming around her, chasing each other. They have the same color hair and tail as her. They must be Damarian's twin brothers, Syd and Syndin.

Damarian's family. I can't believe I'm here.

Doria's gaping at my tail, her jaw practically sweeping the bottom of the ocean. "Your legs…" Her eyes move to mine. "You are a child of the sea?"

The boys stop playing and gape, too. So does her friend. If I were a turtle, I'd hide in my shell.

"Um…yeah," I say lamely.

The four of them continue to stare at me. Fiske stays silent by my side. Some of the nearby merpeople stare, too.

I swim forward. "Where's Damarian, Doria?"

She hesitates. The twins exchange a glance with each other, then with their sister. Even Doria's friend looks uncomfortable.

"What?" I ask.

Merman's Touch

"You should not have come," Doria says, her tone dead serious. We haven't had that much interaction, and I wouldn't call us friends, but I've never heard her talk like this.

"Why?" I move closer. "Because of the reb—"

"No!" She holds out her hands and looks at me like I told her humans are about to invade the ocean. "Do not speak it."

Syd and Syndin's eyes are the widest I've ever seen. Not that I've seen them before. Doria's friend looks like she's about to pass out.

"Come," Doria says, grabbing one of the twin's arms and throwing him over her back. She looks at me. "Follow me."

I swim forward, then twist my head back toward Fiske. His eyes are on me. I give him a thankful nod, and he returns it before leaving.

Doria is a good distance away. As I try to catch up, I watch the way her sapphire tail pumps behind her. The matching, smaller tail of the twin on her back floats just above hers. His arms are locked around her neck in a tight hold. The other twin holds her hand as they speed toward the direction where I imagine their house is.

There is beautiful coral all around me and many caves. Do the merpeople live in them? I don't see any fish around, or crabs, or other creatures. Damarian told me when we first met that he, his father, and brother went out hunting for food. I wish I could slow down and admire everything, but Doria is moving way too fast.

When I finally reach them, she has slowed down, her gaze pasted on the spot in front of her. I follow it. There's a cave. Two large great white sharks guard it on each side. Their eyes are bolted on me.

"Is that…where you live?" I ask.

Doria's eyes stay on the cave for a few more seconds before she turns to me. "You should not have come."

My heart and stomach twist. "Why do you keep saying that?"

She looks at my tail. "I do not understand how it is possible." She tightens her hold on the twin and moves a little closer to the cave. "Father and Mother will want to speak with you."

I freeze. Damarian's parents. I knew coming to the merpeople colony meant I would meet his parents, his family, but now it's becoming a reality. What if they don't like me? Syren's not exactly my biggest fan. But I need to push my selfish thoughts aside and focus on the reason I'm here: to help Damarian. Syren liking me is at the bottom of the ladder.

Doria swims toward the entrance and motions for me to follow. My gaze is locked on the two sharks, who don't look too happy to see me.

"They will not harm you," Doria says.

Taking a deep breath, I follow closely behind her as we enter the cave. There is no door, just an opening that seems to lead to a deep tunnel. When we reach the end of it, I find myself in a large, open space. There isn't much in here, just a stone table with matching chairs. Some fish lie on top of the table. Further down, I see other tunnels. I guess rooms.

"Mother," Doria calls.

I swallow, my heart beating so fast I swear it's about to bullet out of my chest.

Someone emerges out of one of the tunnels. But it's not Kiandra. It's a young mermaid, with the same color hair and tail as Damarian and Doria.

Zarya.

It seems like she's about to launch herself at Doria or the twins, but she stops dead in her tracks and blinks at me. "Who is our guest?"

"Never mind, Zarya. Where is Mother?"

Her little tail sways in the water, just as beautiful as the others. She looks a lot like Damarian, and is very adorable. I wish I could give her a

Merman's Touch

hug—it feels like I know her so well.

Another mermaid emerges from one of the rooms. Kiandra. Her hair and tail are different shades of colors from her kids. I guess their colorings either come from Syren or are a combination of both their genes.

Like her youngest daughter, she blinks at me. From the expression on her face, I can tell she knows exactly who I am. Moving toward me at a very slow pace, she studies me, her eyes narrowing at my face intently.

She continues to stare at me.

One of the twins yells something at Zarya, who is swimming away to one of the deeper tunnels, a shiny object clutched in her hand. The twin zooms after her, continuing to shout, followed by his brother.

The room is too empty.

Kiandra seems to snap out of it. "Damarian's mate."

My hand shoots out. "Hi. I'm Cassie."

Her eyes dip to my outstretched hand before returning to my face.

I drop it. I'm so nervous I forgot that merpeople have no idea what a handshake is. I clear my throat, then open my mouth to say something, but then I snap it shut. I have no idea what to say.

Kiandra moves forward again hesitantly. Slowly, she raises a hand and runs a finger down the front of my hair, her eyes warm and soft. "Damarian's mate," she repeats. She turns to Doria. "Where have you discovered her?"

"Where's Damarian?" I ask.

Her head whips to mine. Her face falls. "You have come to search for your beloved."

I nod, probably too vehemently.

Sighing, she turns away from me.

I glance at Doria. "Seriously, what's going on? He's in trouble, isn't he?"

    Mother and daughter lock eyes on one another. It seems like they're having their own private conversation through their eyes. After a few seconds, Kiandra looks at me. "Damarian has been captured."

Chapter Twenty-Five

It feels like the water in the whole ocean has crashed down on me. Breathing heavily through my gills and with my hand on my shuddering heart, I say, "Captured?"

"By the rebels," Doria says, her voice flat, though her nostrils flare.

"How?" I swim closer to them, wishing I could shake all the information out of them. "When?"

Kiandra looks away. When I bring my eyes to Doria, her face isn't exactly friendly. "He was captured as he returned home from land. After meeting with you."

Not only has the ocean crashed down at me, it slammed my body into floor of the cave, smashing all my bones. I falter back. He was captured because of me, because he wanted to see me, because he needed to warn me to stay out of the ocean. If not for me, he'd remain in safety with his family until the situation was resolved.

I cover my face. "I'm so sorry."

The room is silent. All I hear are my sobs, and I feel myself sinking. Suddenly, soft hands take hold of my shoulders. "Do not fret," Kiandra's voice whispers in my ear.

Lowering my hands, I say, "I didn't mean to cause any heartache to your family."

She rubs my back. "Fret not, Cassie. Damarian has chosen you as his mate. You are welcome in our home and into our lives."

By the way Doria's looking at me, I'm not sure how welcoming she is.

I wipe my eyes. "Where have they taken him?"

"We do not know," Kiandra says. "We are currently seeking information."

"I felt him," I tell her.

Her eyebrows shoot up and she stares at me. "You have sensed Damarian?"

I nod.

She and Doria exchange a shocked look.

"We have not been able to sense him," Doria says.

"I thought all the merpeople—I mean, the children of the sea—can sense one another, even on land."

They both nod. "But we are unable to sense him," Kiandra says. "Not even Zarya, who shares a close bond with him."

"That means…that can't mean…"

"He may very well be dead," Doria says, her voice flat again.

My mind yells a bitter, aching shout. "No," I say, backing away. "No…" I don't need tears to know I'm crying. "I sensed him as I was swimming here. He can't be dead."

They don't say anything.

"They want him as king," I say. "Why would they kill him?"

"Perhaps they wish to start a new kingdom." Kiandra shakes her head. "I am afraid the rebels are not even certain as to what they wish."

I'm at the floor of the cave. "I *feel* him," I urge, begging them to believe that there's still hope. "He's alive."

Again, mother and daughter exchange a look. "She is his mate," Doria says.

Merman's Touch

I feel someone behind me. I turn my head and find a tall, muscular merman floating near the entrance to the tunnel that leads here. His gaze is on mine. He looks just like Damarian, except his hair is longer, reaching his lower back.

Syren.

Like his wife, his hair and tail are different shades than his kids'. I guess that answers my question—the children's coloring is a mix of the both of them.

He doesn't take his eyes off me. The way he looks at me…I don't know if he wants to wrap his hands around my throat, or pretend like I don't exist.

Kiandra looks at him with hope. He shakes his head. He must have been out searching for Damarian, but no luck. My shoulders heave.

"Father!" Zarya surges out of the room and makes a short stop right in front of him. She holds out that shiny thing, which I now see is a rock. "Look what Syndin has discovered!"

"It is mine!" One of the twins zips toward her and tries to reach for the rock, but Zarya hides behind her father.

"You do not have a fondness for such objects!" Zarya says. "I wish to add this to my collection."

The kids seem oblivious to what's going on. That's probably best.

"Zarya," Syren says in a clipped tone. "Syndin. Enough."

They stop shouting and slink away. The other twin emerges from the room, coming to a stop near Doria. The three of them stare at the adults in the room.

"Please leave," Kiandra says to them.

With scowls and bent heads, they head toward the tunnels.

"Cassie has come seeking Damarian," Kiandra says to her husband.

"Cassie?" Zarya rushes back. "This is Cassie?"

"Zar—" Doria starts.

"You have arrived!" She blasts herself at me, wrapping her tail so tight around me, I feel it pound. "You have arrived! Did you receive my gift? I have received yours. It is most scrumptious. Have you brought more?" She peers at my hands and frowns. "You have not?"

"Zarya." Syren's tone is clipped again.

She lowers her head and disappears into one of the tunnels with the twins.

Syren swims over to the table and nods toward the fish. "She must be famished."

He's right—I am. The fish looks amazingly appetizing. I don't think I've wanted food this badly before.

Kiandra motions to the table. "Please eat," she tells me.

Doria sits down next to her father. I tentatively swim closer, like I'm approaching one of the Sentinel sharks instead of a merman. I sit down across from Doria. Syren takes a fish, then Doria does. I take a big one. If I was a human, I'd have no idea how to eat this thing. But my mermaid senses must be working overtime, because I know exactly where to begin. As soon as the meat hits my tongue, my whole body moans in pleasure. I never knew fish could taste so good.

Kiandra swims over to the corner of the room, to a pile of oyster shells. She picks out a small one, places a few fish inside, and goes to the room the kids swam to.

The only thing left to my fish is the bones. I should be embarrassed how I ate every last bit, but I'm not. I hope that's because I'm a mermaid. I take another fish.

Kiandra joins us at the table. We eat silently, the only sounds are our chewing. Finally, Syren drops the bones of his last fish on the table. "You are a child of the sea," he says to me.

Suddenly, I lose my appetite.

"Syren," Kiandra says.

"It is not possible." His eyes flash to mine. "It is an abomination."

"She is Damarian's mate," Kiandra says, her voice stern. "His mate."

Syren yanks his eyes away from me, to the table. He grabs another fish and bites into it.

"We—we don't know how," I say, my voice the shakiest it's ever been. "It kind of just happened after...after..."

"You are bonded," Syren says, clearly not happy.

I nod.

He pushes away from the table.

Kiandra springs up. "It was his wish, Syren!"

"What a silly fry," he mumbles, his hands fisting.

"I do not believe now is the appropriate time to discuss this," Doria says. She throws her half eaten fish on the floor. "Damarian is captured. There is still hope he is alive."

Her parents' mouths shut. They both look at her, their chests rising and falling heavily.

Kiandra rests her hand on her husband's cheek. "Doria is correct." She nods to me. "Cassie claims she has sensed Damarian."

"I sense him *now*," I say.

Syren's hands relax at his sides. "You are certain you sense him?"

I nod. "But it's weak. Like I have a bad signal or something. And I had dreams about him the past few nights."

"Explain the dreams."

I swallow. "He was calling for me. And the last one...it seemed like he was in a lot of pain. Like he was being hurt. Tortured."

"Were you able to see anything?"

"It was pitch black."

He rakes his hands through his hair. "It is as I feared."

"The Deep?" Kiandra whispers, her face even more white, if that's possible.

Her husband nods, his lips pressed in a firm line.

"What's the Deep?" I ask.

"It is far below," Doria answers. "Far, far below. Where life is not sustainable for children of the sea."

"They have found a way," Syren murmurs. "It is where they are headquartered. It explains why the Sentinels and Guards were not able to locate them." He fists his hands again and mutters something under his breath.

Kiandra fits her fingers through his. "It will be all right."

"What do they want with him?" I ask.

"We are uncertain," Syren says. He shakes his head. "They are more likely to kill Kiander."

I feel my eyes bug out. "They took Kiander, too?"

All three of them nod. "There was an attack on the palace," Doria says. "There was a lot of bloodshed. Queen Flora was unharmed."

My head is reeling. All of this, the chaos, the war. I feel responsible.

"I want to save them," I say.

They look at me like I fell from the sky and landed in the ocean.

Syren says, "That is absurd."

"You do not know our waters," Kiandra says, her tone much softer than her husband's. "You are not a Guard and do not have the ability to fight, nor to defend yourself."

"You would be killed," Syren says. He rests his palms on the table and leans forward. "Even though it is against the queen's wishes, I have been organizing a private party to locate my sons." His lips form a straight line. "The Sentinels and Guards failed. I doubt I will be successful, either."

"Father—" Doria starts.

He holds out his hand. "There is no other way."

Merman's Touch

His head whips toward the entrance at the sound of movement. So do Kiandra's and Doria's. A few seconds later, someone emerges. Jet black hair, an emerald tail.

"Kyle?" I rush toward him and fling my arms around him. It feels so good to see a familiar face.

His arms tighten around me. "What are you doing here?" He pulls free and scans me from top to bottom. "What happened to you?"

"I know it's weird. It just happened."

"You look great."

I hug him again. The last I saw him, he was swimming away, returning home to the Emerald colony. He hadn't seen his family and friends in two years. A lot of drama happened between us, but I can safely say we're on good terms now.

We both realize at the same time that we're not alone. Turning my head, I see Damarian's parents and sister watching us with the most puzzled expression on their faces.

I drop my arms from around him and move a few inches back. Merpeople don't know what hugs are.

Kyle faces Damarian's family, bending his head slightly. "Syren and Kiandra." He raises his head and nods to Doria.

The three of them return a nod. "Why have you come here, Kyler?" Syren asks.

He looks at me, then back at Syren. "I have heard of the arrival of a peculiar child." He smiles at me. "I knew they were referring to you, Cassie."

News about me is traveling that fast it reached the Emerald colony?

"You're here for Damarian, aren't you?" Kyle asks.

My throat constricts. I nod.

He faces Syren. "I beg of you. Please, allow me to join."

Syren shakes his head. "I will not put you in harm's way."

"There are many of us willing to help."

"I will not argue."

He throws his hands up. "Do not be stubborn, Syren."

Syren sighs, closing his eyes.

"Please," Kyle begs.

Syren turns toward him and nods. "I will meet with Queen Flora and Callen in the morning."

Kyle bows his head. "Thank you." His fingers close over my arm. "May I speak to Cassie in private?"

"Yes," Kiandra says.

He leads me out of the cave and toward an area that is empty. We sit on stones, facing one another. He grins. "I'm so happy to see you."

"Me, too."

He marvels at my tail. "How did *that* happen?"

I blush. At least, I think I do. It's hard to tell in the ocean.

Kyle's eyes fill with confusion. "What?"

How exactly do I tell my ex that sleeping with my current boyfriend caused me to turn into one of his people? I scratch the back of my head. "Well…we…we kinda…"

His eyes widen. "You're telling me mating with a *merman* turned you into a mermaid?"

I shrug. "Looks like it."

He shakes his head, dumbfounded. "Wow. That's crazy. I didn't know that could happen."

I'm pretty sure Damarian didn't either, because I'm positive he wouldn't have slept with me. That thought causes my chest to tighten. I'm so glad we took the next step and grew even closer, despite the fact that I turned into a mermaid. If I had the choice to go back in time and change it, I wouldn't.

"I didn't turn you," he says, rubbing his chin.

Merman's Touch

"You weren't a merman then," I say.

He nods. "Yeah, that's true." He studies the area around us. "What do you think of my world so far?"

"It's okay, I guess. I'm not exactly enjoying it that much, though."

He nods again. "I hear you. You're worried about Damarian."

"His sister claims he got captured after meeting me on land. Do you…" I bite my lower lip. "Do you think that's true?"

His face fills with regret. "The last time anyone saw him was when he left to go to land. He never returned."

"He could be lost somewhere…"

Kyle shakes his head. "While he was on land, they captured King Kiander."

It feels like I swallowed some sand. "How did they capture him?"

His eyes cast downward. "There was a spy in the palace."

Every part of me grows numb.

"You have to understand, Cassie, we are a peaceful race. We don't have many wars. We haven't hurt one another since the battle long ago, where the Sapphires lost the crown."

My chest hurts. "It's all my fault."

He takes my hand. "Don't think like that. Everyone is responsible for his or her own actions. Damarian stepped down from the throne. It was his decision. Kiander stepped up. They should accept it."

"His family thinks he's dead," I whisper.

Kyle hesitates, his face clouded with pain. "Children of the sea can sense one another. Anywhere, anytime. We can't sense him. Or Kiander."

"I can."

He raises an eyebrow. "Are you sure? You don't know—"

"It's him. I know it is."

It looks like he doesn't know if he believes me, but he nods.

"Syren's been trying to organize a rescue party, to search in the deep ocean. Queen Flora says it's a suicide mission. We can't survive down there. If the rebels did indeed take them down there, it's a good bet they're not alive anymore."

"But the rebels survive," I point out.

He raises his shoulders helplessly. "I don't know, Cassie. I wish I could tell you something positive, but no one knows what's going on. No one at my colony is talking."

"What do you mean?" I ask.

He looks a little uncomfortable. "Most of the rebels are from the Emerald clan. The Diamond, too, but mostly from the Emerald." He presses his lips together. "Some of my close friends."

"Why?" I nearly shout.

He shrugs again. "I honestly don't know. The leader of the rebels, Gyron, has managed to convince most of the others in the colony to follow his cause, that the crown should belong to the true king, Damarian. The Diamonds seem to be split in half, those opposing and those for it. The Rubies are the most peaceful colony. They are fine with the way things are."

"And the Sapphires and Violets?"

He shakes his head again. "They just want Damarian and Kiander returned safe and sound."

I wish I could curl into a ball and cry. I didn't know falling in love with Damarian would cause all this conflict. I just wanted to be happy.

Kyle takes my hand again. "It will be okay. If Damarian and Kiander are alive, we'll find them."

"Syren won't let me help," I say.

He rubs my hand. "I understand where he's coming from. You're new down here and don't know your way around, or the way we operate. Bringing you along would only be a…"

Merman's Touch

"A liability."

He shuts his eyes for a second. "I didn't mean it like that, but it would be better if you stay behind. Leave it up to us to go look for him."

I purse my lips. I risked my life coming here so I could save the love of my life. I won't sit back and wait. I won't.

"Pardon me."

My head snaps up and I see Doria floating a few feet away. Kyle nods to her. "Doria."

"Forgive me, but Mother has asked that Cassie return. It is not safe."

"She's right," Kyle says. "If the rebels know you're here…"

I'm as good as dead.

We pick ourselves off the stones and face one another. Kyle wraps his arms around me, kissing my cheek. "I'll bring him back. For you."

I clutch onto him. "Thanks."

Doria nods farewell to Kyle, then motions for me to follow her. We're not that far from the cave, but my skin prickles as I survey the area. I haven't seen a non-sapphire tail here other than Kyle's, but do I know who I can trust? What if a Sapphire is part of the rebels?

"Doria?" I ask.

She pauses mid-swim and glances at me.

"I'm sorry for all of this."

She picks up swimming. "It is all right."

"I know you don't like me that much, and it's cool. I mean, it's fine. But I just want you to know that I didn't mean for this to happen. If there's anything I could do…"

She doesn't say anything. Is she mad? I'm pretty sure she wants to bash my head into the coral. If Damarian had never met me, he would be king and all the merpeople would live in peace. But if that were the case, Damarian would have been miserable. Is that what she wants for her brother? I know she cares deeply for him.

"As I have told you when I came to land," she says. "I do not understand how my brother can have such love for a human. But I do not question it. Though I am upset at the turn of events, I do not blame you."

That's a relief.

"I wish things were different," she continues. "I wish Damarian chose a child of the sea as his mate. I wish he did not spend so many days on land. But circumstances are so, and there is nothing I can do but accept it."

I'm not sure how relieved I should be, but at least she doesn't want to poke my eyeballs out.

Our conversation has been taking place outside her home. I cringe back when I see the way those sharks look at me. Doria follows my gaze. "They are hostile to all who are not my family," she explains. "But as you are Damarian's mate, and a child of the sea, they understand you will visit often. In time, they will no longer be hostile to you."

The thought of being with Damarian and traveling home with him every so often to see his family is like a dream come true. I mean, we need to work out *a lot* of things, but it would be awesome to have that life.

"These sharks guard your home?"

"Yes. We have only need for one, but due to the current circumstances, Father has requested another."

That's good, I guess. Not good that they need another shark to protect them, but good that they're being protected.

I follow Doria into the cave. Kiandra and Syren are sitting at the table, and Zarya is on the floor, playing with what looks like toys. It looks like things found around the ocean, like parts of coral, stone, fish bones, shells, and other things I can't identify. There also seems to be human things too, probably salvaged from sunken ships.

As soon as she sees me, she springs off the floor. "With Cassie's arrival, surely Damarian is here as well."

Doria takes her arm and lifts her onto her back. "I shall play with you."

"Yes!"

They swim away to one of the rooms.

Syren stands. "Is it your wish to remain here?" he asks me. "Or do you plan to return to land?"

"We cannot allow her to return to land," Kiandra says. "She will undoubtedly get killed."

It doesn't look like Syren gives a damn about my safety. "She traveled here in one piece."

"She is Damarian's mate, Syren. She is part of the family."

I'm not in the mood of arguing with Syren or trying to convince him that I'm the right person for his son. But I deserve respect. "Look, sir, I understand you don't like me. But I wish you would accept Damarian's decision and accept the fact that we are together and will be together forever. He's happy with me. If he wasn't, I wouldn't force him to be with me."

Syren narrows his eyes. He's quiet for a few seconds. Then he turns to his wife. "I will travel to Eteria in the morning."

Eteria is where the palace is located.

Kiandra nods. "I hope all will be well."

He swims toward her and touches her arm. "I will retire to bed."

She nods again. He gives me one more look, his expression grim, then swims away to one of the rooms.

Kiandra and I gaze at one another. A part of me feels like I need to apologize to her for causing this to befall her son. But I'm sick of apologizing. I didn't do anything wrong. The people at fault here are the rebels. *They* are the ones who have caused all of this, not me.

Her eyes soften. "Would you like to rest? You must be exhausted."

I feel my guard start to melt away. "Thanks. I am exhausted."

"I will show you to your quarters."

I follow her toward the tunnels. As we pass one, I feel something. Something crawling on my skin, something buried in my heart. I stop and peer inside. There is a large oyster shell in the center with seaweed inside. A few stone pieces are around, like chairs. "Is this Damarian's room?" I ask.

Kiandra swims over to me and looks into the room. "Yes." Her voice is barely audible.

"Can I…can I sleep here?"

She moves her gaze to me, examining me closely. "Yes, if that is your wish."

I nod.

"Very well. I will leave you to your rest. Please do not hesitate to ask for anything you may need."

"Thanks."

She touches my cheek before swimming away.

I swallow a few times, then face the room. This is it, Damarian's room. His most private area. He's not here to give me permission to sleep here, but I know he'd want me to. He'd want to share every part of himself with me.

Slowly, I swim toward the bed. It doesn't look that comfortable, but I guess it must be. Curling my tail around me, I lower myself into it. My body sinks into the seaweed. It feels more comfortable than I imagined.

It smells like him. The rest of his family have the same salt water smell, but his unique scent is buried between the seaweed. I grasp one of them and hold it tight to my chest, imagining Damarian lying here with me.

It's only because of my extreme exhaustion that I manage to fall asleep.

Chapter Twenty-Six

I have the dream again. Damarian yells my name in the same manner. I call back, but can't see or hear him. There are a few flashes of lightning, and I wake up shaking, aching all over.

A face so similar to Damarian's is in front of mine.

"Mother, she has awakened!" Zarya shouts.

A few seconds later, Kiandra peeks her head into Damarian's room. Giving me a sweet smile, she says, "I hope you slept well."

Damarian's bed turned out to be extremely comfortable. Other than the dream, I had a restful sleep. "I did. Thanks," I say.

Kiandra swims into the room and stops a few feet away from me. "Queen Flora wishes to see you."

I gape at her. The queen of the merpeople wants to see *me*? Other than the fact that she is one of the most important people in the ocean, Damarian dumped her for me. Maybe she wants to have my head.

Words tumble out of my mouth—I have no idea what. A whole lot of gibberish.

Zarya giggles as she circles me. "Do not fear. Flora is pleasant."

Yeah, as long as you don't steal her fiancé.

My hands wring together. "Why does she want to see me?"

"She has learned of your arrival," Kiandra says.

Merman's Touch

And probably wants to give me a piece of her mind.

"It is rude to keep her waiting." Kiandra holds out her hand. "It is all right."

I swallow, get out of the bed, and follow Kiandra out of the room. Little Zarya swims at my side, smiling widely. I return it. I know she will be my next favorite person.

"Every time I visit the palace, Queen Flora presents me with a new gift," Zarya says, her blue eyes shining. She pouts. "But Mother says I am not invited this morning."

"I'm sure she'll invite you soon," I tell her.

Syd and Syndin are playing on the floor of the main room. They lift identical faces as we pass. Zarya holds her head high, like she won a prize for swimming near me. Despite the anxiety pumping through my body, I laugh.

As we near the exit to the cave, they both get up from the floor and follow us. When we reach the exit, a merman with a violet tail floats before us. Right next to him is a hammerhead shark. The merman bends his head.

"He will escort you to the palace," Kiandra says.

I nod, my throat dry.

Zarya wraps her tail around me. "I shall eagerly await your return, Cassie!"

This kid is too cute. I know she doesn't know what it means, but I wrap my arms around her and kiss her cheek. "I will eagerly await returning to you."

She beams.

I look at her brothers. "The same to you."

They smile, too.

I stroke Zarya's head and face the Violet. "I'm ready."

He nods, then bends his head to Kiandra in a farewell. "Swim at my side," he instructs me.

I do as he says. The hammerhead shark swims right next to me, its eyes scanning the area. I look back at Damarian's house. Zarya waves before doing a few somersaults. The twins copy her. They're almost like dolphins at a show. Kiandra brings them inside.

Many Sapphires are swimming around, some talking, some eating, little ones playing. As we pass them, they each raise curious eyes at me. I'm not sure if it's because of me or if it's because I'm being escorted by one of the palace Guards. I think it's because of me.

The Violet's eyes are surveying the area, too. He doesn't look different from the Sapphires, other than his tail and hair. It's dark brown. He and the shark move in similar ways, as if they're communicating with one another.

I see the rocks in the distance, where Fiske and I swam through to enter the Sapphire colony. My heart picks up its pace as we draw nearer. I feel safe in the Sapphire colony. I'm not sure if I should, since it's possible there are spies here just like there was at the palace, but being with Damarian's family made me feel protected.

The shark goes through the gap first. The Guard motions for me to go next. Before I do, I take one last look at the Sapphire colony, Damarian's home. The home I desperately want to be my own, too, if things weren't so screwed up.

"Sapphire," the merman says.

I snap out of it and swim through the opening. The shark is waiting right outside, its intent eyes on me. I don't know if I'll ever get used to this. My whole life I've been taught to fear them, and with what happened to Kayla, I don't know if I can ever be comfortable around them.

"Sapphire," the Guard says again.

I swim to his side. Out here, there's a mix of merpeople again. The

Merman's Touch

Diamonds' tails are the color of glass and they have dark red hair. The Rubies have red tails and angelic white hair. Every single merperson has the same color eyes, the color of the ocean.

Like the Sapphires, they stare at me, their mouth agape. Some even point.

My pace has slowed. The Guard looks impatient. Shaking my head, I speed up and try to keep up with him. He makes a left and advances toward another cave, one almost identical to the Sapphire's.

"We are approaching Eteria," he tells me. "Our capital city."

My chest feels like ice. Like before, the hammerhead enters the opening first, followed by me and then the Violet. When we emerge from it, my breath catches in my throat. A beautiful palace stands a few hundred feet away, covered in sapphire crystals. I stare at it for a moment, my eyebrows furrowed. Why is it covered in sapphire crystals? Then it hits me. The kingdom used to belong to the Sapphires.

Hundreds of large sharks swim around, great whites and hammerheads. It makes sense, since the king is a Sapphire and the queen is a Violet.

The Guard swims toward it. I freeze in my place. I'm not ready. I don't know what to think. My body shakes with nerves.

"Sapphire," he says again.

Taking a deep breath, I swim up to him, and we move closer to the entrance of the castle.

He stops a few feet away, his eyes on it. "The palace is not what it was," he says. "Days ago, it would be bustling with activity." His eyes meet mine. "Ever since the attack, many are afraid to leave the palace."

Tears choke up my throat. "I'm sorry."

I don't know if he knows what I'm sorry about, if he knows I'm the cause of all of this. He shakes his head and motions for me to go in.

There is no door here, just an opening like by the Sapphire colony, but there are sharks guarding it. Every single one of them fastens their eyes on me.

The interior of the castle is beautiful. It's made out of different shades of sapphire crystals. Manta rays swim around, carrying fish and other seafood on their backs. As they pass some merpeople, they take a fish off. It's like they're waiters. There are openings on the higher levels—rooms. The merpeople here are Violets and Sapphires, though I see one Ruby tail. And just like outside, there are many hammerheads and great whites swimming around.

The Guard nods to a few other merpeople as we pass. He leads me to an opening in the back, to a large room that has many Guards and sharks. In the distance, I see two thrones, again made out of sapphire crystals. Someone is sitting on one of the thrones. Queen Flora. Two large hammerhead sharks flank her on each side. Like in the main room, manta rays with food on their backs swim around.

She's in the middle of talking to a tall Sapphire with the broadest chest I've ever seen and another Sapphire—Syren. As soon as she sees me, her mouth closes and she pins her gaze on me. They stay there as we move closer, until we're standing right in front of her.

She's beautiful, with long dark brown hair sweeping behind her. She looks different from the other Violets I've seen. She's glowing. I remember Kiander glowing in the same manner when he visited my house after he became king. She doesn't look any older than me. A tiara sits on her head. It looks like it's made out of sapphire, violet, ruby, emerald, and diamond crystals.

"Your Highness," the Violet Guard says, spreading his arms out and raising them over his head, then bringing them together. He lowers his head.

Syren and the other Sapphire do the same. Queen Flora narrows her eyes at me. Oh, right. I spread and raise my arms and lower my head, trying to copy the way they're doing it. My arms are shaky and my head drops too fast. I probably look like a clumsy mess.

The mermen lift their heads and lower their arms. The Guard gestures to me. "I present Cassie Price of the humans."

I wince when her eyes flash with anger. They study my face inch by inch, then lower to the rest of my body, examining every part of me. "Approach me, Cassie Price of the humans," she orders. Her voice is prettier than the other mermaids I've encountered.

The Sapphires move aside. Again, I'm a clumsy mess as I move closer to her.

"Bow," Syren whispers.

Again? I do, and hopefully this time I have more grace.

Flora leans back in her chair, her gaze never leaving my face. "You have traveled far," she says. "From the human land."

My mouth is dry. I lick my lips. "Yeah."

Her eyes narrow. "Why have you come to the sea?"

I glance at Syren. He's floating next to me with his arms folded. I focus my attention on the queen. "I sensed Damarian was in trouble. I came to rescue him."

With her eyes still narrowed, she says, "You risked your life and the lives of my kind. You have entered our waters after your mate cautioned you not to do so. Did you not think his family would formulate a plan to rescue him?"

"Yeah, but—"

"Did you bring humans with you?"

"What? No—"

"How many of them are aware you are here?"

I can't lie to her. "One."

She sits up. "You have told a human?"

"But she's very trustworthy."

She scoffs. "No human is to be trusted."

I look away. I don't want to stand in front of her as she craps on my race, but she's the queen of the merpeople and I need to respect her. "She's been my best friend since I was a kid—a fry. I promise you that you can trust her."

She eyes me for a few seconds before turning to the Sapphires and the Violet. "I would like to speak to Cassie Price in private."

I gulp.

The Violet bows his head. "I beg your pardon, my queen, but I would like to remain here."

She waves her hand. "I shall be all right. Cassie Price and I have a lot to discuss."

All three of them lower their heads and retreat. I want to call after them and beg them not to leave me alone with her. But I tell myself to relax. She won't hurt me.

Once they're gone, Flora gets up from her throne and swims closer to me. I involuntarily falter back. That seems to intrigue her. "Are you frightened of me?" she asks.

I play with my hair. "No. I mean…yeah, I guess."

Her face that's been so serious suddenly lights up as she laughs. "Why?"

"I'm scared you'll hurt me."

"Whatever for?"

"For stealing Damarian from you."

She circles me, once again examining me from top to bottom. "I will admit it was my desire to punish you," she says. I shut my eyes. "But that was how I felt initially." My eyes open. "It was before I met Kiander." Her voice is soft, filled with love.

I stare at her. I assumed both Kiander and Flora married for duty.

Merman's Touch

"You loved him before you mated?" I ask.

She shakes her head. "When he approached me with the proposition to be my mate, I had different feelings toward him. Ones I did not feel for Damarian. I realized it was love and that he was to be my mate." She smiles wryly. "You have done me a service, Cassie Price." Her eyes narrow again. "I however do not appreciate that you are human."

So much for thinking she might actually like me.

She circles me again. "What does a child of the sea see in a human?"

I swallow a few times. "Children of the sea are not that different from humans, Your Highness."

"So claims your mate." She comes to a stop in front of me. "Syren informed me you have transformed into a child due to your mating with Damarian."

Is it normal in this world to talk so freely about one's personal life? "Um…yeah."

"I have not heard of such a thing."

"Am I the only human who turned into a mermaid—a child of the sea?"

She shrugs. "I am not aware of another."

I don't know what to say to that.

She grabs hold of my arm. "Let us sit." She leads me to a small room on the left, where there is a table and chairs made out of sapphire crystals. She sits at the head and tells me to sit on her right.

"You are a human," she says. "Damarian is a child of the sea."

I raise my eyebrows, not understanding what she's telling me.

"You are two different species. It is against nature for you to mate."

I'm about to open my mouth and tell her where she can shove it, but she raises her hand. "Children of the sea mate for life. Since Damarian is tied to you for all eternity, nature had to make it so that you can remain mated." Her eyes intensify. "That is the reason you are now a child of the sea."

I just stare at her as her words swirl around in my head. "You're saying it wasn't the actual mating that caused me to change, but because it's the only way Damarian and I can stay together?"

She nods. "It is what I believe. As queen of the children of the sea, I have the ability to return you to a human. Only a human."

My head springs up and hope fills me. "That's right. You can." Just like Kiander was able to unbanish Damarian and Kyle.

She holds out her hand again. "But if I were to change you to a human—permanently—you would no longer be mated to Damarian."

My whole body deflates as the hope seeps out of me.

"There is more," Flora continues. "As I already stated, children of the sea mate for life. They cannot take another."

My heart lurches as I finally grasp what she's telling me. If she changes me back to a human, Damarian and I can no longer be mated because it goes against nature. Since merpeople mate for life, it would leave Damarian without a mate. He will be single his whole life.

This sucks. So bad. Tears enter my eyes. I'm stuck being a mermaid. It never occurred to me that there might be a way for me to change back to a human and only a human. I just accepted it for what it was. Now I learned there is a way. But it has a price. A very big price.

"You do not have to make decisions now," Flora says. "We have a more pressing matter to attend to."

"We do?"

"Syren informed me that you are able to sense your mate."

I nod.

"Many have not believed my words as true. Father stated it is my deep desire that has made me think I feel my mate."

"You sense Kiander?" I ask.

"Yes."

"Why can we sense them when no one else can?"

For the first time, I see a different emotion on her face. Grief. "They are our mates," she says, her voice low. "Our beloveds. A bond shared with a mate is like no other bond. It is deep, made of intense, eternal love. It cannot be broken easily." Her eyes bore into me. "It is not like bonds human mates share. We share a heart, a body, a soul. And when our bodies become one, so do our minds."

I understand completely what she's saying. I felt so close to Damarian when we were both merpeople. It was something I couldn't explain, something that wasn't tangible. We haven't slept together in these forms, but from what Flora's telling me, it sounds wonderful.

"I did not wish to believe Father," she says. "I know Kiander is alive."

"Then why won't you let Syren gather a party to look for them?"

She shakes her head. "They are in the Deep."

"So?"

"We cannot survive there. As queen of the children of the sea, it is my duty to protect each and every one of my kind. Venturing into the Deep would only cause deaths."

"What else can we do?"

Her eyes suddenly light up, like an idea entered her head.

"What is it?" I ask.

"You sense Damarian."

"Yeah."

"I sense Kiander." She mutters something under her breath. "Is it possible?"

"Is *what*?" I ask, losing all my patience.

"What do you sense?" she asks. "Tell me in detail."

I close my eyes and try to concentrate. "I feel his heartbeat."

"What else?"

"I don't know. I can't explain it. It's like I feel him in my heart. Do you feel the same?"

She nods. "Individually, we may not be able to locate our mates. But perhaps together we might."

"What?"

"I do not wish for Syren to venture into the Deep because he does not know where to look. But if he were to know where the rebels are holding them, perhaps they can save them."

"You think we can locate them together?"

"Perhaps. Are you prepared?"

I'm ready to do anything. "Yes."

Chapter Twenty-Seven

Flora holds out her hands. "Place your hands in mine."

As soon as I do, my eyes flutter closed and my vision gets bright, like someone is shining a flashlight in my face. Gradually, it dissolves until I can see again. I'm chasing Damarian in the park on rollerblades. The place is deserted, of people, birds, everything. I hear his laughter as he speeds farther away. "How are you such a pro?" I call as I try to catch up.

"It is because I am a child of the sea," he calls after me, rolling faster.

"That makes no sense! You shouldn't be walking well, let alone blading."

If I go any faster, I'm going to trip and fall. Coming to a stop, I bend over and rest my hands on my knees, breathing heavily as my chest burns. I scan around, but don't see my merman anywhere.

"Damarian?" I ask.

Complete silence.

"Where are you?"

Nothing.

I push away the alarm gathering in my heart. "This isn't time for games." Something rustles in the bushes nearby. I whirl around.

"Damarian?"

Something jumps out and tackles me to the ground. Damarian splatters me with kisses. I slap his shoulder. "You scared me."

"I apologize." He kisses me again. "I am really enjoying myself. Are you?"

"Of course. As long as you're with me, I'm the happiest person alive."

He rests his forehead against mine. "Your feelings match mine."

My fingers comb through his hair. "You'll never leave me, Damarian, will you?"

"Never, my love. Nothing can ever keep me from you."

My hands pull on some strands. "What if we were miles apart and it was raining fire?"

He fingers my bottom lip. "I would risk getting burned."

"What if there was a tornado keeping us apart?"

He nuzzles my nose. "I do not know what that is." He gathers me in his arms, dipping his head to plant more kisses on my face. My head rolls back and my eyes close. His lips are warm, inviting, and they taste like salt water.

"You taste good," I mutter.

His chest rumbles as he laughs. "It does not compare to how you taste."

That makes me laugh. I untangle myself from his arms and get to my feet. "Catch me if you can, merman."

I race away. Only a few seconds later, I feel him behind me, and less than a second after that, his arms come around me and lift me, flipping me upside down so that my hair nearly sweeps the ground. It reminds me of the time I tried to race him in my pool. There was no way I was going to win—I was no match for a creature from the sea. And it seems I'm just as unskilled on land.

Merman's Touch

"Do you have to show off?" I tease.

"Yes, for I enjoy seeing the fire in your eyes."

He lowers me to the ground and leans against a tree, tugging me close. He puts both hands on my waist and bends forward to press a kiss on my throat. Then he strokes my cheek. "My Cassie," he murmurs.

I return the stroke. "My Damarian."

His fingers take hold of one of my braids and starts undoing it. Even though he's done this many times, every experience feels new, like it's the first time. Romantic and special. When he's finished with the second one, he brushes his fingers through the strands, raising his hands until they massage my scalp. A soft moan escapes my mouth.

Slow music starts to play. It sounds like a symphony. At first, I think it's in my head, due to Damarian skimming his lips up and down my neck. Then I realize it's real. I look to my right and left but don't see anything. All of the sudden, we're no longer wearing rollerblades. Damarian wraps his arms around me and starts to sway to the beat of the music.

I gaze into his eyes. "Where did you learn to do this?"

"From the TV. Do you enjoy it?" He presses his lips to my ear.

"Mmm. I like it a lot." I lock my arms around him. "You never cease to amaze me."

He kisses my forehead. "Your feelings match mine."

Firecrackers shoot in the sky. Damarian and I continue swaying to the music. "Thanks," I tell him. "For being in my life. For saving me when I wiped out surfing. But most importantly, thanks so much for coming back after you returned home the first time." I brush some hair out of his eyes. "And thanks so much for always coming back when you visit your family."

He takes my hand in his and twirls me around. Then he dips me.

Before I have a chance to blink, he throws me into the air and catches me in his arms. He kisses me before saying, "You do not have to thank me. It is enough that I hold you in my arms."

He lowers me to the ground and spins me around so my back presses into his chest. With his hands around my stomach, we continue to sway to the music. Every so often, his lips run up and down my neck, sending chills all over my body.

"I love you," I whisper. "Forever."

"And I love you," he whispers back. "For all eternity."

He lays me down on the grass and settles on top of me, putting his weight on his elbows so he doesn't hurt me. I wrap my legs around him and pull him closer to me. The sky gets dark and stars twinkle in the sky.

"I don't know if I've ever been this happy," I tell him. "We have our whole lives ahead of us, Damarian. I'm so excited to share every part of it with you."

"As am I."

He kisses me passionately, causing every part of me to throb. As I close my eyes, I feel like I'm rising to the sky, floating on a cloud. When I open them, I see we're flying, heading to.... "Space," I say, smiling up at him. "The place you want to explore."

We're out of Earth's orbit and continue floating. I show Damarian the planets, the moons, our satellites. He watches everything with intrigued eyes. "Your world fascinates me," he says. "I cannot wait to learn all I can."

"And I can't wait to learn all I can about yours."

Suddenly, we plummet to Earth, down and down, heading toward the ocean. We land on my surf board. The waves, which started out flat only a few seconds ago, turn more violent, perfect for surfing. Damarian's arms are clasped around me as we ride the waves. I'm

Merman's Touch

wearing my royal blue bikini and Damarian has matching swim trunks on. Water splashes at us from all different directions.

"This is incredible!" Damarian shouts. Keeping one hand on my waist, he raises the other one and spreads it out. "It is like flying."

We ride the most massive wave I've ever seen. We don't wipe out, just continue sailing forever. The wave never ends. Damarian turns me around and holds me close. We should topple over, but we don't. We stare into each other's eyes as we continue to sail, experiencing a deep, magical moment.

The surfboard disappears and we drop into the water. The waves turn calm. Damarian's legs kick against mine as he treads. "Legs," I say. "You have legs in the ocean."

He stares down at himself, his face surprised, fascinated. Giving me a sweet smile, he drags me closer to him, placing my legs around his middle. I don't feel the stickiness of his tail, but skin.

Damarian's lips find mine. "I never imagined I would experience this with you," he murmurs. He falls on his back and spreads out his arms. I'm sitting on top of him, resting my hands on his chest and staring into his beautiful eyes. As merpeople, we shared a unique bond in the ocean. Now as humans, we share another bond, different but just as deep. We're not in his world now, but mine.

No one is around. No boats, nothing. It's like Damarian and I are in our own little world, where no one can keep us apart. I lie down on him, resting my lips on his jaw. "I can stay here forever."

"How I long for it," he says softly.

We float in the water like this, talking, laughing, kissing. The waves carry us deeper into the ocean. A blue whale soars in the air, startling us. We tip over and crash into the water. Laughing, we break the surface.

The whale swims closer to us. Reaching out my hands, I touch it. It feels soft, smooth, and warm. Damarian rests his hands on it, too, and it takes off, diving deep into the water. I'm not a mermaid, but I can breathe and see clearly. My legs kick after me as the whale swims. Its massive tail is so graceful as it pumps him forward. Damarian and I lock eyes on one another and smile. "Have you done this before?" I ask, surprised I can talk underwater.

He shakes his head. "These creatures like to keep to themselves."

My legs transform into a tail, without any pain. When I glance at Damarian, I see his familiar one. Together, in sync, the three of us leap out of the water. We soar high in the air, and I swear I can almost touch the sky. I stay suspended in the air for what feels like forever, in slow motion, my arms spread out, my face raised to the clouds. The whale is between us, but somehow, Damarian and I lock hands.

We dive into the ocean and leap again, doing this a few more times. The whale swims away, and I'm in Damarian's arms. "We were in my world," I tell him. "Now we are in yours." I gaze up at him. "Total freedom, without anything or anyone getting in our way. It's what we've always wanted."

"There is more," he says against my mouth. His lips sweep across it. "More I would like to share with you."

I touch his cheek. "Show me."

Taking my hand in his, he submerges underwater, pulling me along. We pass the fish, the frogs, the seaweed, the turtles, the rays, and all the other creatures. Our hands run along the coral, our tails wrap around each other. Damarian takes me by the waist and spins around in the water, showering me with kisses. We somersault, we leap out of the water.

Then he takes my hand and leads me further deep.

The temperature drops. The area gets cold. I feel pressure by my ears, pressure I've never felt before. "Damarian?" I pant as my ears ring.

"You will love it," he tells me, clutching my hand tighter and towing me along.

"Damarian," I groan. "Stop. It hurts."

We swim further into the ocean. The place is ice cold and pricks my skin. Glancing down at my hands, I see they are blue.

"Damarian!"

He continues pulling me along.

"Where are you taking me?"

We slip through an opening in the water. The area gets pitch black.

"Damarian?" I call frantically, reaching for his hands. I don't find them.

"Cassie!" his voice calls.

"Where are you?" I shout, squinting, desperately searching for him. But I can't see a thing.

"Why did you come?" he asks, his voice weak, defeated.

"Damarian." There's a sob in my voice. "Where are you?"

"Stay out of the sea, my love," he whispers. "Out of the sea."

"No! I came to find you. Tell me where you are."

There's a flash of lightning. He shouts out in pain.

"Damarian!" I surge forward, but knock into something hard. Like a big piece of stone. My fingers trace it. It's smooth. "Damarian," I whisper.

"Out of the sea, my sweet Cassie." His voice is barely audible now.

Another flash of lightning, another cry. But this time, my own cry explodes out of my mouth. It feels like I'm getting electrocuted. My body twists and turns, my tail throwing me around. This is nothing compared to how I feel when I shift from one form to the other. I didn't think I could feel any pain worse than that, but I do.

I lift weak hands toward the wall and bang my fists on it.

"Damarian…"

Suddenly, I'm shooting in the air, and that same light blinds me. When I open my eyes, I find myself on the floor of the palace, a violet tail in my face.

Two Sapphires and a Violet rush inside. They lift Flora, then me. "I…" I sputter. "I know where they are."

Chapter Twenty-Eight

"As do I," Flora says.

The three mermen stare at us.

"They are indeed in the Deep," Flora says. "Together with Cassie Price, I know their precise location."

Syren says, "We must search there at once."

The other Sapphire shoots his arm out, blocking Syren from leaving. "It is not simple."

Syren throws the other guy's hand off him. "I will travel to the correct location and free my sons."

"I'm coming with you," I say. Every part of me is shaking due to what I've just experienced. I have no idea what it was. Not a dream, but not reality either. It's as though Damarian and I created our own world through our minds. Our own perfect world. Until he showed me where he was being held.

Syren folds his arms across his chest. "Do not be absurd."

"I'm the only one who can lead you there. Please, let me join you."

"You will only be a burden."

Even though I'm still shaking, I straighten myself out and swim close to him, until I'm a few inches away. With the most firm voice I can muster, I say, "Damarian is my mate. You don't understand how much he means to me, and I don't give a damn what you think. Damarian is alive and he needs my help. I'm the only one who can sense him and lead you right to him."

Syren presses his lips together. He knows I'm right, but doesn't like it. He glances at the other Sapphire. "I will lead a party to the Deep, Callen. Will you provide me with any of your Guard?"

Callen bows his head to Flora. "My queen. I have sent scouts as far deep as possible. The waters are dangerous. It is too cold, the oxygen levels are low, and the pressure can snap our bones."

Saliva gathers in my mouth.

"Furthermore, it is uncharted territory. We do not know what creatures live there." His voice drops an octave. "It is rebel ground, my queen. We will be at a disadvantage, presuming we manage to find a manner to survive."

Flora swims to the table and sits down on one of the chairs, rubbing her forehead. Callen goes after her, bowing his head as low as possible. "I will do as you ask, my queen."

She looks up, her eyes moving between the two mermen. "What do you advise, Syren?"

"Training," he says, moving closer and lowering his head. "Combat."

She tears her eyes from him. "We have not engaged in such activity in moons, not since the great battle. We lost hundreds of lives." She shakes her head slowly. "I will not change our ways."

"Times are not what they were, my queen," Syren says. "We no longer live in peace. If we do not halt these rebels now, they will grow stronger, grow in masses. We must train soldiers. I am afraid we have no other option."

Flora's gaze moves to me. "Look at what war and bloodshed has done to the humans," she says. "They know no peace."

Merman's Touch

I can't really argue with that, though I do want to defend my people. As I'm about to open my mouth, she holds up her hand, silencing me.

She drops her eyes to her tail. "What would Kiander do if he were present?" she whispers.

Callen crouches down so his tail is folded. He takes her hands in his. "He would seek your counsel, for you are a fair queen, a capable queen. One who loves her subjects dearly."

My heart goes out to her. She's so young, but has the responsibility of all the merpeople on her shoulders. I have so much respect for her.

She's quiet for a few minutes, like she's contemplating every detail every choice, every outcome. The three of us wait silently and patiently. She gets up from the chair and turns her back to us for a few more seconds. Then she nods to the Violet. "Send notice throughout all the colonies that we are to invade the deep waters, Morteran. All volunteers who wish to train in battle should seek Callen or other members of the Guard." Sadness enters her eyes. "It is not an easy choice, nor one I like, but it is the choice I have to make."

Morteran nods. "At once, my queen."

"I shall lead the training," Syren says.

"What about me?" I ask.

Syren's eyes flit to mine. "You shall remain home until Damarian is returned to you."

"Hey, I don't know what century you live in, but in my world, women don't wait around for someone else to search for their mate. They go out and find them."

"You are in the sea," he says, his voice the sternest I've ever heard. "In the sea, you do as children of the sea do."

"Enough!" Flora says. "Syren, Damarian is your son, but he is also the mate of Cassie Price. You would react in a similar fashion if

Kiandra were captured by the rebels." Her voice wobbles. "If I did not have a duty to my kind, I would join the party to search for my beloved." She swims closer to him and touches his arm. "She is the sole one with the capability to lead you to the correct location."

Again, I can tell he knows the queen is right, but he doesn't like it. "I fear she may be a liability."

"Her love for Damarian will only make her an asset."

Syren is silent for a bit before doing the merpeople bow. "As you wish, my queen."

I give Flora a thankful nod. Despite the fact that I took Damarian from her, that I'm a human, and that she doesn't really trust me, we've bonded and I feel like she'll always have my back.

"Do hurry," Flora says. "I do not know how much time we have."

Syren and I follow Morteran out of the palace. The hammerhead that brought me to the palace swims forward—it was waiting out here, probably guarding the palace while its master did business inside. And then a large great white shark swims to Syren's side. I now notice it's one of the sharks that guarded Damarian's home.

"It is unnecessary for you to escort us home," Syren says to Morteran. "I will manage."

"It is the queen's orders that I protect the human."

I want to tell them that I don't need any of them to protect me, but now's not the time to get prideful. This is a foreign land to me, and since my life is in danger, I should use all the protection I can get.

The journey back to the Sapphire colony is quiet. When we reach the cave, Morteran nods and leaves. The great white parks itself back in its place, its eyes studying the area. When we enter the main room, Kiandra rushes over. "Any word?"

Syren looks at me. "She and the queen have managed to locate Damarian and Kiander."

Merman's Touch

Kiandra's eyes shine. "They have? Are they alive?"

Syren looks at me again.

"Yeah." I swallow. "But weak. There might not be much time."

"We must leave at once," Syren says, taking hold of her hands. "I do not know how long our journey will be. Queen Flora will provide you and the fry with the proper protection." He touches her cheek when her shoulders sag. "Do not fret. All will be well. I will rescue our sons."

She nods, but I see her shoulders trembling.

"And I'm going, too," I say.

Kiandra's faces me, her eyes alarmed. "It is too dangerous, Cassie."

"I know, but I'm going."

Kiandra looks at her husband.

"It is the queen's orders."

Kiandra swims closer to me and rests her hands on my cheeks. "You are brave. You are a fine mate for my son."

My eyes trek to Syren, wondering if he agrees with his wife. He doesn't look at me.

"Please eat," Kiandra says, leading me to the table. "You as well, Syren." She disappears into the other room to call for the younger kids. "Doria shares her time with Hareta."

Syren frowns. "I do not appreciate her out in such dangerous waters."

Kiandra shrugs, trying to hide a smile. "She is your daughter, Syren."

Zarya and the twins join us at the table. I don't know how meals usually are at this table, but right now, it's quiet and very awkward. I watch the way Zarya picks at her fish before throwing it aside and trying another. I smile. A picky eater.

The twins seem well-behaved—well, for the first ten minutes.

Soon, they're throwing fish guts at one another.

"Syd and Syndin," Kiandra scolds. They sit straight and continue eating quietly, though they smirk at one another.

When the kids are done with their lunch, Kiandra tells them to go to their rooms. Once they're gone, I say, "Do they understand what's going on?"

Kiandra sighs. "As the days pass, it grows more difficult to shield them from the truth. Zarya thought Damarian was on land with you, but now that you are here, she questions his whereabouts."

"What did you tell her?"

Her lower lip quivers. "That he will be with us shortly."

"And the twins? They're a bit older than Zarya and probably sense something is wrong."

Kiandra nods. "Yes. Syd in particular. He is mature for his moons and is very intelligent. I fear he is fully aware of the events, though he chooses to keep quiet."

I reach out and pat her hand. "I know where they are, Kiandra. With the help of your husband and the many others who will search for them, we'll bring them home. Safe and sound." I don't know if this is a promise I can keep, but I will try my damn hardest.

She nods, giving me a small smile. "Thank you."

***

Snuggled in Damarian's bed among the seaweed and his scent, my mind buzzes with everything that happened today. I have no idea what time it is, but I went to bed early because I'm so exhausted. It's most likely due to that dream—or whatever it was—I had about Damarian. Did he experience it as well?

It's obvious it all took place in my head, since most of it was impossible, like Damarian and me swimming in the ocean as humans. Surfing. Did Flora have a similar dream? It seems like it was catered to me and Damarian specifically, our experiences and desires. Maybe what Flora shared with Kiander was something special to them.

It felt so real. Every touch, every kiss, every romantic word we said to one another. My hand wraps around some seaweed. How I yearn for him to be with me right now.

I wonder what tomorrow will bring, if Morteran will be able to gather enough merpeople willing to risk their lives to search for Damarian and Kiander and to battle the rebels. These are people who hardly know war. I'm pretty sure the rebels are well versed in combat.

A part of me is pretty confident that many will join, since it's their king they'll be searching for. But I know how scary it is. They seem like a close-knit species that care about each other, so I'm hopeful.

I feel someone in my room and sit up. Zarya is standing in the doorway, her big blue eyes hesitant and curious. "Hey," I say.

She moves a few inches into the room. "May I sleep with you?"

"Of course." I scoot over in the oyster shell. She smiles the biggest one I've ever seen and zooms toward me, knocking her head into mine. We both grab hold of our heads and giggle. I put my arm around her and hug her. She's the closest thing I have to Damarian.

"Syd claims it is difficult to be a human."

I raise an eyebrow. "Oh, really?"

She nods vehemently. "He says it is most difficult to walk on those…legs? And that humans are not as beautiful as children of the sea. He also says you have no room on land for your wastes, therefore you throw them into the sea."

I tickle her. She giggles, trying to swat my hands away. "Well, I won't argue that children of the sea are definitely prettier than humans. But he's wrong about walking on legs. It's pretty easy."

"Your language is so peculiar."

I tap her nose. "That was my reaction when I first met Damarian."

She bounces in the shell. "Please tell me the tale of how you and Dammy fell in love."

She calls him Dammy? I really like it.

There's the sound of rustling, then the twins pop into my room. Zarya folds her arms and scowls. "You are not invited."

One of the twins—I think Syndin—pushes his chest out. "You are too much a fry to command us."

Zarya glares at him. I tighten my hold on her. It's comforting to see them behaving just like human kids would. I really love finding all these similarities between us.

Syndin throws something upward, then catches it in his hand. "I believe you have forgotten this."

Zarya rockets toward him and tries to grab it from his hand, but he's too tall and dangles it over his head. "It is my gift to Cassie!" she whines.

A gift for me? She's such a sweetie pie.

Syndin rolls his eyes and drops it. Gathering it carefully in her arms, she returns to me and lands in my lap. "Father has told me this is very rare coral." She holds it out to me. It's the most exquisite thing I've ever seen in my life. Bright colors of green, yellow and orange in the shape of tree. "Explorers have discovered it."

"Thanks, Zarya." I kiss the top of her head. "But are you sure you want to give it away?"

She nods eagerly. "I have one more in my collection." She beams. "Is the other coral I gave you alive?"

I bite my lip. How do I tell her I honestly don't know? With everything that happened over the past few days, I totally forgot about it. "It's in my pool filled with sea water," I say. "Thanks for giving it to me."

She beams again.

Merman's Touch

Syd moves closer. "What is it like to live as a human?"

His brother punches his arm. "Syd wishes to live on land."

"That is not so!"

I motion for them to gather around. Zarya cuddles close to me as her brothers sit near us on the floor. Growing up, I wanted siblings very badly. I remember how I begged for one for my seventh birthday. It feels good to have Damarian's brothers and sister in my life. I mean, assuming everything goes well and we rescue Damarian and Kiander and destroy the rebels and I can finally have my happily ever after.

I wonder if Syren would have me thrown into the Deep if he knew I'm about to tell his youngest kids about humans. But the truth is that I'm a human, and if I finally get to have my happily ever after, we'll be spending lots of time together. I can't change who I am. It would be awesome if they'd be able to visit Damarian and me on land.

"Humans are difficult, complex creatures," I tell them. "We make lots of mistakes and we'll make a lot more. But we're really good people."

"Why do you throw your wastes into the sea?" Syd asks, a hint of betrayal in his eyes.

"We're trying to put a stop to that."

"You steal our fish," Syndin says.

"There's enough to feed all of us," I tell him.

"Tell us a fascinating tale," Zarya says, tugging my arm.

I think for a few minutes. "Okay. We have cars. Vessels to transport us from one location to another. When you swim in the sea, do you ever grow tired?"

The three of them nod.

"We get tired on our legs, too. And it would take months to travel really long distances. That's why we have so many means of transportations. Trains and planes."

"What are those?" Syd asks.

"Planes are like birds. We sit inside them and fly."

Their mouths fall open.

"Have you ever been a bird?" Zarya asks.

I nod. "Once, when my mother and I went on vacation to Los Angeles." It was one of a few vacations I had as a kid.

They all exchange astonished glances.

"What else?" Syndin asks.

"We can create light."

"Like the sun?" Zarya asks.

I nod. "Your eyes can see in the dark, but humans can't. We used to use fire, but now we have lights."

"Fire?" they all ask.

I laugh silently to myself. Of course they wouldn't know what that is. "It's like the opposite of water. It's a source of light, also used for cooking. It's really hot and burns you."

They stare at me like I'm speaking a foreign language. Again, I laugh to myself.

"What else?" Zarya urges.

"Well, you have so many edible creatures in the sea. We have so many on land."

"Unintelligent creatures," Syd said. "With flesh you can devour."

"Yes, but we don't eat the meat fresh. We use fire."

I see their heads swarming with all the information they just learned. If any of them would relay what they learned to their father, I know he'd yell at me. But my hope is that the kids are interested enough in human life to come visit. Not that I want to put their lives at risk, but I really want them to be part of Damarian's life. I feel like I've taken so much away from him.

Doria swims into Damarian's room. "Forgive the intrusion, but

Merman's Touch

Father searches for Syd and Syndin."

"What is his request?" Syndin asks.

"To hunt."

They both grumble.

There's a hint of a smile on Doria's lips—something I've hardly seen before. She taps Syd's shoulder. "Do not keep Father waiting."

With more grumbles, they leave the room. Doria's eyes fall on the little mermaid slumped against me, her eyes shut tight, her breathing steady. "Sorry," I say. "She must have fallen asleep."

Doria settles down near the oyster shell. "It is all right. Zarya tires easily."

The kid uses up way too much energy.

"Doria?" I say, keeping my voice down so I don't wake Zarya.

"Yes?"

"Do only males hunt?"

She shrugs. "That is the manner it has always been. The males hunt while the females care for the young. But times have changed." She averts her gaze to her tail. "Father has always hunted with Damarian and Kiander. But they no longer dwell here."

"So you hunt with him?"

She nods. "It is not something I enjoy, but it is a duty I must perform. As well as help Mother care for the little ones. Father is teaching Syd and Syndin to hunt, but it will be a while before they master the skill."

That explains why she's so eager to get out of the house, even though it's dangerous.

"What about you?" I ask. "Is there someone special? Someone to sweep you off your feet— uh, I mean your tail?"

Her eyebrows shoot up. Clearly, she doesn't understand the expression. "There is no one."

"No one you like? There has to be someone."

Something flickers in her eyes. It's gone so fast, I wonder if I imagine it. "There is no one," Doria repeats.

She's totally lying. Why, though? Maybe it's because she's embarrassed to be crushing on someone. Or maybe it's because it's someone her parents don't approve of. "I'm sure you'll meet him soon," I assure her.

She doesn't say anything, her gaze on floor. After a bit, she looks at me. "Mother tells me you are to join the search party to locate my brothers."

I nod.

She runs her hands up and down her tail. "Father refuses to allow me to join."

That doesn't surprise me. As strict as he is, Syren loves his kids very much. He would do anything to keep them out of harm's away. Even though he made it seem like I would be a nuisance if I came along, I suspect there was another reason—that he didn't want to risk the life of his son's mate because if something were to happen to me, Damarian would be crushed. Not to mention alone for the rest of his life.

"I wish I could put myself to good use," Doria says. "Like you."

I reach for her hand and am surprised when she lets me take it. "But you are. Maybe you won't actually be going with your father and the others to search for your brothers, but you'll be so useful here. Someone needs to hunt for food for your family. Someone needs to help your mother take care of the kids. Someone needs to be a support system for your mother."

Her eyes brighten as she considers my words.

"So you see," I say. "There are many other ways you can help out."

I expect her to narrow her eyes, to yell at me, tell me I have no right to come here and tell her what she should do or how she should feel about herself. But instead, she leans forward and grabs me, pulling me into her arms.

I'm so shocked, I sit completely still.

"Did I make an error?" she asks. "Is this not what humans do as a sign of affection?"

I laugh and return the hug. "You're fine."

She leans back. "Thank you, Cassie." Her voice is sincere. "I do not have others I can speak to."

"Not your friends?"

"They do not understand."

"Well, I'm here if you ever need to talk."

Her eyes scan every feature on my face. "You are all right for a human. Damarian has chosen well."

"Thanks."

She sits here for a few more minutes before getting up. "I shall leave you to your rest. I understand you have a tiresome day ahead of you."

I nod, my body filling with anxiety.

She rests her hand on my shoulder. "It will be all right. Father will allow no harm come your way."

I nod again. "Thanks."

After lifting Zarya in her arms, she leaves. I pull some seaweed over myself and close my eyes tight. I'm scared as hell to train and fight the rebels and venture into the deep, dangerous water. But I push it all aside because I don't care about myself right now. I care about Damarian and Kiander. I'm not leaving this ocean until they're safe.

Chapter Twenty-Nine

Kiandra tells me to eat because I'll need my strength today. For the first time since I've entered the ocean, I have no appetite.

Syren left early this morning to meet with Callen to gather as many merpeople as possible who are willing to join the search party. Hopefully, they'll return with a large army and we can start training. Every second we waste puts Damarian and Kiander's lives more at risk.

When I'm done eating, Zarya pulls me into her room and shows off all of her toys. She's a good distraction.

After what feels like days but is only a few hours, Syren finally comes home. The adults meet in the main room, eagerly waiting to hear the news.

"Twenty," he says.

My heart sinks. That's such a low number. "Don't they want to help save their king?" I ask.

Syren shakes his head. "We are not accustomed to war. Many do not wish to put their lives in jeopardy. They have families."

"So do you. And Kiander one day." And hopefully, Damarian, too, but I don't want to think about that. Though, I guess now that I'm a mermaid, having children with Damarian may not be such a scary thing. I quickly shake my head. I am *not* thinking about this right now.

Merman's Touch

"Human rulers sometimes draft people for war," I say.

"Draft?" Doria asks.

"Like force."

"No," Syren says. "Absolutely not."

Yeah, I didn't think so.

"I guess that's it, then," I say.

Syren nods. "Yes. We are to meet with the others shortly." He nods at the food on the table. "You will need your strength."

"Father," Doria says.

"No."

"But Father—"

"I will not allow it, Doria." He swims closer to her and touches her cheek. "I will not put you in harm's way," he says softly.

I see in her eyes how she wants to demand he let her go. But I also see the fear in them. The terror.

"We will locate them. I assure you."

She nods reluctantly.

Syren swims over to his wife, takes her hands, and wraps his tail around hers. "I will bring them back to you."

She rests her head on his chest and they stay like that for a little bit, until Syren forces himself away from her. He calls the younger kids into the room, and kisses the top of their heads, telling them to behave while he's away.

"Are you exploring the sea?" Zarya asks, eyes wide with excitement.

Syren puts on a smile. "Yes, my darling."

Syd frowns, eyeing his father suspiciously. He probably knows exactly what's going on.

"I wish to come!" Zarya says.

"Not now, Zarya."

"But Father!"

"Zarya."

She pouts. He kisses the top of her head again. "We will see you shortly."

She looks at me. "Cassie is leaving with you?"

Her parents exchange a look. "Yes," Kiandra says.

"Why?"

"It is because Damarian and Kiander are lost," Syd says.

"*What?*" Zarya cries.

Syren gives his son a look. "Damarian and Kiander are well." He pats Zarya's head. "Behave, all right?"

She nods, then rushes to me. "You will return, will you not?"

"I will," I assure her. "Don't worry."

She grins.

Syren heads for the opening and nods at me. I say goodbye to the rest of Damarian's family and follow him out. The great white swims forward. Syren rubs the top of its head. Then he goes to the second one and touches the top of its head, closing his eyes. He's communicating with it. After a few seconds, the shark lowers its head and moves closer to the entrance of the house. Like it's protecting it.

"Come," Syren says to me.

The other shark swims between us as Syren leads me toward the exit. But we don't leave the merpeople colony. He brings me to a large open area that is devoid of fish and other creatures. Merpeople are gathered there, tails of all colors, though most are Sapphires and Violets, which doesn't surprise me. There is one Ruby and a few Diamonds and Emeralds. They are comprised mostly of men, but I see a couple of women, too.

Sharks swim around as well.

Surveying the merpeople, I recognize two of them: Callen, head of the Guard, and Kyle. Kyle waves when he sees me and swims over. "Hey, Cass." He gives me a hug. A large tiger shark follows closely behind him.

"Not such a big turnout," I say.

"Yeah, but we honestly didn't expect many to volunteer. That's okay. We'll take the rebels down either way."

The tiger shark is only a few feet away from me. My stomach swirls around as the image of Kayla's severed arm and bloody body bounces in my mind. I know it's not fair to blame this shark for something it didn't do, but I can't help it.

"You have a shark," I mutter.

"Yeah."

"How does it work? Does every merperson get a shark when they reach a certain age or something?"

He shakes his head. "Generally, each home is assigned a shark as protection. Depending on status and other factors, heads of households can have their own private shark. For example, if someone is an explorer, he will have his own personal shark. Though some sharks choose what master to serve. Like Fiske."

"Fiske?"

"Yeah. He grew attached to Damarian."

"And your tiger shark?"

"Recently assigned to me by Queen Flora because I joined the search party."

I scan the area, watching the sharks swim around. "And all these?"

"Will be assigned to their masters."

My heart pounds in my head. That means I'll be getting one, too.

Kyle smiles. "Hey, they're not so bad. And they won't hurt you."

I eye a bull shark whose eyes are pasted on me menacingly. "Can they catch my human scent or something?"

"I doubt that. You're one hundred percent mermaid now."

"I don't like the way he's looking at me."

He follows my gaze and chuckles lightly. "Bull sharks are pretty aggressive, more so than the other sharks. Bullies. Just ignore him."

My gaze moves to the great white sharks. They're all massive, with crazy sharp teeth. One of them will be my protector. I don't know if I should sigh in relief or hide in a cave.

A Sapphire and a Violet join us, each with a shark, and then Syren and Callen swim to the middle of the area. "I believe all who wish to search for my sons are present," Syren says. He eyes the merpeople floating around. "As we have informed you earlier, this is a difficult task we ask of you. My sons' lives are in peril. The life of the king is in grave danger. It is a dangerous mission we are set to embark on, but it is a mission we must do." He swallows. "There will be warfare, there may be death. If you are not up for the task, I advise you to leave."

He waits for people to go, but no one does. He bows his head. "You have my thanks." He raises his head. "Let us commence training."

Callen starts assigning sharks to the merpeople who don't have one. My heart races as I watch the number of great whites grow smaller and smaller. Will I get one? What if there aren't enough left? Maybe Syren has no intention of letting me come along?

When there is only one left, Callen and Syren make their way toward me, the shark trailing behind. It's large, maybe a little larger than the others, with the most intense eyes I've ever seen. It wants me for lunch—I know it does.

"Cassie." Syren gestures to the shark. "Callen and I believe this shark is best suited for you."

Yeah, because it'll eat me two minutes into training.

"She enjoys doing as she pleases," Callen says. "Many have

reported her for her refusal to adhere to orders. But it is my belief that she will listen to you."

Great. This is just awesome. I'm left with the problem shark.

"Okay, I guess," I mumble.

"If she refuses to listen, we will assign you a different shark," Syren says.

When they're out of earshot, I face Kyle. "Am I being punished or something?"

He shakes his head. "Trust Callen. He knows what he's doing."

I fold my arms. "What's Syren, anyway? Is he a member of the Guard?"

"Sort of. He was King Palaemon—the former king's—most trusted advisor. Ever since they made the agreement to set up their kids. He oversaw the Guard. But as soon as Kiander took the thrown, he dismissed his father."

"Why?"

"I'm not sure. But I think it's because he wanted his dad to spend more time at home."

My skin prickles when I feel the shark staring at me.

I back away. "I think my life is at stake."

Kyle laughs. "Don't be scared. Talk to her, get to know her. See if you guys can get along."

Right, like it's so easy. I face the shark. I heard that one rule to showing an animal who is master is by letting it know who is master and who is servant. I've never had any pets, other than the marine fish my mom bought for me who hadn't lasted more than a week.

I move a little closer to the shark, my heart thumping so hard my ears ring. Reaching out, I slowly rest my hand on her head. Like Fiske, her skin feels rough. *Hi*, I think in my head. *I'm Cassie.*

She continues to stare at me.

I swallow the saliva nearly choking me. *Do you have a name?*

Shoney.

Its voice scratches the inside of my head. Biting back a groan, I smile. *Shoney. I like that name.*

She shoots me a look that says she doesn't give a damn whether or not I like her name.

"Now that you are all acquainted with your shark," Callen says. "It is time you connect your minds."

Say what?

Everyone seems to know what they're doing. I look helplessly at Kyle. "That's how you and your shark communicate," he says. "Through your minds. You develop a deep connection."

I don't know if I can do this.

Looking at Syren, I find him watching me. He swims over. "Place your hands on your shark," he instructs. "Feel her energy flow through you."

I rest my hands on the top of Shoney's head and close my eyes. My eyebrows come together as I concentrate—on what, I have no idea. But nothing happens. Opening my eyes, I see the shark's eyes on me. She looks bored, yet slightly amused.

Okay, I say. *I get it. You like to have fun. You don't like to listen to authority, but would rather do your own thing.*

I see something flash in her eyes. My body perks up. Maybe I'm making progress here.

I'm like that, too, I continue. *I don't like doing what other people tell me either, and I don't like anyone getting in the way of my happiness. I fell in love with someone different. People may think I'm crazy, but I'm happy.*

She's looking at me differently now. Like she's actually listening to what I'm saying.

With me, I won't order you around. I'd like to be your friend. Together, we can accomplish many things. I play with my hair. *I have no idea what I'm doing, but I need to save the man I love.*

Something passes through me, sending a jolt up my spine. My vision gets blurry for a few seconds, and then I'm looking through eyes that aren't my own.

I stumble back. I see myself gawking at me.

I *am* Shoney.

After blinking a few times, I'm back to myself. She gives me a smug smile. I take a deep breath and let it out slowly. Okay, I can merge my mind with a shark and see what she sees. Totally normal.

Callen moves to the center of the area. "Let us begin training. My hope is that we do not spend too much time, for it is imperative that we rescue our captured brothers."

Syren leads everyone out of this area and out of the colony. He and Callen bring us to an area with many sea life. I've never seen so many different creatures in one location. It's like a buffet.

At first, we just stand there, but after a few seconds, Callen's shark shoots forward and snatches one of the fish in its mouth. A second later, it goes for another and another, its razor-sharp teeth chomping. But Callen is not just standing there watching the show. It looks like he's the one in the control, like he's the one telling his shark exactly which fish to eat.

They're sharing a mind.

The shark stops and returns to Callen, staying at its side.

Syren swims forward. "Sharks will feed on their own will, but they will listen to their masters if they instruct them. The object of this exercise is to order your shark to feed on whichever fish you choose. When you have mastered the skill, we will be able to search for the rebels and attack them in the same manner."

Now I understand what we're doing. Merpeople don't have

weapons to use to attack their enemies. They have sharks. By being connected through their minds, sharks will know exactly who their masters want them to attack.

I glance at Shoney, who looks at me. I can already see the defiant look in her eyes.

We'll make a good team, I tell her.

She turns her head away from me and stares straight ahead.

"You may begin," Callen says.

I motion for Shoney to follow me away from the others, to an area with a lot of fish to practice on. From the look in her eyes, I know she's not in the mood for any work.

So do you have any brothers and sisters? I ask.

She narrows her eyes like she knows what I'm trying to do.

Um…okay. Let's do this.

With a blank expression on her face, she swims toward a school of fish. Concentrating hard, I tell her which fish I want her to eat. She goes in the opposite direction and gnaws on a fish of a different species.

"Shoney, not that one!"

Everyone stares at me, including my shark.

I'm definitely blushing.

I surge to Shoney and touch her face. *Look, I know it's hard to take orders from someone. I thought we spoke about this before and came to an understanding.*

No response.

I told you I think we can make a good team. I gesture to the others who seem to be hitting it off very well. *I can tell you're one competitive shark. What do you say we show them who the real winner is?*

Shoney rushes to my fish and snaps her mouth over it.

Awesome!

Merman's Touch

Once again, I'm in her mind and see what she sees. But at the same time, I'm also in my head, seeing everything through my eyes. I tell Shoney what to eat, how fast to go, when to stop. When she's actually listening, she makes one hell of a hunter. She's amazing.

Once she's done, I swim over and wrap my arms around her, rubbing my cheek against her rough skin. *You're awesome, Shoney. Thanks so much for listening to me.*

She nuzzles me.

Two merpeople enter our practice arena, a female Sapphire and a male Violet. They incline their heads to Callen and Syren. "What have you learned?" Callen asks.

The Sapphire moves forward. "The deep water is indeed uninhabitable. Venturing there will surely kill us."

Syren's face drains from every last hope he had.

The Violet moves forward. "But we have made a profound discovery. We now understand how the rebels live down there."

"How?" Callen asks.

"With a specific species of fish," the Sapphire says. "One that can survive in the Deep. It latches onto its host and provides it with the nutrients necessary to survive."

Everyone in here starts whispering at once. I can't believe what I'm hearing.

"I have never heard of such a thing," Callen murmurs.

"We do not know what creatures live in the Deep," Syren says. He moves his eyes to the scouts. "Are they friendly?"

They shrug.

"We must do everything in our power to make them our allies." He nods to everyone. "We have trained enough. Now it is time we battle."

Chapter Thirty

We're moving deeper into the ocean. The temperature drops lower, and it's getting a little harder to breathe. Kyle swims to my left and Shoney is at my right. It makes me a little less nervous. Only a little.

I have no idea what's going to happen, if we'll be able to convince those fish to help us. And if we do, will we be able to fight off the rebels and save Damarian and Kiander?

Syren, who is at the head of the group, makes a sudden stop. My limbs grow heavy as fear settles in my stomach.

Something jumps out. A blue shark. It snaps its mouth at Syren, missing him only by a few inches. Syren's great white lunges at it, catching it in the middle and crunching it. It cries out as it struggles to break free, but the great white has it in a death hold. Blood pours out of it, causing some of the sharks that belong to members of our party to bolt to it, each vying for a bite. All of the sudden, more sharks leap out at us, tiger sharks, bull sharks, even a few great whites. They charge at the sharks that were heading for the blue shark. I gasp as one by one, they're killed.

Looking to my left, I see merpeople hiding behind coral or rock with triumphant smiles on their faces. The rebels. I mostly see Emerald and Diamond tails.

Merman's Touch

"Attack!" Callen shouts.

My hands reach for Shoney as she darts toward them, but all I get is water. No…I don't want her to fight. I don't want her to get hurt. She's supposed to listen to me!

My eyes widen as I see the way she rips into those sharks with her teeth. Bones crack, blood fills the water. She's like a ruthless beast, snapping and mauling, twisting her body to avoid attacks. She saves a few of her comrades who are seconds away from being killed.

I just stare at her, my jaw probably hitting the ocean floor.

Something moves in my peripheral vision. I freeze, watching in slow motion as a bull shark charges at me. It opens its mouth wide, ready to rip my face off. I yell.

A great white storms at it, catching it in its mouth, digging its teeth deep into it, then tossing it aside like a useless rag.

"Shoney," I breathe.

She turns around to face me. *I am not a pup. Do not treat me like one. Have faith in me and I will protect you.*

I clutch my thumping heart with two hands. Then I grab her and hug her close to my chest. "You're right," I pant. "You are absolutely right. I'm sorry."

She nods before returning to the action. But there's not a lot of action left. Sharks are dropping to the bottom of the ocean, their blood filling the ocean like red ink, bits and pieces of them floating around. I look at the members of the search party. My heart constricts. Some of them are wounded. Some of them have lost their sharks. Some are dead.

The rebels must have fled.

I rush over to Kyle who's holding an unconscious female Emerald in his arms. "Kyle," I say.

He raises his head. I don't see tears, but I know he's crying. "It—it was a tiger." There's no hiding the betrayal from his voice. "I can't believe a tiger shark would do this to an Emerald."

I pat his arm. Kyle looks around. "I...I can't believe any of this. Most of them are from my clan. *My* clan. The shark that attacked her belongs to my neighbor's family!" He tightens his hold on the mermaid in his arms. "I didn't know her, but she's part of my extended family." His voice is so choked I can barely hear what he's saying. "I-I knew what was going on was pretty bad, but to kill this ruthlessly, and to members of my own clan?"

He's in my arms. I don't know what to say to comfort him. I just rub his back.

Most of the others are looking at us, some holding other wounded merpeople. Syren swims forward. "Yes, Kyler. You are correct. What the rebels have done, it is not who we are. Our kind does not hurt one another. We will put an end to this and continue living peacefully, as we've done all these moons since the great battle." He studies the wounded. "We must return them to their families. We must..." His voice wavers. "Inform the families of those who have perished."

I glance at the Emerald in Kyle's arms. She's lost too much blood. There's a high chance she won't make the trip home, if she hasn't died already. Tears enter my eyes.

Syren nods at some members of the Guard who came along with us. "You will escort the wounded to the colony. They will need assistance. Would anyone like to join them? It will be a difficult journey."

A few people move forward. I raise my hand.

Syren shakes his head. "We require you here, in the chance you sense Damarian."

I nod.

Four head home, taking the wounded and dead with them. That

Merman's Touch

leaves us with only twelve people.

"We should rest," Callen says. "Tomorrow, we will draw closer to the Deep." He inspects the area. "But here is not an ideal location. The rebels may return. We must travel to a safe location."

I hold out my hand to Kyle. He gives me a small, thankful smile and grasps it.

We travel for a long time before settling down in a cave next to an area with a lot of ocean life. Syren claims the rebels are less likely to attack in a heavily populated area. The sharks stand guard outside.

A few merpeople bring in fish, and everyone chows them down like this is the last meal we'll ever eat. When every fish is gone, we lie down on the floor of the cave. I have no idea if I'll be able to get any rest tonight, but I need to. I'm exhausted from all the traveling and from the attack of the rebels.

Kyle lies down next to me, his eyes focused above.

I scoot closer. "Are you okay?"

He nods. "I'll be okay. Been through worse. Okay, maybe not."

I pat his arm, then lie down and stare toward the surface. It's so far away. "We'll kick their asses," I tell him.

He nods, though I see the uncertainty in his eyes. "You know, I never thought we'd end up like this. You and me, fighting side by side." He laughs softly. "I didn't even think we'd see each other again."

I sit up and put my weight on my elbow. "Why did you join?"

"The search party? Well honestly, Kiander and Damarian have been great to me, especially Kiander. If not for him, I'd still be banished and never see my family." He laughs again. "I was getting just a bit too bored of being a human."

I slap his shoulder. "It's not so bad."

"Maybe. But it's never fun when you're alone."

Something gets stuck in my throat. Damarian's face flashes before me. I turn to my side and shut my eyes tight.

Kyle rubs my back. "I'm sorry. I shouldn't have said that. You'll be with Damarian very soon."

I roll back over and force a smile. "Thanks."

"I'll do whatever it takes to save them."

We're both quiet. I turn to my side again, trying to get some sleep. But all I manage to do is toss and turn.

"Kyle?"

"Yeah?"

"Do you have anyone special in your life?"

He lies back down and scoffs. "Me? Nah. Haven't found anyone yet."

"No mermaids have caught your eye?"

He shakes his head. "Maybe human girls have ruined love for me."

I slap his shoulder again. "I'm sure you'll meet the right one soon. Hey, is it weird for merpeople to choose mates from a different clan?"

"It's perfectly okay to do that, though most choose mates from their own clan. Each one has its own personality, so they may not mesh well with another clan."

"What personality does each clan have?"

He thinks for a few seconds. "The violets are aggressive, that's why most of the Guard is comprised of Violets. The Diamonds are humorous, maybe a little too humorous. The Rubies are peaceful and try to avoid all conflict. The Emeralds are confident, though maybe a bit too confident. And then there are the Sapphires."

I raise my eyebrows. "Do you have something against the Sapphires," I ask, half teasing, half serious.

"No." He holds his hands out like I'm about to pull out a gun and shoot him. "They're caring and understanding. And very loyal. But I'm sure you know all about that."

Merman's Touch

I certainly do. Damarian is everything I've ever wanted in a guy, plus lots more.

"It's so amazing, learning about all of this." I feel my face fall. "Though I wish it was under better circumstances."

He squeezes my hand.

We lie back down and stare at the surface. I feel Kyle watching me. "What?" I ask him.

"Do you miss land?"

That question stumps me. I've been so caught up in everything down here and so worried about Damarian that I never sat down to asses my own feelings.

"I miss it a lot," I tell him. Leah, my mom, my dad and his family, my students. My legs. The feel of the sun on my skin, the soft wind blowing through my hair. And the food, even though lately all I've been craving is fish. "I don't even know how long I've been gone," I say. "No one knows where I am, other than Leah."

He grins. "Ah, Leah. That girl. She's a tough one."

I smile. "Yeah." The best friend a girl can ask for. I miss her terribly.

"You'll see them again soon," he says. "With Damarian at your side. I promise."

I really hope so.

Chapter Thirty-One

In my dream, Damarian's cries are louder, slamming into me like a bulldozer, jerking me from my sleep. I spring up, my heart speeding, my body shaking. Around me, everyone is asleep. I hug my upper arms.

I see someone at the entrance of the cave. The only other person here who can't sleep, either. His back is pressed against the wall, his long golden hair hanging over his body like a curtain. Syren.

Pushing off from the ground, I head toward him. Based on how his shoulders stiffen, I can tell he knows someone's coming, and that the someone is me.

I sit down opposite from him. He's staring straight ahead, toward the Deep. I study it. It looks close, but I know it's farther than it seems. It's completely black, like a never ending hole.

Syren turns his head, and our eyes meet. "I am not surprised you cannot sleep," he says.

"I had a dream of Damarian again." I rub my arms. I'm not too cold, but I know I would be if I were human. "I felt him stronger than I had in the past."

Syren gazes out toward the Deep again. "That is likely due to your close proximity to him."

I'm closer to Damarian. I hug my upper arms again, wishing I were hugging him.

Syren and I sit in silence, watching the activity outside the cave. The sharks circle around, their eyes intense and vigilant. A few randomly grab some fish. The place is alive. All the other creatures go about their usual lives, blissfully unaware of the turmoil going on in the merworld.

Syren shakes his head like he can't stand the thoughts going through his mind.

"We'll find them," I tell him.

He shakes his head again. "How I have been a disappointment to my fry."

I don't know what to say to the man with the hard shell, the one who was never a fan of me or my union with Damarian.

"Perhaps I have failed them as a father," he continues.

"This isn't your fault," I say.

His gaze is still on the area outside the cave. "A father behaves in a manner he believes will only benefit his fry. I was too stubborn and did not see reason. I should have listened to my mate."

"None of this is your fault," I repeat.

"Perhaps if I were a better father, this would not occur."

"This is no one's fault but the rebels."

"I have made promises I could not keep. I promised to place the true king on the throne." He shakes his head. "Had I succeeded, my son would have not been happy."

I move a little closer. "Damarian is a great guy, Syren. An amazing guy. Part of the credit should go to you."

He finally looks at me. "You are kind, Cassie. Kind for a human. I understand why Damarian has such a love for you." His focus is back on the outside. "I pushed duty over love. I did not see reason when Damarian proclaimed his love for you. I believed him to be a fry.

Juvenile." He looks at me again. "I did not wish to hear his thoughts of love." His fists clench and unclench on his lap. "When I have fought for love myself."

I stare at him. "What do you mean? You and Kiandra?"

He nods. "We grew up together, our homes side by side. I did not admit my feelings to her." He smiles lightly. "Not until her father suggested a mate for her." His eyes move to mine. "She had no will to mate with him, for she knew I deeply desired her. And that she desired me." His smile widens and his eyes soften. "I pleaded with her father to let me mate with her. I did not surrender until he agreed."

I feel a warm smile capture my face. "That's very romantic."

He nods, a shadow creeping over his face. "I did not allow my son to experience love."

Somehow, I end up sitting right next to him. "Everyone makes mistakes. We're just human—I mean, we're just flesh and blood. When we make mistakes, we need to learn how to make amends."

He nods. "How correct you are. Only in dire circumstance do we recognize the errors of our ways." He gets up from the floor and floats before me, all business-like. "You require rest. Tomorrow will be a difficult day."

I nod. "Good night, Syren."

He bows his head.

***

After eating, we exit the cave. The Guards who left to bring the wounded back home have returned, without the others. Our count is now sixteen.

Like I feared, the Emerald mermaid died on the way. As we swim toward the Deep, I ask Kyle what merpeople do with their dead. He tells me there are a few members in every clan who are in charge of the dead bodies. After loved ones say goodbye, they bring the bodies deeper into the ocean and let them fall. Their bodies become part of the ocean. In a way, they never leave.

"Be vigilant," Callen says when we're close enough to the Deep that I can see some creatures swimming inside. I feel Damarian more intensely now, and my heart yearns for him.

"Cassie." Syren holds his hand out toward me.

I swim forward.

"I would like you to join me as I speak to the fish that will help us survive down there."

With my heart pounding in my ears, I nod.

Callen and another Guard flank us on either side as we approach the opening to the Deep. The rest stay behind to keep watch.

"We are not familiar with these species," Syren says to me. "They may be poised to attack."

I nod because no words can leave my mouth. My heart beats so fast I feel it in my tail. The electrical pulse of Damarian beats through my body. He's so close.

Syren's fingers tighten on my hand as he gives me a reassuring smile. My heart rate slows down a little.

We swim forward until we're right outside the Deep. I peer over the edge. It's like looking down into a volcano. I can't see the bottom. But what I do see is hundreds, maybe thousands of species of fish, ones that belong in a sci-fi move. Some of their bodies are so transparent I can see their insides. A few are lit up like they have tiny beads of lights attached all over their bodies. Many of them don't have any eyes.

"They have unique bodies," Callen says. "It is how they survive in cold conditions with no source of light."

"They're beautiful," I say, mesmerized as I watch them swim.

"We must locate the species that can assist us," Syren says.

"Perhaps—"

A tiger shark shoots toward us. Toward me. Syren shoves me aside, and my head knocks into coral with so much force that I black out for a few seconds. When I open my eyes, my sight is blurry and my head rings.

Sharks are attacking us. Lots of sharks. I see the others are in battle. Kyle's arm is bleeding.

The same tiger shark charges at me. I try to run away, but my tail is stuck between coral. No matter how much I yank, it won't come out.

The shark is only a few feet away.

I'm going to die.

I close my eyes. The only person on my mind is Damarian.

Something explodes all over my face and chest. My eyes snap open. I'm covered in shark guts and blood. Shoney is right in front of me, blood and flesh dripping down her mouth. She saved me.

Thank you, Shoney.

She inclines her head and returns to the action.

When it's over, Callen helps me out of the coral. This was battle number two. We've lost three people and five have been injured, including Kyle.

"They will send larger armies," Syren says.

"Our sharks are better trained," Callen says.

Syren shakes his head. "We will be unable to withstand a larger assault." His eyes move to mine. "We must hurry. Are you injured, Cassie?"

I rub my forehead, "Just my head."

"Are you well enough to seek the fish?"

I nod. Even if my tail was sliced off, I would go with him.

I swim over to Kyle, who's hugging his arm. "Are you badly hurt?"

He forces a smile, but winces. "Barely a scratch."

Merman's Touch

Ignoring his protest, I lower his arm from his chest and gasp. There's a large cut starting from his elbow to his wrist. It looks really deep.

"I'll be fine, Cass."

I glance at the other injured merpeople who are getting ready to return home. "Go back," I tell Kyle.

"Never."

"Don't be stubborn."

"I'm going to help rescue Damarian and Kiander."

I fold my arms. "I'm guessing Emeralds are extremely stubborn?"

He grins.

"Fine," I say. "But get some rest." After giving him a quick hug, I make my way to Syren.

"Are you sure you are well?" he asks. "Forgive me for pushing you."

"It's okay. You kind of saved my life. Thanks."

He bows his head, then tilts it to the side. I step closer and widen my eyes. Two Guards are holding down a Diamond merman.

"You caught one," I say.

"Yes. He will provide us with the answers we need." Regret enters his eyes. "Even if we will need to acquire it forcefully."

Bile rises in my throat. He'll have no choice but to torture him.

"I do not wish for the others to see what I am to do," Syren says. "Perhaps you would not like to witness it, either."

I nod. "Thanks. Let me know if you find anything."

I return to Kyle, who looks a lot better than he did a few minutes ago. I examine his injury. It seems to be healing, though it looks painful.

"I told you I'm fine, Cass." He smirks. "When was the last time you looked at your face?"

Rolling my eyes, I wipe away the gunk from my eyes, nose, and mouth. "A shark exploded all over me." I glance at Shoney, who is with the other sharks, keeping watch. "My shark is pretty bad-ass. I'm lucky to have her."

"You'll never find a more loyal creature than a shark," Kyle says.

Kayla's bloody body and arm stump enter my head. I wonder if Kyle and the rest of the merpeople know about the attack. Would they even care? I don't bring it up because I don't want to start anything. Not when we need to put all of our focus on finding Kiander and Damarian.

Shouts are heard. Everyone's bodies grow tense, their eyes darting in all different directions. Callen holds his hand up and informs us that everything's okay. Bile rises in my throat again. Syren is torturing the Diamond.

The shouts grow louder, more frantic, laced with pain. It's so hard to hear.

"What's going on?" Kyle asks.

I swallow a few times before saying in a shaky voice, "They captured one of the rebels. They're trying to extract information from him."

Kyle's face gets dark. "Look what all this is doing to us. Torturing?"

"He has no choice."

"I know. It's just terrible."

We sit in silence, and I try to block out the screams. By now, everyone knows exactly what's going on, and they have similar reactions. Torturing a fellow merperson is not something they do.

After a few minutes, I hear groaning, and then nothing. Syren motions for me to come. Every cell in my body fills with dread. Did the Diamond die?

Merman's Touch

As I approach, I see the Guards carrying away the half conscious, bloody Diamond.

Syren's eyes seem to match the tortured yells of the Diamond. "I now have the knowledge required to appease the fish. Let us go."

Chapter Thirty-Two

Once again flanked by Callen and the other Guard, Syren and I are back at the opening to the Deep. I keep looking around, expecting more rebels to jump out at us. The others are not too far away, ready to fight and defend if necessary.

Syren picks a stone with a jagged edge off the floor and positions it over his other hand. Without hesitating, he slices his palm. Blood seeps into the water. Leaning over the opening, he thrusts his hand inside and waves it around.

Nothing happens.

I'm about to ask him what's going on when a hiss slips through his lips. He jerks his hand out of the Deep. Two fish hang from his hand. They are about three inches long, with skin that looks like little balls of light attached together by a piece of thread.

They start sliding up his arm, one nestling on his shoulder and the other one on his upper chest. They're like leeches.

"Do not fear," Syren tells me. "They will not drain your body of blood." He picks up the stone and slices his other hand, then sticks it into the Deep. He leaves his hand in there longer than the last time. After about a minute, he releases a few hisses and pulls his hand out. A dozen more of those fish are attached to his skin, sliding to different parts of his body. His whole body starts to glow, growing more and more transparent.

I just stare at him. He's like an ethereal ghost.

Syren hands me the stone. "The puncture will sting."

"Okay." With a shaky hand, I take it from him. I'm not queasy about blood, but I've never cut myself before. And what happened to Syren scares me, to be honest.

But I need to do this. It's the only way to survive down there, the only way to save Damarian and Kiander.

After taking a few seconds to clear my head, I dig the stone into my palm. I count to five before cutting myself. Holding back a wince, I shove my hand through the opening of the Deep. My heart thumps loudly in my chest as I wait for the fish to bite me.

I don't expect it to hurt this much.

When I wrench my hand out of there, one fish hangs off me. It doesn't hurt anymore. I can see its mouth latched onto me. The feeling…it's hard to describe. It's like energy flows through me, giving me life.

Syren nods at my other hand. Counting again to five, I slice my second palm, then quickly push it into the opening. I need to get as many of these fish as possible. I'm not too keen on slicing any more parts of my body.

I feel one bite, then another, followed by a few more. My hand gets numb for a few seconds. When I pull it out, seven fish are latched onto me. They start moving to other parts of my body, and once again, I feel like energy is being pumped into me.

Warmness spreads through me. I glance down at my hand and see it looks exactly like Syren's.

The others move toward the opening to the Deep and start cutting their palms and dipping them into the water. One by one, they turn into light creatures. The sharks come next. Then we're all set.

Callen swims forward. "I will enter the Deep first."

Syren rests his hand on his shoulder. "Be vigilant."

Callen does a quick nod before diving in with his shark. The rest of us wait.

And wait.

And wait some more.

We exchange glances. Did the rebels get him?

It seems like forever before his head pops out of the opening. "I did not encounter any rebels," he reports.

"That is no assurance that they are not present there," Syren says. "Are we able to survive down there?"

"Yes."

Syren faces us, telling us to be extra careful. Then he takes my hand. "When you enter the Deep, your sense of Damarian will most likely grow more powerful. We must locate him as soon as possible."

I muster everything I have to give him a confident nod.

A few members of the group dive in with their sharks. Tightening his hold on my hand, Syren tugs me closer to the opening. Together, and with our great whites by our sides, we jump in.

At first, all I see is darkness. But then it's like a light switch goes off in my head and I can see everything clearly. The many unique sea creatures swimming around, the ocean floor and rocks beneath.

A pulse goes through me. Damarian. He's so close I can almost touch him.

"Which direction?" Syren asks.

I point to my left and our party heads that way. Every part of me prickles with fear, anticipation, and nerves. This is it. If we can fight off the rebels, it won't be long before Damarian will be in my arms again. Before I can feel his warm, sweet loving lips on mine.

Merman's Touch

A sharp jolt of electricity sparks through me. It starts at my back, then moves to every part of my body. I groan and twist in different directions as the pain grows more intense. I feel my tail shove Syren away.

They're torturing Damarian. They might be killing him. Maybe they learned we're down here and decided to screw their mission and just kill Damarian and Kiander.

The pain stops and I'm left shaking. I find myself in someone's arms. Opening my eyes to slits, I see it's Syren. "We…need to hurry," I force out.

Syren cuts my arm with a piece of stone, and a few seconds later, a fish bites me. Energy flows through my veins. After making sure I'm okay, Syren asks me where Damarian is. The pulse is the strongest it's ever been. Blinking a few times, I see something in the distance—a large cave. It almost looks like a building

Raising a trembling hand, I point to it.

Everyone intakes a breath. The building isn't the only thing in the distance. A group of rebel merpeople are, too. And they're headed this way.

Syren pushes me behind him. "Be prepared," he tells us.

A tall, skinny merman swims forward, a massive tiger shark at his side. A few more follow, like they're his bodyguards.

Syren moves closer. "Gyron."

Gyron smiles. "Syren."

He must be the leader of the rebels.

Gyron's smile gets bigger. "I understand you learned of the Yoki fish. Marvelous creatures, I must say."

"I will attempt to speak with you in a peaceful manner," Syren says, his tone the most serious I've ever heard.

If Gyron's smile were any wider, he'd have no lips. His eyes trek to mine, curious. "The human. You have brought her here. She is a child of the sea."

Saliva pools in my mouth.

Syren keeps me behind him. "Release my sons, Gyron. There is no need for violence."

With his gaze still on me, he cocks his head. "She is the cause of all this. A wretched human, meddling in our affairs, tearing the king from his throne."

"Kiander is king," Syren stresses. "He is a fair one. Do not be foolish."

He cocks his head the other way. "Ah, so you approve of the union between this human and your son."

"Yes," Syren says to my surprise. He didn't even hesitate. "Cassie is a good mate for my son."

Gyron laughs like he can't believe what he's hearing. Spreading out his arms, he faces the rebels behind them. "Have you all witnessed what Syren, of the royal Sapphire clan, has just claimed? He approves of the union between his son and a *human*." He spits the last word. "Humans! They destroy the sea and her creatures. They throw their wastes into our home." His hand shoots toward me. "This is the mate he wishes for Damarian, the one who is destined to be our king." He shakes his head. "The Sapphire clan is corrupted. Perhaps it is time we choose a new king."

"We are free to choose our mates," Syren says.

Gryon glares at him. "A king thinks of his subjects before himself."

Syren pushes forward. So does Gyron. They stare each other down.

The tiger shark right next to Gyron opens and snaps its mouth. Open and snaps it. Its amused eyes are pinned on me. Why the hell is it looking at me like that?

She was scrumptious. The female human fry.

Merman's Touch

My chest freezes up. I move a little closer. "What did you just say?" I ask the shark.

Syren holds out his hand, telling me to stay back.

"*What did you just say?*" I repeat, my voice rising an octave.

It snaps its mouth again. *I have not tasted anything quite as delicious as her.*

"You bastard!" I lunge at it, slamming my fist into its mouth. The force is so strong that the shark tumbles back like a tomahawk.

At once the place goes crazy. Sharks charge at other sharks, merpeople flee. As a hammerhead zips toward me, I raise my tail and slam it into its middle. Another tiger is a few inches away. I stab my elbow into its face. Its teeth graze my arm.

Syren grabs me by the waist and hauls me away. "Do you wish to be killed?" he shouts. He deposits me on the side. "Do not move from this location."

My arm stings from the shark's teeth, but that's not enough to stop me. I shoot forward, ready to strike, when I hear Damarian's voice in my head. *My love, do not put yourself in harm's way.*

"Damarian?" I ask.

Please.

He's alive and conscious and knows exactly what's going on. "Damarian!"

I don't hear him.

"Damarian?"

Nothing.

My body fills with newfound vigor. Concentrating hard, I focus on Shoney, merging our minds into one. Swimming toward her, I hold out my fists in front of me. *Together*, I tell her.

She nods.

A tiger storms toward us. Without having to say a word to each other, Shoney and I rush to it. She bites into it while I slam my tail into its other side. When a blue shark comes from behind, I shoot my arm backward, getting it in the head.

We do the same to the other sharks coming toward us.

As the battle rages on, the number of sharks on the rebel side diminishes. They are so shocked to be left defenseless that they are paralyzed in place, not sure what to do.

They run.

Kyle swims over to me. "Cass, are you crazy?"

My chest rises and falls wildly, my mind swimming with the realization of what I just did. Hitting sharks with my fists? I must be losing it.

Syren moves forward, a firm look on his face. "That was reckless."

I lower my head. "I know. I'm sorry."

"You are the mate of my son," he says. "You are my responsibility."

"I'm no one's responsibility. Just my own."

"Her heroics saved us," Callen states. "We would all be perished if not for her."

A mangled cry escapes my lips as my body feels like it's getting electrocuted. I sink toward the bottom of the ocean.

Kyle and Syren catch me. "Cassie, what's wrong?" Kyle asks.

"It's Damarian," I gasp, my eyes rolling back. "He doesn't have that much time left."

Chapter Thirty-Three

Kyle throws me on his back. "Let's go."

With every step we take, I grow weaker and weaker, like someone is sucking out my life. Syren cuts me, attracting more of the Yoki fish to latch onto me, but it's no use.

"Stay with me, Cassie," Kyle says, gently slapping my cheeks.

The area around me spins. I can barely lift my head.

"Is she dying because of Damarian?" Kyle asks Syren.

"She will not die," Syren says, his voice choked up. "What she is experiencing is the…the loss of her mate."

No! No! I want to yell it, but I'm so weak.

"We're too late," Kyle says.

"One does not lose hope," Syren says.

We speed up until we reach the wall of the cave. Kyle lowers me to the ground. "Where's the entrance?" he asks.

Through my blurry vision, I see them touching the wall, looking for openings. After a few seconds, Syren is at my side. "Cassie." He touches my face. "Be strong, Cassie. Do you know if there is an entrance to the cave?"

My head rolls back. An image enters my mind. "Your fingers," I mutter, my voice barely audible. "Bring them down across the wall.

Then upwards, then toward the left."

He lifts me into his arms and dashes to the cave. He does what I tell him and the wall moves to the side. We hurry in.

At least five rebels are inside. After transferring me to someone else, Syren sends his shark to attack. A few minutes later, the rebels and their sharks are dead.

Syren returns to me. "Which direction?" he asks me, his voice eager but patient. I point to the right.

The cave is huge.

I lead Syren to where I sense Damarian, and then I see him lying on the floor with Kiander next to him. A net is thrown over them. They're not made out of lights like us. They look normal.

The sight of Damarian ignites something in me. I free myself from Syren's hold and rush toward him.

"Stop!" he says.

I freeze.

His eyes are shut tight and he's lying face down on the ground. I gasp when I see his body covered in wounds. They look like burn marks.

"Damarian," I whisper.

"The...the net," he manages to say. "It is electrified."

Tears pool in my eyes. Glancing at Kiander, I find him also covered in wounds. I fall flat on my stomach and slide my hand underneath the net. Damarian's hand grips mine. "Cassie." A smile crawls onto his face. "My sweet Cassie. You are here."

"You called for me."

"No. I did not wish for you to enter the sea."

"I heard you," I tell him, squeezing his hand. "In my dreams."

His eyes open for a few seconds before closing. "I have seen you in my dreams as well." His eyes flutter again. "How I wish to see your face."

"We're going to get you out of here."

He shakes his head. "Cassie…I am afraid I must part with you."

"What? No! Stop. You're *not* going anywhere."

"You feel it," he whispers. "In your heart."

More tears enter my eyes. I rip my gaze away from Damarian and look at his dad. "We need to get rid of this damn net."

"It is not possible," Damarian says. "There is no way to destroy it."

"Damarian."

"We must…" He swallows. "We must say goodbye."

I raise my hand to snatch the net off him, but someone grabs my arm. "No." It's Syren. "It will kill you."

"Please," I beg him, feeling Damarian's pulse growing fainter and fainter. "Do something. Don't let them die."

"I will do all I can." He instructs two Guards to search the area for anything that can help us.

Syren swims as close as possible to his sons. Looking from Kiander to Damarian, a pained expression on his face, he says, "Damarian."

"Father." Damarian's voice has more life to it. "Father, you are here as well."

"Please forgive me for all I have done." He looks like he wants to apologize to Kiander, too, but he's unconscious.

Damarian shakes his head. "It is no bother."

The Guards return, telling Syren that they couldn't find anything. My head spins as my insides churn. "There has to be something we could do," I say in a choked voice.

Syren holds unsteady hands over the net. I'm about to yell at him, when Callen zooms toward him and tackles him to the ground. "There must be another way!"

"No." Syren fights to free himself from Callen, but he won't let him go. "Release me."

"You wish to sacrifice your life for your sons."

"Do not, Father," Damarian mutters, his voice the weakest I've ever heard. I stick my hand underneath the net, and his fingers find mine. "Cassie," he whispers. "Remain with me…please."

"No," I cry. "Someone do something. Please."

My own life seems to be draining out of me. Memories start to play through my head. The first time I saw Damarian unconscious on the beach. How I brought him home and splashed cold water on him. How he woke up for the first time, shocked that he was a human. How cute he was when he learned to walk for the first time. The utter fear I had when he nearly died because he needed sea water. The friendship we shared before he returned home, the heartache I felt when he was gone. How happy I was when he returned.

I can still feel his lips on mine, his hands on my body. I can hear the romantic things he said to me, the promises we shared. How we fought everything and everyone, just so we could be together.

Something sparks between our hands, so strong it nearly blinds me. I'm tossed to the side, knocking into the opposite wall. My whole body throbs. Raising my head, I see the net is no longer stretched over them.

"Damarian?" My limbs still aching, I push myself off the ground and throw myself over him, careful not to touch his wounds. I kiss every part of his face. "Damarian."

With weak arms, he snakes them around me, pulling me to his chest. "Cassie."

"What the hell just happened?" I ask Syren, who is crouched next to Kiander.

He looks just as bewildered as me. "I am not certain. There was electricity between your hands. It caused the net to break and dissolve."

I blink at my hand. What on Earth?

Merman's Touch

I don't have too much time to dwell on it because something doesn't feel right. Life is still draining out of Damarian.

"He's not getting better," I say.

Syren touches Damarian's chest. "His heart is weak." Moving back, he studies his sons. "They are not receiving the sustenance such as we are. The net must have kept them alive." He grabs two stones from the floor and tosses one to me. "Carry them," he says to the few mermen who came with us into the cave. Two lift Damarian's arms over their shoulders and drag him toward the entrance. Two others do the same to Kiander.

They lower them to the ground. I get down, taking Damarian in my arms. His breathing is labored, his gills expanding and contracting very fast, like they're working overdrive. Syren and I cut Damarian and Kiander's palms and shove their hands outside. After a second or two, they groan. We cut their other hands and the same thing happens. When Damarian's body is lit up like mine, he slumps against me. His breathing grows more even.

"Cassie," he murmurs.

I press my cheek to his, squeezing him tight, but not enough to hurt him.

"We must leave," Callen says. "We do not know how long these fish will sustain us."

Damarian and Kiander can't swim on their own. Kyle, who's been outside the cave all this time, rushes to grab one of Damarian's arms.

"Have you caught sight of any rebels?" Syren asks the Guard who was in charge of the outside party.

"Not one."

He nods to everyone. "It is time we return home."

Chapter Thirty-Four

As soon as we emerge out of the Deep, the fish unlatch themselves from our bodies and rush into the black water. Our skin turns back to normal.

I glance at Damarian, who is still being carried by Kyle and another Sapphire. I thought he'd start to get better once we left those waters, but his head lolls to his side and his eyes are barely opened. Kiander looks the same.

Are they going to die?

I swim over to Syren, who's gazing at his sons with a concerned expression. "Are they going to be okay?" I ask.

His eyes don't leave them. "I have never seen wounds such as these."

"What were they made from? Those nets?"

He shakes his head. "I do not know."

"What...what are we going to do?"

He finally looks at me, a determined look in his eyes. "We journey home and heal them."

I nod, my chest hurting. After risking my life to come here, will I just lose Damarian?

We head home. There are no rebels around. I'm not sure how

Merman's Touch

many we killed, but I know there were a few survivors, including their leader Gyron. They could be regrouping now.

Shoney swims at my side. I smile, rubbing her fin. *You did good.*

She inclines her head. *So did you.*

Traveling back home seems to take forever. I keep glancing at Damarian, trying to determine if his condition has gotten worse, but he looks the same.

We finally make it to the colony. The merpeople swimming around gape at us as we bring in the wounded mermen. A Guard member rushes ahead of us to inform Kiandra and the rest of the family of our arrival.

When we draw closer, I see her outside. Her eyes widen with pure shock when she takes one look at her sons. The mermen hurry into the cave and place Kiander and Damarian on the stone table. I take Damarian's hand. It's colder than it should be and his eyes keep fluttering.

"What has happened?" Kiandra gasps.

Syren lightly touches a wound on Kiander's lower back. "They were tortured," he tells her. "I have not seen wounds such as these. They are not healing."

She hurries to a large oyster shell and pulls out sea plants, then returns and dabs one of Damarian's wounds. A soft, weak hiss leaves his mouth. She does the same to Kiander.

"Where are the fry?" Syren asks.

"Doria has taken them to play."

The room gets quiet as Kiandra cleans more wounds.

Syren tells the mermen they can leave. All of them besides for Kyle lower their heads and exit.

"You may take your leave as well, Kyler," Syren says.

"Would it be all right if I remain here? I wish to see Damarian and

Kiander get well."

Syren nods. "Very well."

We're all quiet again. Kiandra continues rubbing plants on her sons' wounds.

"I don't get it," I say, my gaze dead locked on one of Damarian's burn marks, waiting and hoping to see signs of healing. "Why did they hurt them? Didn't they want Damarian to be king?"

Darkness clouds Syren's features. "Perhaps they wished to torture Kiander until Damarian conceded." His eyes move sadly from one son to the other. "Perhaps they grew upset when he refused."

"He would never concede," Kiandra says, dabbing more wounds. "For he is mated to Cassie."

They, along with Kyle, look at me.

"What does that mean?" I ask.

"You are Damarian's mate," Kiandra says. "If Damarian agreed to take the crown, you would be queen."

It feels like the wind got knocked out of me. "*What?*"

"Unless they wished to kill you," Syren says.

"Damarian would be left with no mate. No heir to the throne."

"Perhaps they assumed mating with a human is not mating," Syren says.

Meaning, if they killed me Damarian would still be able to take another mate—a mermaid. They would rule.

"But that would be taking a big chance," I say. "What if killing me left Damarian with no mate for life?"

They're quiet, until Syren says, "Damarian would be the true king. Upon his death, if he has no heir, kingship would transfer to the next in line. Kiander."

I fold my arms as anger boils inside me. "So either way they would end up with Kiander as king."

Merman's Touch

"Yes. Or his fry."

How ridiculous is this? I brush some of Damarian's hair out of his face. He's fast asleep now. "Let's assume they're still sticking with their plan. They know about me now and that I'm a mermaid—a child of the sea. Will they do anything with me?"

Kiandra and Syren exchange a glance. Kyle looks a little uncomfortable.

"What?" I ask.

"Many consider you an abomination," Syren says in a low voice. "A human turned child of the sea…it is not natural."

So even if we get rid of the rebels and all is fine in the ocean, I might not be welcomed here. I sit down on one of the chairs, my head spinning.

Kiandra sits near me, taking my hand. "You are Damarian's mate, Cassie. You are our family."

"You don't see me as an abomination?" I glance at Syren. He called me that when I first came to the colony.

"We do not," Syren says.

A sigh of relief escapes my lips. They don't know how much that means to me.

"If it's any consolation," Kyle says. "A lot of my clan didn't know how to treat me when I returned to the sea." He takes the other seat near me. "But we're very accepting people, Cassie. You'll feel welcome here in no time."

That makes me smile. "Thanks, Kyle."

"Syren of the Sapphire clan," a voice says from outside.

Syren's body stands to attention. "The Guard," he says, then swims out. When he returns, he's followed by a few members of the Guard. And Queen Flora.

Kiandra and Kyle launch off the chairs and do the merpeople bow.

I stumble out of my chair and copy them.

Flora waves her hand, telling us to be at ease. Her gaze falls on Kiander, who's lying unconscious on the stone table. Her entire face fills with pain.

One of the Guards swims forward. "My queen, this is not a sight you should see."

She holds out her hand, shushing him. Hesitantly, she swims to Kiander and runs the back of her fingers down his cheek. "What is causing him to be ill?" She looks at Damarian. "What has happened to them?"

No one says anything.

Her gaze moves to Syren. "Have they been tortured?"

He nods.

Her eyes flash with fury. "Have you eradicated the sea of these beasts?"

"Many," Syren tells her. "There were survivors. I imagine they will regroup and gather more followers."

Her gaze is back on her husband. "I want each and every one of them captured." She looks at one of the Guards. "Search the waters day and night. They will pay for what they have done to their king. We do not tolerate treason."

"Yes, my queen." The Guard bows before leaving.

She lowers her head to Kiander's, resting her forehead against his, her eyes shut. "He is a breath away from death," she whispers.

My stomach coils. I look at Damarian. He's probably at death's doorstep, too.

"Why do they not heal?" Flora demands.

"We are not certain," Syren says.

"I could not treat their wounds," Kiandra says.

"No," Flora says as she studies the burn marks, her voice far away.

"These are not average wounds. They will not heal on their own."

"My queen, are you familiar with wounds?" Kiandra asks.

Her hand traces a large mark on Kiander's chest. "I have an interest in healing. No, these will not heal without assistance."

"From what?" Kiandra asks.

She doesn't seem to know the answer to that.

Kyle swims forward, bowing his head. "My queen, if I may?"

"Yes?"

"When I was a fry, I grew ill. An elder at the Emerald colony fed me a unique species of plant. It eliminated the disease."

Flora's face brightens. "Is the Emerald with us?"

Kyle shakes his head. "She perished many moons past."

"Orja," Syren mutters, rubbing his chin.

"Pardon?" Flora asks.

"Legends," he says. "Myths. Tales that are told to fry, of a mystical plant capable of healing all illnesses."

"It is not a myth," Kyle says.

"Where do we locate this plant?" Flora asks.

No one seems to know the answer to that.

She nods at another Guard. "Travel to the clans. Make inquiries of this mystical plant. This is an urgent matter."

He bows and leaves.

"I only hope that we are not too late," she says.

***

I don't leave Damarian's side, not even to sleep. My hand is laced through his. Even though he's colder than he should be, his heart pumps blood throughout his body. I feel it. "Stay strong," I whisper. "Hang on just a little longer."

We haven't heard back from the palace yet. We don't know if the Guard's been successful in learning anything about the Orja plant. We don't even know if it exists.

"Cassie?" Zarya comes out of her room and lowers herself onto my lap. With my hand still clutched in Damarian's, I wrap the other one around her and hold her close. "Will Dammy and Kiander be all right?" she asks. Her parents told her that Damarian and Kiander were out exploring when they got injured.

I kiss the top of her head. "We're doing everything we can to make sure they will be."

Zarya lays her head on my shoulder. Having her in my arms like this comforts me, makes me feel less alone. Less scared. Sliding her hand into mine, she places something in my palm. I study it. It looks like a gem from a piece of jewelry. Probably from a sunken ship.

"Thanks," I tell her.

After a bit, she grows still in my arms. "Good night, sweetie," I whisper.

Soon, I find my own head starting to bob

Someone touches my shoulder. Doria. "You should sleep. You must be exhausted."

"I don't want to leave him."

With every second that passes, it feels like he loses more of his energy. I want to be here if he…if he…I can't even think it.

Doria leaves and returns with some seaweed. She arranges it across two of the stone chairs, creating a bed. "Thanks," I tell her.

She smiles, then reaches for Zarya. "Good night, Cassie."

"Good night."

With my hand still in Damarian's, I lie down. I feel sleep starting to take over. The last thing on my mind before I black out is that I'm going to do everything in my power to save the man who has my heart. I'm not giving up without a fight, not after everything we've been through.

Chapter Thirty-Five

Syren, Kiandra, and I swim to Eteria. Flora requested a meeting, specifically stating that I should join as well. Every cell in my body is on edge. The Guard must have learned something important.

Syren's shark accompanies us, along with Shoney. There has been no sign of the rebels since our attack, but we're not risking anything. Syren swears they're regrouping and gathering more members, though Kyle told us everything seemed to be in order back at his colony.

We enter the palace and are led to Flora by one of her Guards. She's sitting on her throne, talking to a male Violet with similar features as her. Palaemon, her dad and former king. When she sees us, she gets up and swims toward us. "Syren. Kiandra. Cassie." She turns to her dad. "Father is more versed in healing plants."

"The Orja plant is no legend," he says. "It indeed has profound healing abilities. But it is not easily located."

Flora nods to the Guard standing on the side. He's the one whom she sent to find information about the Orja. "Inform our guests of what you have discovered," she tells him.

"A child of the Ruby clan claims the Orja plant is located a far distance from the colony. The length of time to travel to the location is one day."

A day? Damarian and Kiander could die by then. All the hope I had inside me rushes out.

Syren lays a hand on my shoulder. "Do not fret, Cassie." He directs his next question to the Guard. "Are you certain there is no closer location?"

He shakes his head. "This is all I learned."

The room gets so quiet I can hear every tail whooshing in the water.

"It is what we must do," Syren says. "If that is the only option."

"Father," Flora says.

Palaemon inclines his head. "There is an element to the Orja plant. It only reveals itself to those in dire need of it."

Neither Damarian nor Kiander is in any condition to travel. I don't think there's an ounce of hope left inside me.

"Or to one who has a close bond to the one in dire need of it," Palaemon continues.

My body perks up like I've been zapped.

"It is my greatest desire to search for the Orja plant," Flora says. "But I cannot. You, Cassie, are the one with the strongest bond to Damarian. And you, Syren and Kiandra, are the ones with the second strongest bond to Kiander."

Syren, Kiandra, and I exchange glances. Syren pats his wife's arm, then mine. "I am ready and willing to travel far to acquire this plant."

"Me, too." I would travel anywhere to help Damarian.

***

Because the rebels are still at large, four members of the Guard are set to leave with us.

Kiandra wraps her tail around mine and kisses my cheek, telling me to be careful and thanking me for doing this. I say goodbye to the kids and Doria, then take Damarian's hands in mine. Bending close, I kiss his forehead. "I'll be back soon."

He stirs and squeezes my hand. I brush my lips lightly against his.

"Let's go," I tell Syren.

Together with our sharks, the six of us leave the mercolony. Syren told me earlier today that we will be traveling at an extremely fast pace. I don't have a lot of experience swimming at such speed, and I'm worried I'll need to rest a lot, but I push those thoughts away. I'll use up every last bit of my energy if I have to.

I don't have a clue where we're going, but Syren seems to know. We swim in silence, each of us focused on the task at hand.

I'm not sure how many hours pass before my limbs feel heavy. My pace has slowed down, and I find myself in the back of the pack. Shoney comes over and tells me to hold onto her fin. Giving her a thankful smile, I grab on.

"I am sorry," Syren tells me when we catch up to the others. "The journey is quite tiresome."

"I'll be okay," I assure him. "I just want to get the plant and heal Damarian and Kiander."

Hours pass and it gets dark. We rest for a few minutes and eat, then go on our way. When Syren finally stops and tells us this might be the place, every part of me feels like jelly.

He instructs the others to stay back while he and I seek the plant. Putting my arm over his shoulder and wrapping his around my waist, we swim to an area with a lot of coral and plant life. As we pass through the many species, I study each one, wondering how exactly we're supposed to know which is the Orja.

The area is so quiet.

"Are we supposed to say something?" I whisper.

Syren looks just as clueless as me.

"Maybe if we channel our thoughts to Damarian and Kiander, they might sense how much we need them and they'll come out."

"That is a magnificent thought," he says.

I close my eyes and think about Damarian, imagining him wounded, putting the images of his burn marks in the front of my mind.

Nothing happens. The area is dead quiet.

Suddenly, something sounds in my ears. It's like a light howl of the wind. Opening my eyes, I see pink plants floating toward us. They move closer and stay suspended in the water.

I'm about to reach for one, but it jumps at me. The others do the same. I watch in horror as they cover every inch of me. It feels like little needles pricking my skin.

Syren growls. Glancing at him, I see the plants covering him, too.

They're dragging us toward the bottom of the ocean.

"Syren!" I yell, twisting my body, trying to shake them off. But they're stuck like glue.

Syren doesn't answer. He twists his body in the same fashion. Are these plants going to kill us?

"Think about Damarian and Kiander!" I tell Syren. "Put everything you have into this."

Ignoring the pain, I shut my eyes tight and press my lips together. I think of Damarian, of him lying half-conscious on the stone table. I think about what he means to me and how much more we need to explore and experience together. How despite all the odds, our love for each other can withstand every obstacle that's thrown in our path.

They continue dragging me to the ocean floor.

"Damarian," I whisper. "I love you."

They stop. Slowly, I open my eyes. The plants are no longer on my skin, but float before me and Syren. They don't appear hostile anymore.

Merman's Touch

With a hesitant hand, I reach for one, praying it doesn't attack me again. My palm closes over it. It doesn't prick me, but feels spongy. I reach for some more. Syren does the same. After a few minutes, the others dissolve.

We hurry home, not paying attention to how tired our bodies are. Nothing matters now except for getting these plants to Damarian and Kiander.

When we reach the Sapphire colony, I feel like I'm going to collapse. Mustering every ounce of strength I have left, I follow Syren into the cave. The mermen's situation hasn't gotten better—in fact, it looks like it got worse. A lot worse. They look like they're in comas.

We hand the plants to Kiandra, who stuffs them into their mouths. Nothing happens. Damarian and Kiander continue lying there like dead logs. Then Kiander stirs, followed by Damarian. Light seems to creep onto their faces, and the wounds heal before my eyes. It's not long before they look healthy again.

"I shall inform Queen Flora at once," Syren says, but not before he kisses the top of his sons' heads.

Kiandra and I help them into sitting positions. But they don't really need help. They look just as new. After telling Kiander how glad I am to see he's okay, I squeeze Damarian to my chest, never wanting to let go. Not seeming to care that we're in front of his mother, he slowly and gently brings his lips to mine. It's a kiss of passion, of longing, of the days lost. His lips skim lower, to my neck, then back up again, meeting mine in nothing but urgency. Like we need to make up for all we've missed.

We would go on for hours, if not for Flora showing up. She and Kiander wrap their tails around each other and nuzzle their noses. It's a great sight, seeing how happy they are to be together. Ever since Damarian gave up the throne for me, I carried around some guilt, that

Flora lost the man she loved and that Kiander was forced to be king and marry someone he didn't love. But I realize now that these two love each other very much, and that meeting Damarian changed the lives of four people, not just two.

Chapter Thirty-Six

Damarian and I cuddle up in his bed. For the first time, we have a chance to share it. Our lips never leave one another, our hands don't stop exploring. We talk to each other between kisses, saying how much we love each other and how alone we felt when we were apart.

"I thought I was going to lose you," I whisper.

Damarian buries his face in my hair. "Never, my love. I will never leave you." His fingers lock with mine. "I survived because of you," he says. "When I closed my eyes, I saw you. I felt you in my soul. If not for you, I would have perished."

I give him a long, deep kiss. "Did we share a dream? When Flora and I tried to find you, I had a dream. It was wonderful." I tell him about it.

"Yes," he murmurs. "It was a world we created together. Thank you for locating me, my love."

My fingers trail up his arms as we continue to kiss. After a few minutes, I pull back. "What happened in the cave? How did we get rid of the net?"

Damarian shifts in the bed, looking uncomfortable.

"What is it?" I ask.

"There was an incident when I was a fry."

"What kind of incident?" I ask, my heart starting to speed up.

He touches my cheek. "I have not told anyone this. It frightened me as a fry."

"I won't tell anyone if you don't want me to."

He lays his forehead against mine. "All these moons, I assumed it did not occur but only in my head. I understand now that it is not the case."

My heart is now pounding. "You can tell me," I say softly.

"It was a game of squid wars. Kiander and I versus two fry. I am not certain how it occurred, but I became trapped in the coral. I shouted for help, but no one heard me for I was far from the colony." He takes a deep breath and lets it out slowly. "I was frightened. I hit the coral in the hope that I could break it, but I did not have the strength. As I attempted to strike the coral again, as strongly as I could, electricity shot out of my hand. It destroyed the coral, releasing me." He kisses my temple. "An incident such as that never occurred again. It was forgotten, until today."

I stare at him, not blinking. "So…you can shoot electricity from your hands?"

He shakes his head. "I do not know. However, I am certain I could not have done it if you were not with me."

Is he saying he thinks I helped him create that electricity? But how could I when I wasn't there the first time?

"Children of the sea have abilities?" I ask.

He's quiet for a few seconds before slowly shaking his head again. "If every child of the sea had such an ability, there would be no need to keep it a secret."

"So you think only some merpeople have abilities?"

He shakes his head for a third time. "I believe I am the sole child to have this ability."

Merman's Touch

I stare at him, feeling my jaw fall. "Why only you?"

"Because I am the true heir to the throne. As fry, we are told stories, stories of the imagination. I never believed them to be true. There is one that is told by many, of a great king with the ability to cause electricity in the sea." He looks down at his hand. "Perhaps these stories are not tales fabricated from the imagination. Perhaps…perhaps they are indeed true."

I gaze at my own hand. "And me? You said you were only able to do it because of me."

He nods slowly. "Because I was weakened. When your hand clutched mine, you provided me with strength."

I think back to the battle we had with the rebels, how I managed to hit the sharks like I had super strength. Does that mean I have an ability, too? I tell Damarian about it. His eyes widen in surprise. "Perhaps it is because you are my mate."

"You mean…the true queen of the merpeople." A lump as big as my fist forms in my throat.

Damarian hugs me close, trailing kisses down my neck. "You are not queen of the children of the sea. Flora is."

"But if you're the true king—"

"No." His lips continue to press kisses into my skin. "You are Cassie Price. I am Damarian of the Sapphire clan. We are lovers. We will remain together for all eternity. Nothing else is relevant."

"Dammy?"

We both lift our heads to find Zarya standing there, watching us with eyes the size of the stone chairs in the main room. We quickly untangle ourselves from around each other. I think the merpeople need to seriously rethink the lack-of-doors-in-rooms situation.

"Zarya," he says.

"You are well!" She bolts toward him, throwing herself into his arms, her tail whipping into my face. She wraps it around his.

Damarian kisses the top of her head. "How I have missed you."

"As have I. Have you learned anything as you explored the sea?"

Damarian exchanges a look with me. He doesn't know that she's not aware of what really happened to him. I motion with my eyes that he should go with the flow. Shaking his head, he says, "I am afraid I have not."

She frowns. "Will you bring me along the next time you explore the deep sea?"

He taps her nose. "Not until Father believes you are old enough."

She pouts.

"The hour is late," Damarian says. "Why are you not asleep?"

"I wished to sleep with Cassie." She beams at me. "I did not expect to see you in here."

He strokes her cheek. "Perhaps we shall return you to your shell."

"Will you sing?" she asks. "Please."

He kisses the top of her head again. "All right."

The two of them get out of Damarian's bed. "I shall return shortly," he tells me.

"May Cassie come as well?" Zarya asks. "Come, Cassie!"

A warm feeling invades every part of me. She wants me to help tuck her into bed. I feel a large smile capture my mouth. "Of course I'll come."

We swim to Zarya's room. The shell is smaller than Damarian's. She dives headfirst into it, her whole body disappearing under the seaweed. Her head pops out, then her hands, which she folds over her stomach. She smiles widely.

Damarian sits down next to her. "What shall we sing tonight?"

She scrunches her eyebrows together. "I do not know. You choose!"

Merman's Touch

He pulls some of the seaweed up to her chin and starts to sing:

"The sea is so vast with creatures inside,
From the deep black waters to the sandy tide,
Tell me, young fry, are you an explorer today?
What beautiful sights have you observed on this day?"

Zarya continues the song:

"I have searched the waters far and low,
To all the secret places that most do not know,
But I have learned a fact that is only true,
The place I call home is where I am with you."

Damarian kisses her forehead. "And now, my young explorer, it is time you sleep."

"Good night." Zarya's head turns to me. "Good night, Cassie."

I head over to her and kiss her forehead, too. "Good night, Zarya."

With a content smile on her face, she turns to her side.

Hand in hand, Damarian and I leave her room. "You're so sweet with her," I say. "It's lovely to watch."

He wraps his arm around my waist and tugs me close.

Something blasts at us, so fast it looks like a blur. A second later, there's another blast. At first, I think we're getting attacked, but then I see sapphire tales and golden hair.

It's the twins.

One of them—I think it's Syd—hides behind us while Syndin tries to catch him. As Syndin dashes behind us, Syd comes in front of us. All the while, they are yelling at one another. I can't help but laugh how similar they are to humans.

Damarian grabs Syndin by the waist and throws him upside down over his shoulder. He does the same to the other. That doesn't seem to stop the fighting—their hands slap at each other.

"It is quite a shame you are quarreling," Damarian says. "For it was my desire to play squid wars."

Simultaneously, they both stop.

"Please!" Syd says. "Let us play!"

Damarian gives me a smug smile. "Do you wish to play, Cassie? It is quite difficult to beat Syd and Syndin, for they have an extremely strong bond. But as they are quarreling..."

I've always wanted to play squid wars ever since Damarian told me about it. It's like the human version of paintball.

Still hanging upside down from Damarian's shoulders, Syd and Syndin narrow their eyes at one another. "We will triumph," Syndin says. "Even though my brother shares a face with the lump fish."

Syd tries to slap him. "Your face is identical to mine."

"It is not!"

I swim forward and press my hands on their chests, forcing them apart. "Game on, mermen. Game on."

***

Damarian and I are wedged tightly together between two rocks. The space is so tiny I'm amazed the life is not getting squeezed out of us.

Syd and Syndin are good. Too good. This is our fourth game, and they lead two to one. I take full responsibility for the first loss since I've never played before. I blame the second loss on my squid, who refused to shoot ink at the twins. They won't cut me any slack but treat me like I'm a pro.

Damarian's lips dip to the side of my neck. "This is quite wonderful," he says.

"Mmm." I don't know if we've ever been this close before. It feels really nice.

The squid in my hand starts moving around. I tighten my hold on it. "I don't think this squid likes me."

He chuckles and is about to say something, when we hear movement. He puts his finger on his lips. If I twist my neck, I can see through a small crack in the rock. I point to my eyes and then to my ears, telling Damarian I'll tell him when it will be the best time to attack. He nods.

Syd and Syndin are swimming back to back, their squids held in their hands like guns. They seem to have a weird twin telepathy bond where they know exactly what the other one is thinking.

As I'm trying to find the perfect time to jump out at them, I feel Damarian's lips graze my jaw. I'm about to motion for him to stop because we need to kick their asses, but it feels so good, and I find myself melting into him.

A soft moan escapes my lips.

Crap.

Peeking through the hole, I don't see the twins. Maybe they left? I strain my ears, but I don't hear anything.

Suddenly, black ink shoots at me. I squeeze my squid, squirting my own ink, but I have no idea where I'm aiming.

"We are triumphant once again!" the twins say, surging upward and slapping their tails together in a high five.

Damarian is also covered in ink. I give him a face. "This is all your fault. We totally had them."

Laughing, he pulls me closer and whispers in my ear, "You are competitive."

"Well, no. I mean…maybe."

His chest rumbles as he continues to laugh. "It is 'hot.'"

That causes my stomach to flutter. "You are hotter. And I see you haven't forgotten human phrases."

"Let us begin the next game!" one of the twins whines.

Damarian and I squeeze ourselves out of the rocks, and I raise my squid. "It's on, boys."

We lose this game, too.

Chapter Thirty-Seven

With interlocked hands, Damarian leads me out of the merpeople colony. There have been no signs of the rebels, but everyone's guard is still up. Flora made it perfectly clear that the threat is not over and that we will not rest easy until we know every last one is captured and reprimanded.

I have no idea where Damarian is taking me. He told me it's a surprise. Wherever it is, it's far away from home, but not too far that we need to worry about the rebels.

We dive deeper, underneath a row of rocks. It looks like it leads to nowhere, but Damarian twists his body to the left and dives between a gap that can fit only one person at a time. He makes sure I get through before continuing. There's an opening to a cave in front of me.

"Most are not aware of this cave," he tells me, then leads me inside. This cave is completely different from the ones the merpeople live in. It's darker with green coral all around. The contrast between the dark blue water in here and the green coral makes the whole place look exquisite. As we move further inside, it slopes upward, like we're climbing a mountain. There isn't a lot of space to move around.

Damarian lets go of my hand and lowers himself on the mountain. He pulls me to him, pressing my back to his chest and wrapping his hands around my stomach.

"This place is beautiful," I say.

"It is where I go when I wish to be alone."

I lean my head on his shoulder. "Thanks for showing it to me. I love it."

His lips tickle my ear. "It is where I remained when I fled from home."

My head twists to look up at him. When my mom stayed home for a few days, Damarian had to return to the ocean. But he didn't want to go home because his father was pressuring him to marry Flora and become king. He stayed here.

I reach to kiss his lips. "Your dad is much more understanding of us now."

He nods. "He has spoken with me last night. I believe our relationship has much improved."

"I'm so happy for you."

He sits up and lowers me to the ground. My skin sinks into the coral. It's very soft on top and hard underneath. "I am so happy that you are here with me." He lifts both my hands to his mouth and kisses the back of them. "When I was captured, I did not know if I would be able to see you again. It caused my heart to ache."

I cup his cheek. "I felt the same way."

His hands slide underneath me, lifting me to his body. "I love you, Cassie Price."

"I love you, Damarian of the Sapphire clan."

He shifts over so that he's sitting and I'm on his lap. "Do you have a location where you travel to when you require solitude?" he asks.

I think for a few seconds. "I don't think so. I usually surf when I'm upset."

His eyes fill with regret. "Cassie, forgive me. You will never have the opportunity to surf."

I put my finger on his lips. "That's okay. Look at this." I gesture around. "Look at us. We're here together in one of the most beautiful places I've ever seen. What more can I ask for?"

He smiles and positions his lips over mine. They move closer, slowly, making my heart race with anticipation. Unable to wait any longer, I press mine to his. His mouth moves over mine with vigor, strongly, passionately. Electric. I fall back on the coral and yank him down with me, tangling my fingers in his hair.

Everything we've felt these past few days are shown in these kisses—the fear, the worry, the hope. The relief and happiness that we are finally together again.

We whisper and moan each other's names as our lips continue moving over each other with all the energy and love we have. We've been through so much together, but our love for one another reigned supreme and no matter what else we need to face in life, I know we will get through it.

After a few more minutes, maybe hours, of making out, we fall back on the coral and stare at the ceiling of the cave, which is also lined with coral. "I can stay here forever," I say.

"As can I."

"We totally should. Away from everyone else where we will be alone."

He brushes some hair off my cheek. "Is it not your wish to return to land?"

"I do want to go back. I miss everyone." I look into his eyes. "But I don't want to face everything. Life. It's easier to just stay here."

He's watching me closely, like he's trying to understand what I'm saying. "Is it your wish to remain in the sea?"

To give up my human life? I shake my head. "No, I don't want to give up being a human. Even though I'm afraid to face a lot of things, I want to. I want to become a stronger, more confident and independent woman. I want us to share both of our worlds."

He nuzzles my nose. "That is my wish as well. I wish to live in the sea with you, as well as live as a human with you. To work and provide us with pay, and enjoy your world."

I giggle before kissing him. "Provide us with money."

He grins. "I know. I enjoy causing you to laugh."

He lowers his mouth to mine.

Chapter Thirty-Eight

My stomach burns. I'm yanked out of my sleep and spring up, knocking into Damarian and forcing him to roll off of me.

"Cassie?"

My palms dig into the coral and my head hangs low as I find it difficult to breathe. Clutching my chest that's starting to ache, I shoot my other hand out to Damarian. He grabs it, trying to look into my eyes, but my shoulders are slouched so low they're nearly touching the coral. "Cassie, what is wrong?" he asks, his voice laced with worry.

It's hard to breathe. I open my mouth wide to draw in oxygen, but that's useless because I get oxygen through my gills. I can't see them, but I feel them opening and closing rapidly. Violently.

Damarian takes hold of my face and stares into my eyes. A look of terror flashes across his face.

"What?" I ask, my voice weak.

"Your eyes. They are no longer the color of the sea, but the color of land."

It takes a few seconds for me to grasp what he just said. My eyes are turning back to my natural color—brown. Glancing down at my hands, I see they are no longer webbed. And my skin seems to be more peachy.

I'm turning back into a human. And I'm thousands of feet in the ocean.

Damarian must realize it, too, because he scoops me in his arms and bolts toward the entrance of the cave. My head flops on his shoulder as my chest continues to ache, my lungs begging for oxygen. My gills must be disappearing.

Why didn't we consider this? Damarian can't be on land for too long because his natural form is a merman. No matter how many years he lives on land, he will always need to dip himself into sea water at least twice a day. The same is happening to me. My natural form is a human, and I need to return to land. Apparently not every twelve hours, but at least once or twice a week. And it explains why I don't need to swim in sea water as often as Damarian, because my true form is a human.

Flora told me I changed into a mermaid because it was against nature for me and Damarian to mate in different forms. But I guess my body requires me to sometimes be a human, too.

"You will be all right," Damarian murmurs, his lips grazing my temple. "I will return you to land. I will reach the sandbar as quickly as possible." He presses the back of his fingers into my forehead, my cheeks, my neck. "You are warm," he says, his voice breaking. "To warm for a child of the sea."

"I...I don't think..."

"No. No, Cassie. I will not lose you."

The average human can hold his or her breath for no longer than a minute, maybe two. If I undergo a complete transformation, we won't make it.

My whole body is shaking uncontrollably and I can barely keep my head up or my eyes open. Damarian tightens his hold on me and gives me words of encouragement and hope, telling me to hold on because we're going to make it and I'm going to be okay. Forcing my eyes open, I look at the surface. We're not even close.

As my eyes flutter closed, I see shadows. Forcing them open again, I look around but don't see anything. My eyes close again, and the only thing I feel is the movement of Damarian's body as he rushes to bring me to land. The only things I hear are the water and our tails as we zip away.

Something knocks into us. I fly out of Damarian's arms and tumble in the water, coming to a stop a few hundred feet away. My head pounds and my chest is on fire, my limbs so weak they can no longer support my body. I sink toward the bottom.

"Cassie!" Damarian yells, racing toward me. Two Emeralds, with their sharks at their sides, block his path. He tries to push past them, but they grab hold of his arms and shove him back. The sharks open their mouths wide, baring their teeth.

I continue to sink.

"Move aside!" Damarian yells.

They fold their arms and don't budge.

"I said, move aside!" I've never heard him this frantic.

"Is she going to perish?" one of them says in a humorous tone. He waves his hand. "A measly human? She is an abomination. It is better if she is dead."

Damarian tries to push past them again, and again they shove him back.

"Please," Damarian pleads. "You may do as you please with me, but allow me to return her to land."

They snicker.

"Please!"

They continue to snicker. Even the sharks laugh.

My tail touches the floor. I open and close my mouth desperately, tying to breathe in oxygen. But it's futile.

With an enraged shout, Damarian slams his body into the Emeralds. They are propelled backward like he blasted them with a grenade.

Damarian zooms to me and snatches me off the ocean floor. With his tail pumping and pumping, he shoots toward the surface. He must realize that the most important thing I need right now is oxygen. Maybe if I have that, my body will hold out long enough for us to get to land.

"It will be all right," he tells me.

But it's not. Because a Diamond stands in our way.

"Move aside," Damarian says in an authoritative tone.

I'm wheezing. I don't know how much oxygen I have left.

The Diamond stays put. Damarian must not have enough strength to shoot another invisible grenade, because he makes a sharp turn and continues to swim to the surface.

An Emerald blocks our way.

Damarian turns the other way, but there is another Emerald. And another, and another. We're surrounded by at least twenty-five merpeople, each with a shark.

"Damarian," I whisper, panic taking hold of me.

His body is trembling. He's exhausted, probably because he's using every ounce of energy he has left to bring me to the surface.

He spins in different directions, trying to find weak spots in this merblockade.

There isn't any.

My chest gets as stiff as a board. I've run out of oxygen.

About the Author

Dee J. Stone is the pseudonym of two sisters who write adult and young adult novels. *The Keepers of Justice series, The Merman's Kiss series, The Cruiser & Lex series, Falling for the Genie, Emily's Curse*, and *Chasing Sam* are now available on Amazon. You can email them at deej.stone@yahoo.com or follow them on Facebook and Twitter.

Made in the USA
Columbia, SC
10 January 2025